THE HUNTED

LINDA COLES

Blue Banana

Published by Blue Banana

Chapter One

WHAT IS an acceptable age to kill your first victim? Jackie pondered that very question as she sat outside the woman's house in her car. She couldn't simply let it go, couldn't let any of them get away with it; it would never do. She opened the driver's side, stepped out, and walked towards the front door.

She was about to find out what that number was.

Chapter Two

"JACKIE! What a pleasant surprise, I wasn't expecting you just yet. Come on in!"

As the curly blonde-headed woman waited in the open doorway and smiled back brightly, she let the lethal syringe slip down the inside of her shirtsleeve into the latexed palm of her hand, which was out of sight behind her back. The blonde leaned forward to give the other woman a quick peck on the cheek in greeting, and at the same time, slipped the protective cap off the syringe needle, all out of view. The other woman turned and started her way down the hallway towards the lounge area chatting as she went about nothing in particular, not that Jackie was even paying attention. Instead, her focus was on what she was going to do next. The other woman's words sounding to her ears like she was talking under water, the bubbles masking the words making no sense at all. The thin plastic syringe was now set and ready to kill, and it felt heavy in her hand. Even knowing it would only take a moment, it seemed like a lifetime to the inexperienced woman, and she wanted it over. She'd never thought of herself as a killer, yet was about to cross the line and become one. With the other woman's back still to her as they entered the lounge area, she quickly took her opportunity to strike. The blonde knew it wouldn't need much, just a quick jab, the plunger and a couple of drops of the fatal liquid would do the rest. Well, they would do the first part. The easier part. Jackie raised her right arm in preparation, syringe at the ready and slammed it forward into the back of the woman's right arm, the plunger depressing quickly. The woman hardly had time to feel or react.

"What the ..." Her words were lost. Jackie watched the other woman crumple down onto the floor at her feet, like her whole body has lost its bones, a pile of dying flesh slumped obscurely on the wooden floor, her eyes glazing over in near death. Jackie knew it wouldn't take long for the liquid to activate and she stood and watched in awe, never having seen someone in the throes of dying before. And definitely never witnessed a murder before. She checked her wrist-watch, the second hand moving slowly around the clock face. A minute passed, then another, and one more just to be sure. She double-checked her watch again; then she checked the woman's pulse. Nothing. The first part of her task was done, the easy part. It was what she had to do next that she wasn't looking forward to.

"It's your own fault. You chose to do what you do, and I'm choosing to do what *I* do," she reasoned with the lifeless woman as she moved her still-warm body into position, laying her out on her back on the floor. She reached into her bag, pulled out the insanely sharp, smooth-edged hunting knife she'd brought with her and laid it beside the woman.

"I'll use your towels, if you don't mind. It was too risky bringing my own. Shall I help myself?"

Was she really expecting an answer? Obviously not, but talking to the woman somehow gave her comfort for the task ahead. Stepping over the prone body, Jackie headed to the bathroom to look for a couple of towels, and then changed her mind and headed back out to a cupboard she'd noticed in the hallway.

"I really don't want to use your best white ones, so I've taken your beach towels I found in the hallway cupboard. Seemed to make more sense. And they are probably a bit bigger anyway." She laid them both around the woman's shoulders on the floor.

Jackie stood to look at the arrangement in front of her, a feeling of queasiness starting in her stomach. Knowing her body all too well, she knew she'd need to be prepared, just in case the inevitable happened.

She absolutely couldn't leave any evidence, so she stood up and left the lounge, entering the small kitchen in search of a plastic rubbish bin liner.

"Better grab two, just in case. Don't want to leave a drop somewhere if there's a hole in the bottom of the bag." Opening the cupboard door under the sink, she found what she was looking for, a roll of white refuse bags. She tore off two and inserted one inside the other for extra protection. Satisfied the bags would be secure and nothing would leak out, she made her way back through to the lounge, and her first victim. And the task.

"Okay, I think I'm ready. Can you tell I'm a bit nervous? It's my first time you see, but I suspect it won't be my last. People like you will always be around I expect, and that will keep me busy. No doubt I will get better at this, get more used to it, not think about it so much."

She knelt down beside her victim's head, towels around her shoulders as she lay there, and took the hunting knife in her hands.

"Here goes."

Holding her head up slightly by her hair, Jackie slashed quickly from left to right and made a wide incision across her friend's throat with the smooth blade. The blade went through her skin like the proverbial knife through butter, the blade as sharp as a new scalpel. Dark red blood slowly seeped out of her gaping neck wound into the towels, their presence doing their job of soaking the excess up beautifully. Even to a vet, the sight of so much blood, human blood, made her stomach roll and she was glad she had been prepared with the double-lined plastic bag. What she hadn't expected was how violently the sight would affect her. Making a grab for the bag, she held it high to her mouth and rapidly emptied her stomach as it spasmed excruciatingly several times, depositing the contents inside it, her body not able to control itself after the revoltingness of what she'd just done. When she was sure her retching was over, her stomach empty, she tied the bag up and slipped it gently into her own bag, ready to dispose of when she left. She sat back on her heels, catching her breath, gasping.

"Damn, I could do with a glass of water right now, but I can't, not yet anyway," she said to her victim. "I'll just have to wait. Good job I'd stopped your heart first off, otherwise it would have been a whole lot messier, and I'd probably be a whole lot sicker, and we couldn't have that. And, I've still got part three to do yet. No rest for the wicked, eh? Now, if I could just get your phone—where is it?" Jackie looked around the small room, scanning the surfaces but couldn't see the woman's phone resting anywhere visible. She stood up, her legs a little wobbly, but gained the strength she needed as she moved across the room.

"Strong as an ox! Well, apart from my stomach, that is." She chatted away to the woman like they were gossiping over coffee, as nothing of any consequence had happened. She walked over to the big comfy leather chairs on the other side of the room and spotted what she was looking for. "I'm going to have to look in your bag. Sorry for the intrusion, but needs must."

Digging deep into the woman's handbag she felt the familiar smooth surface of a smartphone and pulled it out. Pressing the home button, she activated the screen.

"I'm glad to see you still don't bother with a passcode. I noticed when we were out, at the Italian restaurant, stroke of good luck for me. Not that it would have mattered that much, I'm pretty much buried in most of your life now anyway, been following you and your movements for a while. It's amazing what you can learn about someone being their friend online. You've been really useful to me; did you know that? I'm guessing not. And now I'm following your death too. And so will your other friends shortly."

She took the phone and tapped the settings icon on the screen and when she'd found what she was looking for in privacy, turned location services to 'off.'

"Don't want people knowing where I am when this gets posted now do I, not that stupid."

Clicking the camera icon on the screen, she prepared to take a photo.

"I'm going to lift your head up now and take a pic. A rather different kind of selfie from what you'd normally see, not the pouty type you usually post. This one will be shall we say, more attention-grabbing?" Holding her up by the hair, she took a picture of her half-severed head, taking care not to add anything of herself into the frame.

"Don't want to be in this particular selfie, now, do I?"

When she was satisfied with the image she'd taken, she put the phone into her own bag to deal with later and felt remarkably calm and satisfied at what she'd done.

"Right, I think I'm done. I'll just wipe the knife off. Mind if I grab another plastic bag to wrap it in? I don't want blood in my lovely new bag; I bought it especially for the occasion." She headed back off to the kitchen for another bag, then returned and wiped the knife on the edge of one of the towels beside her head. She was all set. Checking around the room one last time to make sure she'd not moved anything or left anything unnecessarily, she rolled her latex gloves off her hands and then stuffed one inside the other, dropping the small bundle into her bag along with the neatly secured vomit.

"Well, thanks for being such a sport and being my first. Apart from being ill, it was easier than I'd expected it to be. Sorry about the mess, but needs must. It'll be interesting to see what happens next, with your friends, and of course the police, but unfortunately, you'll never know. Anyway, I'm off now. Think I'll take the back door, if you don't mind. Fewer people about."

With one final glance around, Jackie made her way to the rear door through the kitchen and out into the small back garden.

"Bye-bye," she called inside quietly like good friends would have done, then closed the door and made her way down the path. She opened the little gate at the bottom and casually walked along at the rear of the row of properties' gardens and emerged from a communal side entrance further up. Before she entered the full view of the quiet suburban street, she slipped the blonde curly wig off her head and into her bag, fluffing up her own short auburn hair as she walked. To anyone who noticed her, she looked like any other young woman taking a walk and mixed in with the suburban surroundings easily.

Chapter Three

TWO WEEKS earlier

Fiona was good at her job. Too good. Which made her a small fortune on the side even though it wasn't legit. Legit? Who was she kidding with such a word? It was downright illegal, and if she got caught again, it would probably land her a spell inside this time. Fiona had been lucky last time she'd been found out. The charges had all fallen through due to a lack of any real evidence and she'd simply lost her job, but she'd managed to find another position in another town not long after. Keep changing her location and her identity was proving expensive, so with her current job, she'd vowed to take more care, more precautions, and not be too greedy. Though the job as a bookkeeper at a hotel and restaurant complex wasn't particularly well paid, being just outside Croydon, it was good and local into the bargain. And she needed the money. And the hotel owners wouldn't miss a few extra thousand each year, and that was how she reconciled it in her own mind. Reconciled—definitely a bookkeeper term, how apt. Over the years, she'd developed quite a few simple scams; the current one she used topped up her bank balance up nicely each month and was almost foolproof. Almost, because you really needed to know where to look to find it. She'd buried it nicely, though no doubt a forensic computer scientist could locate it if they had access. Since no one suspected anything, she was safe for now.

"Here we go," she said warmly. A few clicks of her mouse in the right places and her account was topped up again for the month, with no one any the wiser. Over the two years, she'd been working at the hotel, she'd amassed a tidy sum, and it had paid for her expensive hobby, something she couldn't afford to take part in without the added income. She flicked her thick sun-kissed mane off her shoulder as she rose from her seat and went out to the break room and fancy coffee machine to make herself a cup. Adrenaline was already starting to pump through her veins at finalising the monthly transaction and the feel of it thrilled her as it always did. And coffee would add to that, the caffeine pushing the adrenaline harder, her high even more euphoric; it made her giddy with excitement. Each time she did it, each month she transferred the money, the buzz was absolute. She had begun to crave it, wanting the months to roll around quicker so she could experience the thrill of it all over again, feel it inside of her veins, strumming away, and had been sorely tempted to do it more often. But greed could land you in a whole heap of trouble, and she'd restrained herself from it.

The strong coffee tasted good as she sipped it from her mug and stared out of the window that looked out to the staff car park and the back of the hotel complex. From her vantage point, she could see Isabel, her boss's wife, dressed in all her usual finery, all perfect long shiny hair and red nails, getting into her sports car ready for her weekly trip. Michael wasn't with her—never was. They rarely went anywhere together, though Fiona knew for a fact where Isabel was going, and it wasn't more shopping like Michael thought. No, because today was Tuesday. For the last six months, Isabel had driven off every Tuesday morning at 11.30 precisely and had come back mid-afternoon, looking just as good as when she had left earlier, but with a certain rumpledness about her, a look that was so subtle, only a woman who had been there herself could detect it. Fiona knew what she was up to, that she had a regular lover. She just didn't know who it was. Maybe Michael knew what she was up to, though she very much doubted it; he was too busy wrapped up in his own world to notice the telltale signs. Isabel started her engine, and it purred like a big cat as she manoeuvred her car out of the parking space and to the main road out front. With a couple of loud revs, she was gone, leaving Fiona to check her watch, knowing full well what the time was. And when she'd be back.

"See you about three o'clock. Enjoy yourself!" she called through the window, though no one could hear her sarcasm.

She took her mug of coffee back to her desk, feeling her heart rate increase a little more as the caffeine penetrated her blood and went back to reconciling the hotel's transactions for yesterday. The month was turning out to be one of the busiest they'd had so far this year, with each month getting better than the last one, and Fiona wondered why the owners were such cheapskates in hiring 'professionals' for certain tasks. It wasn't like they couldn't afford someone better qualified. Take her own position, for instance; a business of this size really should employ someone a little more competent than the services of 'Fiona, the bookkeeper.' But while they were having great months and were happy with the hotel's income, they were blissfully unaware of their deeper financials, and the report that she went through with them both each month was nothing more than what she wanted them to see. If only they'd spent a little time looking in more detail they'd have seen that things were not quite as they should be. But no matter, Fiona wasn't about to spill all her illicit activities—and in the absence of annually audited accounts, they'd never find out. So she kept up her very lucrative skimming.

It was nearly lunchtime when her office door opened and Michael stood leaning against the frame, smiling.

"Hey Fiona," he said seductively. No doubt he appreciated Isabel's departure each Tuesday whether he knew where she was going or not.

"Hey yourself," she replied smiling sweetly at her boss, watching as he sauntered over to her desk, checking if anyone was behind him before bending down to plant a slow kiss on her neck, pushing her hair to one side as he did so.

"Mmmmm, you smell good."

Fiona laughed lightly at the compliment and offered her neck up for another kiss. "What can I do for you, Michael?" she asked teasingly.

"Oh, I wish we had time for what I'd like to do for you, but right now I need a breakdown of the bar takings this month for a meeting with a drinks rep in a couple of hours." He pecked her neck lightly again. "Can you get them ready for me?" he said, making his way lower down her neck. Another peck.

"Not a problem. I'll get them organised. Oh, and don't forget, I've got some time off coming up soon—Friday, in fact. And I'm going away."

He carried on nibbling. "Damn, I'd forgotten about that. Do you really have to go, now?"

"Yes, I do," she said, enjoying the nibbling.

"Then I'll just have to manage. Not sure I can do without you for seven whole days, though." He was teasing her rotten, blowing little kisses onto her shoulder, though Fiona knew he was just using her body like she was his. As well as his bank account.

"I'll make sure everything is up to date before I head out. You know that."

"That's not quite what I meant, and you know it," he said, winking at her. Yes, she did. Their relationship, for want of a better word, had been going on almost as long as she'd been working there, an instant spark having ignited between them both, though it was nothing more than good fun for each of them. Both in relationships, the little extra together gave them what they missed out on from their respective partners. He bent again and kissed her hard and full on her lips in a brief and desperate attempt to satisfy his craving for something a little rougher than what Isabel provided. Fiona pushed back with her lips in response then, realising where they were, broke off abruptly before someone walked in, someone who'd tell Isabel what they were up to. Michael might not care whether Isabel found out, but Fiona didn't want to lose the goldmine she'd been working.

"You'd better go, Michael. Anyone could wander in here and see us. And besides, Isabel might be back soon."

He knew she was right although he also knew it wouldn't be Isabel, not yet. She'd not been gone long enough. He straightened up, rearranging himself as he did so, ready to leave, reluctantly.

"I'll get those reports to you within the hour, okay?" she said, smiling dismissively as nothing had just taken place.

"Fine, then. I guess I've no choice; I'll be in the bar." And off he went, somewhat petulant, used to getting his way and leaving her office door wide open. Fiona watched him retreating away down the corridor. One thing she could say about Michael—he was incredibly generous. In more ways than one.

Chapter Four

PUTTING her key in the lock, Fiona once again wondered what she'd find on the other side of the front door. The familiar click and the door swung open, so she stepped into the small hallway and closed the door quietly behind her. Flicking off her shoes she padded her way down towards the back of the house and the kitchen, hoping that just for a change, there may be some resemblance of a meal being made, though her nose told her the answer that deep down she already knew. She sighed heavily as she entered the room, her eyes confirming what her nose had already told her. Deflated again, she wondered why she bothered. She glanced into the living area from the empty kitchen and saw him lying there on the sofa, where he spent so most of his time these days passed out, and from the empty Jack Daniels bottle on the coffee table, it had been just another day at the office for him, every day the same.

Martin was in the middle of yet another downward spiral, a journey of self-destruction, and while Fiona was trying to be supportive, she was getting to the end of her tether, sick of it. Sick of the negativity, sick of the half dead body she shared her bed with, and sick of the smell of him quite frankly. Stale booze, bad breath, and even worse body odour was not a concoction that made her feel good, and understandably so. But to leave him in the lurch while he was in such a bad way would be heartless and that's why she'd chosen to hang around, at least for a while longer anyway. But she'd been thinking about moving on from him, asking him to leave, though she hadn't said anything yet. He was never going to change for her, or for them; he was never going to get cleaned up and make something of himself. And if she kicked him out, where would he go?

They'd been seeing each other for as long as she'd been working at the hotel, that's where they had met in fact. He had been part of the very small management team when he'd been accused of misconduct with a guest's daughter. It seemed she'd been a little younger than her stated twenty-two years and while she was still considered a grown-up, a woman, Daddy had taken offence when he'd found them sat together, out on his balcony in the early evening sunshine wearing very little clothing and smoking dope. That had led to not only an argument, but Martin had lashed out at the man and given him a black eye. All in all, it had been a stupid situation to find himself in, and he'd ended up getting the sack. Isabel and Michael didn't know at that time that Fiona and Martin were even dating, or should she say that Martin had moved into her house. She had been pissed at him for his indiscretion, but since her own dance card had had a few extra signatures on it at the same time, she wasn't going to call him out on it.

They'd drifted along for a while together and put the whole sordid incident behind them, but he'd found it hard to get another job after leaving his position under a very dark cloud. Somewhere along the line, he'd hit his funk, and never having any money except for the government benefit, his mates had ditched him from their lads' nights out because they were sick of his sponging. Fiona knew he'd taken the odd note from her wallet and had continued to turn a blind eye rather than have it out with him and make him feel worse, but as she looked at him passed out yet again, she knew the situation had to change soon.

She picked up the empty bottle and took it straight outside to the recycling bin, balancing it on top of a pile of other empties. It saddened her to see what he had consumed since the last collection only last week. How he could afford it she'd no idea, he wasn't taking that much from her purse and suspected he had started shoplifting and helping himself. He hadn't been caught, not yet, but the risk was very real. Then what would happen to him? A short stint in a cell wasn't going to help change his state of mind though a longer stint in jail probably could. If his access to booze were taken away, surely he'd have to dry out? Either that or join the other desperate inmates taking hand sanitiser for the meagre alcoholic content they did have access to and the rather nasty side effects that came with such a dangerous practice. With nothing to be said or done right at that moment, she headed upstairs and changed into jeans and a T-shirt, then went back to the kitchen and made spaghetti carbonara for one.

"Good morning." Martin stood in the doorway looking sheepish, three days of bristly growth around his jawline, hair tousled in all directions. He looked like he needed a long hot shower and Fiona could smell the stale booze and body odour from where she sat at the kitchen table. It disgusted her.

"Morning," she said tersely, trying hard to keep the tone lighter than had escaped her mouth but only half caring of the effect it might have. "Did you sleep?"

"Not bad, thanks. Any coffee going?"

"Help yourself; I've just got one." *I'm not your sodding servant. You can make your own you're quite capable—when you're sober, that is.*

From over the top of her glasses and laptop screen, she watched him make his way over to the coffee machine, feeling a hint tetchy that her morning quiet had been broken already.

"What are you doing?" he asked as he poured milk into his mug and piled two heaped spoons of sugar in, giving it a noisy stir; the sound grated on Fiona just a little bit more, adding to her annoyance at him. She closed her laptop screen down and gave him her full attention. He sipped his coffee, waiting for her reply.

"I'm going away for a few days. I've got some time owing from work so I thought I'd take myself off and see Mum for a few days. I'm assuming you won't be coming?" Fiona knew damn well there was no chance of Martin visiting her mother with her, they'd never seen eye to eye from the first moment she'd introduced them, and she had told

Fiona that she didn't particularly like him, didn't trust him. Perhaps she should have listened to her mother a bit more back then because looking at the dishevelled man that stood in her kitchen now, she found she was actually repulsed. But Fiona didn't intend to go and see her mum anyway, but he didn't need to know that. She'd been planning to go away for a while, and without Martin, and do the one thing that was her true passion, the one thing that thrilled her, the one thing she was scamming and saving hard for, the one thing she was putting herself in danger for.

"No, I won't, but you enjoy yourself."

I'm planning on it.

Fiona stood and gathered her things into her handbag, slipping the laptop into a carry case ready to leave.

"So when are you going? Soon?"

"Yes, I'm going in a couple of days—Friday morning, and I'll stay the week. I've squared it at work so I've got a bit of tidying up to do there before I leave, so I might be late home tonight. Don't want to leave them in the lurch."

"Okay. I'll see what I can amuse myself with while you're gone." He was sarcastic at himself, and they both knew all too well what he'd be up to for the week—nothing but sleeping and drinking. What a damn waste of life.

"Right, I'm off to work. I'll see you later," she said, and headed out of the kitchen towards the front door, leaving Martin to his syrupy coffee. At least he was up this morning. He didn't usually rise until late morning or, on a really bad day, around lunchtime.

Her car was parked out the front, and as she sat in the driver's seat ready to leave, she scanned the row of houses where she lived, the brown stone walls of identical properties, all identical to the ones on the street next door, and the street next door to that. It was depressing, her life at the moment, and she craved more, much more. The engine fired and sounded somewhat different to Isabel's purring sports number, but she had better things, better pleasures to spend her hard earned on. Thoughts of her upcoming trip were fresh in her mind as she navigated the traffic driving towards the hotel. A few days of peace with a few healthy spikes of adrenaline were just what the doctor ordered, and maybe she'd have an idea of what to do about her depressing relationship with Martin while she had time to think. It couldn't go on the way it was, but how could she let him down gently? The guy was at an all-time low, needed a friend and some support, but she was getting weary of his negative and booze-filled presence. Why was it down to her to look out for the loser? A few minutes later she pulled into the hotel staff car park and could see Michael hovering in the back doorway. He gave a slight wave and a coy smile as she pulled up so rolled her window down as he approached the driver's window and leaned in.

"Hey."

"Hey yourself. Are you waiting for me?"

He leaned in closer and whispered, "I want you. Now, preferably, but Isabel is out later. Fancy getting together when she's gone? I'll make it worth your while." He licked his lower lip lightly so only she could see it, knowing full well it would do the trick with her. Fiona thought for a moment, about her planned trip and Martin. What the heck. She deserved some fun and if Michael was offering her some, then why not. She lifted her eyes at him and said, "sounds naughty, Michael, text me the room number and what time, and I'll be there," then opened the car door and sashayed across to the hotel entrance and went inside, a wry smile on her face that only she knew was there. She desperately needed the trip away and under the circumstances a couple of hours rolling around in bed with Michael she could do, since it was Michael who was paying for it.

Chapter Five

THE SEATS in premium economy were so much better than in 'cattle class,' Fiona mused as she accepted a glass of wine from the flight attendant and took a sip of the cool, almost clear, liquid. One day she'd go all the way and book first class, but right now, the trips were expensive enough. Perhaps if her next job paid a little better in benefits, she'd make a move up to the next level, but right now, she was just glad to be on her way to Zambia—alone. Martin, bless him, still thought she was going to her mother's for a week and would no doubt by now be almost passed out, lay sprawled on the sofa with yet another half-empty bottle of Jack Daniels, its contents pickling his organs from the inside out. Glad to be out of the depressing environment for a few days, she thought ahead to what the trip might hold, though she felt a small knot of regret that she'd lied to him about where she was going. The vision of him lying on the sofa shot back into her mind, and she shuddered involuntarily at the thought. A nearby attendant noticed it.

"Can I get you a blanket, Madam? Are you a little chilly?" she inquired helpfully.

"No, I'm fine, thanks. Someone must have just passed over my grave," she said, smiling. The attendant apparently hadn't heard the old wives' tale and looked a little startled. Fiona smiled again to put her at ease and briefly explained. "They say that when someone walks over where your grave will be one day, that's when you shiver for no apparent reason."

The flight attendant smiled awkwardly and moved on to the next passenger to serve them drinks. Fiona sipped at her wine and savoured the relaxing gentle hum of the aircraft as she closed her eyes and put her head back on the pillow for a few moments. This, travelling in style, was one of the perks of Michael and his bank account access, and well worth the risk. Not wanting to spill her wine, she sat back to attention while she placed the glass safely in the drinks holder in the armrest, accidentally touching the man sat beside her in the twin seats.

"Oh, sorry, I didn't mean to bump you," she apologised.

The man lowered his magazine as Fiona spoke, and she caught his eye. He spoke in soft and welcoming tones.

"No problem." He smiled genuinely and put his magazine down on his tray table. Fiona couldn't help but see the front cover. Her heart skipped a beat as she glanced at the front-page image, one of a lion that had been shot and posed with its hunter, in this case, a middle-aged man, beaming at the camera next to his trophy. The man sat next to her noticed her glancing and spoke.

"You're not going to get all upset on me, are you?" he asked warily.

"Quite the contrary. I suspect a lot of people on a flight to Zambia at this time of year could be going to do the same thing. Is that what you're going to be doing out there, big game hunting?"

The man looked relieved she wasn't going to start a speech on how horrific hunting big game was, and he visibly relaxed a little. "I am, yes. I try and get across each year for a week or so, my man time alone" he said, raising both sets of fingers and making speech marks in the air.

She smiled, knowing just what he meant, a bit of time doing exactly what he wanted, not having to think about anyone else for a time.

"How about you?" he said. "Is that what you're doing in Zambia too?"

"Yes, the same. And just like you, a bit of 'me' time, away from work and the humdrum of daily life. I've been hunting for about eight years now, though this is only the second time in Zambia." The man smiled at her, his eyes meeting hers again and he offered his hand in introduction.

"I'm Aaron Galbraith," he said, offering his hand. "Nice to meet a fellow sports person with the same interests!"

Fiona took his proffered hand and shook it firmly. "And I'm Fiona Gable. Happy to meet you too. Are you headed out to Luangwa?"

"The very same!" He sounded delighted. "And the very best, I might add. Hoping to find a lion preferably, but buffalo will suffice if I don't get quite so lucky. Not that I can take them home. My wife wouldn't have them in the house."

"You'd have to have a pretty big place for all your trophies if you've been hunting a while."

"I have a place up north, actually, in the Lake District, a holiday home for when I want a bit of man time. And I hunt a bit up there, though much smaller animals—not like what we're going after on this trip. I keep a good selection up there. Well, as many of them as I can anyway—as you say, you'd need quite a big place. And my wife doesn't go there very often, so it's pretty much my getaway when I'm not working and want some fresh air."

"And what sort of work do you do, Aaron?" she enquired.

"I'm a pilot, so I get quite a bit of down time, though I am officially on leave at the moment. Flying takes me all over. And you?"

"Company accountant," lied Fiona. *Bookkeeper* wouldn't have sounded quite so grand, and he may well have wondered how she afforded such trips. Better to lie from the outset than cause intrigue. And it wasn't far from the truth so she wouldn't need to remember too much to keep her story straight.

"Well, Fiona," he said, raising his drink to her, "here's to a successful hunting trip, and maybe the first of a few celebratory drinks together!"

She picked up her glass and clinked it gently to his. Her pale eyes caught his dark ones, and both sets twinkled just a little. "Cheers!"

How convenient, Fiona thought, sat next to a fellow hunter going to the same place. She stole a look at his profile as he turned back to read the magazine that had started the conversation off, and noted, not for the first time, that he was quite good-looking, the 'tall, dark and handsome' type. She guessed he was in his mid-forties, about ten years older than herself, though she was not sure why she'd made that observation. Obviously something had registered in her subconscious. Taking the hint that he was happy reading his magazine, she once again closed her eyes and rested her head back, letting random thoughts enter her head. Martin couldn't have been further from her mind right at that moment.

It was nearly eleven hours and a good deal more conversations about hunting later that Fiona found herself exiting the airport with Aaron. They headed over to a waiting taxi and on to their accommodation. She gave the driver the address, and they both sat back to admire the hot and dusty scenery, dotted with wild animals, as they drove for a couple of hours out to the complex. Conversation came easily as they enjoyed each other's company. As they neared their destination, Fiona could see the familiar tall chain link fence that often surrounded the hunting complex, as a way of keeping the animals enclosed and away from poachers. A member of staff stood waiting in the entranceway as the vehicle pulled up and they both got out, Fiona stretching her arms behind her as she did so.

"I've had enough travelling for one day; I hope the bed is reasonably comfortable, though I shouldn't have any difficulty if I had to sleep on a fencepost tonight. I'm done in!"

Aaron helped her with her luggage, and they ventured inside to the small reception area. A gentle breeze was blowing through the traditional windowless wooden building, the thatched roof their protection should it rain.

"Join me for a drink before dinner?" he enquired after they had checked into their respective rooms. "May as well get to know each other a little better if we are going to be staying here for the week."

She couldn't help but like his smile, but also couldn't fault his forwardness, so self-assured. And his dark good looks made him something rather nice to look at, even though he was already spoken for. Still, that didn't stop them from enjoying each other's company before dinner. She thought for a moment, and then said, "Why not? Sounds nice. I'll see you in an hour? Give me time to freshen up and unpack a little."

"Perfect. Until then." He surprised her by taking her hand in his, giving the back of it a light kiss and bowing slightly. She smiled warmly in response, a little amused.

Interesting . . . Maybe that was just his gallant way?

Fiona gathered her bags and headed out down the path towards her chalet to freshen up, wondering about the tall-dark-and-handsome man making himself known to her, being so forward, so friendly. A man she wouldn't mind finding out more about, a man called Aaron Galbraith.

Chapter Six

THAT NIGHT over drinks that turned into dinner, then dinner that turned into nightcaps, Aaron and Fiona shared war stories and conquest re-enactments spanning the eight years or so they'd both been hunting. It seemed Aaron was trying to fill gaps in his collection if only with photographic evidence rather than physical evidence hanging at his place in the Lakes, and he regaled Fiona about the ones that had got away.

"I'd have liked to have been the one to take Cecil the lion rather than the dentist guy, but it wasn't to be—he beat me to it. Though he set off a bit of a shit-storm in the process, I might add." Aaron took another sip of his whiskey, and Fiona picked up the conversation.

"Perhaps not the brightest thing to have done in retrospect. I mean with that particular animal, and all the hoo-ha that went with the licensing of it. The internet went berserk with it. It had a massive effect on his business and personal life, I gather. Glad that one wasn't me. Though that said, it is a life goal of mine to kill a lion."

"I wouldn't have minded, I don't think. I'd have bagged the prize and taken the rap. Not sure about the bow and arrow, though. I prefer a clean shot. More humane, quicker. Don't like to make them suffer."

Fiona nodded her head in agreement. He carried on.

"I don't suppose *my* employer would have been too fond of the publicity either. And you just never know where your photos end up anymore with social media as open as it is. When I first started hunting big game, photos stayed in your camera until you got them developed and hung them on your wall or put them in an album, not like today."

Fiona laughed. "Now you sound old; you didn't use an old Brownie camera, did you?"

"Now you're taking the mickey!" he said, laughing at himself. "No, I did not! And I'm quite happy to post them online, in moderation though. And in any case, I don't always get the trophy. No kill, nothing to show, nothing to take a picture of. And as you know, you might hunt for three days straight and not even see what you are after, never mind shoot it."

Nodding, Fiona said, "I've had a bit of stick in the past but nothing major and it doesn't stop me from wanting to hunt. People just don't understand it, what it feels like to hit your target. The thrill of tracking the animal, getting it in your sights, it's something special, isn't it? I find it quite addictive."

"It is for sure," said Aaron. "It's sport, no different from duck shooting or fox hunting. Helps to keep the population under control too."

She sipped her whiskey. The glass was just about empty. "And my partner couldn't care less either way, so I've nothing to worry about." *Not that he knows I'm even here.*

Fiona stifled a yawn and glanced at her watch; it had been a long day.

"It's getting late, and I'm done in, so I'm going to turn it. Early start tomorrow. Thanks for a lovely evening, Aaron, and if I don't see you in the morning before you head out good luck." She rose and stifled another yawn.

Aaron stood as she did. "And thank you for joining me. It's been fun. And good luck to you tomorrow too. Maybe we can swap stories again tomorrow night if we have a successful day?"

"Sounds good. Let's hope I've something to share."

Unexpectedly, he bent forward and gave Fiona a light peck on the cheek, and she caught his eye and slight smile before she turned to

Chapter Seven

THE HOT AFTERNOON sun shone down brightly as Fiona and her personal hunter crouched down in the undergrowth. They'd been following their tracker for some hours, and this was the first bit of luck they'd had all day. Off in the distance, a buffalo was now in her sights. It was the closest she'd ever been to one in the wild and wanted to watch it a while from the safety of the brush though she was conscious she'd miss her chance if she left it much longer. Her PH nudged her arm and said something in not much more than a whisper, pointing his thin brown finger to the left of the beast up in the distance. That's when she noticed it. Next to the animal they were watching was her young calf, with a lighter tan-coloured coat than its dark-skinned mum. It stuck out in the dusty dry conditions and looked more like a baby cow than a baby buffalo.

"Damn!" she mumbled out loud, knowing full well she couldn't now take the adult beast with her rifle. "Just my damn luck!"

"Shh!" her PH urged, not wanting to spook the animals. The mother raised her head slightly, listening for sounds and not liking what she was picking up. She ambled back towards where they had come from, her calf close by her side for protection. Fiona watched as they both sauntered off away from her and she consoled herself she'd done the right thing by not taking a shot and leaving a calf to fend for itself and almost certainly die. Those were the rules, written or not.

When the two animals were far enough away, Fiona and her guide made their move from hiding in the dry brush and carried on their way, tracking, in search of something else. She'd wanted to do it the old-fashioned way, to track them for hours, and her opportunity with the buffalo had come a lot quicker than she'd expected though not meant to be. But luck was on her side that day because it was only an hour or so later when she again found a target—another buffalo, this time, without its young. And this time, it was going to be hers. Fiona rechecked her surroundings and was happy with her choice. Crouching back in the dirt, well hidden in the long dry scrub, she prepared her rifle and got into position. The beast was not far off. Through the crosshairs, she could see it as clearly as if it was only a few feet away; the animal was unaware it had been discovered, unaware that a shot was lined up ready to go. Fiona didn't waste any time, and when she was confident of a kill shot, she pulled the trigger. The sharp noise was deafening to her ears, echoing around the dusty landscape, forcing other smaller animals to make a quick getaway. Birds flew away from nearby trees.

"Gotcha!" Fiona shouted as the beast went down.

"Good shot, Ms. Gable. Good shot!"

Fiona and her guide emerged from their hiding place and made their way over to the downed animal which was lying in the dust, a small blood pool evident from the shot. It had died instantly. The two hunters were very aware of their surroundings, making sure there were no other animals nearby that could put them both in danger. Satisfied that the dusty area was clear, Fiona asked, "Will you take a photo of the two of us, please?"

The guide took her smartphone as she crouched down and posed beside the huge head of the downed buffalo, rifle in one hand, a big smile plastered across her face. She felt glorious, powerful even, as adrenaline shot rapidly through her veins, giving her the high she so craved. Finally, she had her trophy, and it didn't matter if she didn't get so lucky again on this trip. At least she'd got one, though it was still her lifetime goal to kill a lion. When the photos had been taken, her guide spoke through his radio to alert the ranch they had a carcass to deal with. Fiona wondered how Aaron was doing. Had he fared so well? No doubt she'd find out later tonight at dinner. Brushing the fresh dirt off her clothing, she smiled.

"What a great day! What a trophy!"

"Yes, Ms. Gable. Very well done, though it's getting late. Shall we make our way back now? The carcass will be dealt with for you, and you must be tired after tracking all day." She nodded in agreement, and a yawn came from nowhere. She'd had an excellent day, but as the adrenaline shot slowly subsided, she could feel her body start to crash a little, a long journey yesterday and the excitement of the day catching up with her and was glad of her guide and their Jeep to get them both back to the relative comfort of the complex. First a long, hot shower to get rid of the day's dust, followed by a cold beer, and she'd feel a whole lot better.

Chapter Eight

THE SHOWER HAD DONE her the world of good and her whole being felt much more relaxed, the adrenaline from the kill now well out of her system. Her thoughts wandered off to Aaron as she towel-dried herself in the outdoor shower just off her room, the thatched roof shading her from the late afternoon sun. Had he had a successful day too, added anything to his collection? She'd heard other vehicles returning after she'd woken from her unintended late-afternoon nap, the quick jabber of the locals shouting and laughing to each other in a language she didn't understand. She'd fallen asleep stretched on the small sofa, which wasn't ideal, but the few winks of sleep she'd grabbed had done her good. Her watch said it was close to 5 pm and her stomach told her it needed filling, so she dressed quickly in clean loose khakis and a fresh T-shirt, leaving her long sun-kissed hair to dry itself in the remaining heat. She applied a little lip gloss, marvelled at what a few hours in the sun could do to a person's colour, and then she was ready to find a drink, good food and company.

Everyone rose early and dined early on hunts; that's just the way it was, and since she was hungry anyway, she didn't mind the early routine. As she entered the little bar area, she saw that a few of the others were already enjoying a cold beer. She ordered one for herself and took a long glug from the ice-cold bottle. The golden contents felt good on her dry throat, lubricating it and satisfying her thirst at the same time. She was vaguely aware of someone calling her name. Turning, she faced a smiling Aaron.

"Hello again." He sounded almost seductive, or was she imagining it? With his dark good looks, he certainly was gentle on the eye.

"Hi, Aaron! Nice to see you again. How was your day?"

"Well, no prizes for me today but I did see a lion, and we tracked it for a while so I'm going back out there tomorrow to see if I can't get it then. You?"

"Nearly had two buffalo, but only bagged the one. Had to let the other go because she had her young calf with her. So, yes, I'm pretty pleased with my day."

"Congratulations. Well done. You taking the carcass back with you or just the head?"

"We brought it back here but I'm not sure I'll take it back home, not even the head. God knows where I'd put it in my small house. No country house for me, not like you. Photos will have to do, I suspect." Fiona glanced over the top of her beer bottle and caught his eyes for a second or two longer than was normal. Aaron picked it up.

"Well then, maybe you could ship it to my place and come on over and see it occasionally."

Not quite sure what to say to his invitation, she settled for a light laugh and took another sip of her beer to avoid adding anything further. Though the thought did please her.

Undeterred, Aaron followed up with, "Have dinner with me tonight? You can regale me with every last detail of your day, and I'll lap it all up, jealous it wasn't me."

How could she refuse? And did she even want to refuse? Those dark eyes were dancing.

"Sounds lovely, and of course I'd love to hear about the one that got away, or didn't come anywhere near, as it were." She was flirting with him now, and they both knew it.

"If you're going to be cheeky about it, I might just change my mind!" But he was smiling as he said it and took her elbow to steer her towards a table in the small dining room, further away from the other hunters present. She allowed him to lead her where he wanted her to go and watched as he pulled a chair out for her to sit.

Seems to be a gentleman, so far, she thought.

They chatted easily over a meal of tender zebra, something Fiona had never experienced before, the yellow fat marbling of the meat keeping it tasty and succulent. And it went well with whiskey, the drink of hunters even though there were some spectacular local wines available. As the night wore on and dinner had long been eaten, the dining room emptied out as other guests made their way back to their chalets for an early night and another early start the next day. Fiona and Aaron sat with the remains of yet another whiskey each, Aaron swirling the liquid around in the bottom of his glass, the conversation relaxingly quiet.

"I think it's time I turned in, too," he said finally, taking the last mouthful of the deep golden liquid and setting the empty glass down on the table.

"Me too. It's been a long one, but a good one," and she stood at the same time he did. She felt his hand at the base of her back as he guided her from the dining room towards their chalets, even though she was quite capable of getting herself back unaided. She hadn't had that much to drink. With an alcoholic partner, she'd seen all too closely what too much could do to a person. No thank you.

Slowly they walked and chatted until they came to her room and stopped outside. He wished her goodnight, then leaned in to peck her on the cheek once again. Knowing that was his intention but feeling a little more flirty than normal from the relaxation of the whiskey, she turned at just the right time, so his light kiss caught her on the lips.

"Oh! I'm sorry! I was aiming for your cheek!" he exclaimed.

"I know, but I figured it was my lips you wanted. You were just being a gentleman. So I gave you them." Her smile was pure seduction.

They both fell silent for a moment. She stood staring straight at him, his eyes searching hers for a clue of what to do next. He clearly didn't want to do the wrong thing. It was Fiona who took charge, sensing he liked to be led, someone else making all the decisions. With her back to the door, she found the handle behind her, turned it and pushed the door open, pulling Aaron in with her other hand. Once inside, she kicked the door closed and led a rather surprised but delighted Aaron over to her bed.

"Get undressed."

She'd gone away to have some 'me' time, and while she hunted big game for pleasure by day, nothing was stopping her from hunting at night, either. And Aaron had made it obvious he would have no problem being her 'prey.'

Chapter Nine

SHE'D HAD a great time at the ranch, had done exactly what she'd wanted to do—got her adrenaline hit and had got laid into the bargain, though that hadn't initially been on her agenda. Aaron had proved to be good company for the few days they were together though his tastes in bed were a little off the scale for her liking, for anything long term. And he was married with a family, so there was nothing longer-term on offer there even if they had been a good fit in bed. Fiona idly wondered if his wife knew about his tastes and suspected she probably didn't, assuming he got his particular kicks by other means. As a working pilot, he probably had a woman in every airport town just waiting for his arrival. Those sultry dark looks would be hard to resist, and there would be no shortage of young attendants lining up for him should the need arise.

Though she didn't know it, Fiona was correct in her assumptions. As she waited at Lusaka airport wishing there was a comfy lounge to pass the time in, she thought about the life she was going back to, south of London. And the man she was going back to. One thing Aaron had shown her was how a real man could be when he wasn't out of his head half the time or smoking pot, and she craved a little normalcy if the truth be told. It had been so long she'd almost forgotten there was a different way of living with a man. And Michael.

Well, he was okay, but again he was spoken for, and fun time aside, there wasn't much else to him. She wouldn't be dating him seriously if he had been available anyway, they were using each other on that score, and both knew it.

Thinking back to Martin, she asked herself if it was time to move on, move him out of her house, get rid of the drunk that lay sprawled on her couch by day and snored heavily at her side by night. The problem wasn't so much whether to or not, but more *could* she turf him out in his current state? He had nowhere else to go, but that shouldn't be her problem, and he did have some family somewhere, though they weren't close. One thing she was certain of, though: she wasn't going to be lumbered with him for the rest of her life. She deserved a little more than that, which meant it was only a matter of time.

She folded the magazine she hadn't actually been reading and made her way over to the departure gate. The Emirates flight home was starting to board. Aaron wasn't on the same flight going back; a shame, really. She'd enjoyed the fun they'd shared, but he'd gone back yesterday, a call into work cutting his trip a little shorter but they'd promised to keep in touch and swapped numbers and email addresses. Whether they did or not they both knew was down to Fiona.

A desk attendant scanned her boarding pass, and she made her way to the waiting plane, where a flight attendant showed her to her premium seat. Fiona buckled up in anticipation of take-off and rested her head back to think a while longer, savouring visions of the good-looking Aaron sitting in the seat beside her as he had on the journey out. Moments later they were gone and were replaced by a mixture of images circling in her head—a drunken Martin, a rough Michael and the eclectic Aaron—and none of it gave her any clue as to what she should do going forward. Perhaps none of them should do. That was another option—forget them all and start again. She hoped by the time the plane landed back at Gatwick she'd know what the answer.

As they cruised high up in the sky on a double-decker aircraft, Fiona took advantage of the Wi-Fi onboard and took her smartphone out. Flicking through the great pictures she'd had taken of the trip and choosing the one of her first kill, the buffalo, she loaded it to her social accounts, adding a brief commentary of where she'd been hunting and added the relevant hashtags. She loved using hashtags; it was incredible how far a photograph could go if you used the right one. With a bit of strategy on her part, she could get people all over the world interested in her hobby. The pictures had come out well: she looked sun-kissed, she looked cool in khaki, and most of all, she looked happy. She clicked Share and posted them. She wondered which of her friends and followers would respond to her first. Someone she knew? Or someone far, far away? Aaron dropped into her thoughts again, and a smile crept across her face. *Why not?* She tapped the Facebook app and searched for Aaron Galbraith. While there were a few as you'd expect, it wasn't hard to find the right one. Right there was the profile picture of the man she'd spent the last few days with, smiling back. His distinctive dark hair and good looks made him stand out from the others. The 'add friend' icon stared at her.

"Oh, what the heck. Here goes nothing." Tap. Request sent. "Too late now." He was probably working, so there was no point in waiting for an immediate response. She put her phone back in her bag and picked up the current month's airline magazine from the pocket in front of her. She flicked idly through the pages, looking for something that might grab her interest. A few minutes later, she was completely engrossed in a story about Italy, a glass of red wine in one hand. In her bag, however, her phone screen was lighting up with responses to her posts. And there was a message from Aaron.

It wasn't until she was waiting for her luggage at Gatwick that she pulled her phone out, and then smiled widely at the screen and the long scroll of notifications waiting there. She let her forefinger do the work, skimming the comments quickly. The pleasant ones resonated in her heart; she let the hostile ones fly right over her head. It was just as she expected, but she had noticed that each time she hunted and posted her trophies, the trolls had got progressively nastier. Or was she imagining it? Certainly, some might consider her hobby distasteful, but then she never understood those who enjoyed train spotting or stamp collecting, and no one bothered to shout them out, did they? No.

Her familiar suitcase trundled towards her on the conveyor belt and she yanked it off, pulled the handle up, and wheeled it towards customs. With nothing to declare except for her love of hunting, she sailed quickly through. She had thought hard about bringing her trophy head back but had decided there was no place in her house for it, with or without Martin there.

Martin. What was she going to do about him?

The traffic was heavy on the M25 as she headed towards home, but when was the motorway ever free flowing? They didn't call it England's biggest car park for nothing, but after the long flight, premium economy or not, she was desperate to be in her own place, feet up, with a mug of steaming hot tea. Sitting nose to tail, her thoughts drifted back to Martin again and the problem at hand. She'd texted him from the airport saying she was nearly home, though having posted the pictures from Zambia, he'd likely know she hadn't been to see her mum in Bath all along, and that in itself would mean a blazing row. She noted she didn't much care, and that feeling told her all she needed to know. Martin had to go, and take his negativity and half-empty whiskey bottles with him. And the sooner, the better.

Chapter Ten

OUTSIDE HER HOUSE, she sat in the driver's seat for a moment watching, running her decision through her mind, the little cogs and wheels turning the issue slowly over and over. While she didn't need to turf him out today, she did need to tell him, to give him a couple of days to sort himself out, but he had to go soon, preferably by the end of the week. The curtain twitched. He was watching her from the lounge, and waiting. She was not looking forward to this one bit. She trudged up the front path and opened the front door.

"Hello!" she called out, but it was met with nothing. She dropped her bags in the hallway and walked into the lounge. Martin was sitting on the sofa, his bags packed and on the floor beside his feet. He was steepling his fingers before him, looking down at the floor in thought.

"Hi, Martin. What's going on?" Putting her keys down noisily on the coffee table, she went and sat beside him, the leather crumpling softly under her as she did so.

"You lied, Fiona. And I just can't actually believe where you've been, what you've been doing. I can't get my head around it." He sounded as defeated as ever.

"I didn't think you'd approve. That's why I didn't say anything. I'm sorry for lying to you. It was the only way to avoid a scene."

"So that's okay then, is it? You did it to avoid a scene? What possesses you? What primal need are you trying to fulfil? Help me here, Fiona, because I'm struggling to understand."

"I enjoy it! It's sport, and I love it. What's wrong with doing something you enjoy?"

"There's nothing wrong with doing something you enjoy, but it's barbaric! And everyone it seems has seen the pictures you posted. They've gone viral, let me add. You've become a target yourself now, a celebrity, but for all the wrong reasons." Martin was straining to keep himself under control, spittle gathering at the corners of his mouth. With a slight void in the conversation as they both took a moment, he added, a bit more calmly, "Tell me why, Fiona."

"I've told you, I enjoy it, and it helps with conservation."

"What!" Martin spluttered. "You're kidding me, right? Conservation?" Martin was as angry and upset as she'd ever seen him. With his drinking, they'd had plenty of screaming rows but this was something new.

"Calm down, Martin. There's no need to yell at me," she said levelly. "Look, why don't I make us a drink, and we can talk more calmly about it." Fiona glanced at the bags waiting by his feet. She nodded in their direction.

"Looks like you've already decided what you're doing about it, though. Where you headed?"

"Stopping at a mate's for a couple of nights." His voice was petulant. "On his sofa."

"Why do that? Why not stay here and sort this out?"

"Because you're not the woman I thought you were!" he screamed. "I can't trust you, and I don't want to be around someone who kills for fun! Don't you get that?" He took a deep breath to steady himself. He'd obviously been working himself up to a row for a while and was hell-bent on letting his anger out.

Fiona stayed silent, thinking it a better way to calm the situation. It was at that moment she noticed he was completely sober for a change.

He spoke again, more calmly now. "Look, I didn't want it to burst out like that, but it's true. It's over, Fiona. I'm out of here. I'm sorry."

Fiona watched from her spot on the sofa as he stood and picked up his bags.

"I guess I'll see you around," he said calmly, a bag in each hand, and made his way to the front door. She heard the catch unlock, the door open and then close again. He was gone. She sat back into the soft leather, somewhat dazed. After a few moments in the quiet of her now empty lounge, she smiled to herself.

"Saved me a job," she said out loud.

He'd gone and done the one thing she had been dreading to do herself—he'd dumped her, beaten her to it. If she had known it was only going to take a hunting picture or two for him to leave, she'd have done it sooner. Fiona stretched out her tanned legs a bit further on the sofa, now vacant at last. Good riddance to his miserable drunken ass. She hadn't bothered enquiring which mate he was going to and realised that, actually, she didn't much care. She grabbed the remote control and channel-hopped until she found something mundane to wash over her and make some background noise in her newfound empty house.

Chapter Eleven

SHE HAD ALWAYS ENJOYED her breakfast routine. It was the part of her morning she cherished: just coffee and a bran muffin, quietly sat at the corner table in 'her' café before heading into the clinic. Every morning was the same if she was on duty, and invariably if not. The smell of hot fresh coffee and freshly baked muffins and pastries was simply the best way to start the day, bar none.

She skimmed Facebook, down through the photos of other people's children and cats chasing vacuum cleaners and then stopped dead at an article on a news site, featuring a picture of a dead buffalo, a woman with long blonde hair crouching down beside it, rifle in hand, a grin on her face. It was evident from the picture she'd just shot it and was now posing alongside her trophy. It made Philippa's stomach roll and, judging by the comments from her friends who had seen or shared it, it had had the same effect on them too.

"How could someone do that for sport—take such a big animal's life for no reason than the thrill of killing it?" she muttered, incredulous. "It's not like it's even for food." As a vet and an animal lover, Philippa abhorred such activities and only just agreed with the concept of line fishing, figuring at least you ate what you caught. Out of morbid interest, she clicked on the comments to see what others were saying, the friends of her friends: Would they feel the same way as she did or were they in support?

"Gross! How could you?" said one.

"Get over yourself. It's human nature to kill animals. Where do you think your steak comes from?" said another.

"Bitch! I should shoot you and see how you like the senseless killing. You should be ashamed!"

And on they went, some in support, but the majority against. She clicked through to the whole article to read the story, driven once again by a morbid curiosity. The article reported that the woman, Fiona Gable, lived in South Croydon and recounted her recent trip to Zambia and her hunting hobby—as well as the storm she'd started by sharing the pictures online. Since Ms. Gable had returned, the offending picture had gone viral, as had the news article. The arguments were getting more heated, the comments more poisonous. Philippa wasn't surprised to see the odd cloaked death threat. She sipped her coffee and scrolled on. The picture had been shared by news sites all over the world, and she clicked on a random one.

"Local woman in kill storm," said the headline. She read on.

A local woman shared her experiences online of big game hunting in Zambia, and the post has gone viral. Many of those commenting on the picture of her crouching by the dead buffalo have expressed their disgust for what they term the senseless killing of endangered animals out in the wild, though she's also had support from pro-hunting groups. Their argument is that it's much-needed conservation, to keep the herd numbers in check and allow younger animals to live longer by culling the older ones. The woman who has drawn the attention, Fiona Gable, from Croydon, is unfazed at the 'kill storm' she's created.

"It's sport," says Gable. "I'm entitled to do it, and will continue to do it, and the nonbelievers will find something else to amuse themselves with as this unfairness passes."

Philippa finished the last of her bran muffin and sat back thoughtfully for a moment. The picture had disturbed her, angered her somewhere deep inside, like a heavy ball rocking low in her stomach, a feeling she had felt for the first time just a couple of weeks ago. Then, another animal story had gone viral and disgusted the nation. This time a couple of youths had chopped the ears off a dog as punishment for losing a dog fight, and taken photos of it, posting them for all to see. They'd been prosecuted and been given a measly fine of £900 but no jail time. The nation had been outraged that thugs so cruel could get away without any real punishment. What fairy-tale land had the judge lived in to think that was perfectly okay to let go? If she'd been on the bench, they'd have been sleeping in a cell for a good few years to come. But she wasn't on the bench and could do nothing about it. Her mind returned to Fiona Gable and her buffalo. No one would be sitting this woman in front of a judge for what she'd done, and she'd do it again: she'd already said so. Since hunting big game wasn't an actual crime, she too would go unpunished.

With the vision of severed dogs' ears and a dead buffalo floating queasily in front of her, she grabbed her bag and left the café. Maybe a busy clinic would take her mind off it, or throw up an idea of what she could do to make a difference. She got in her car and drove the few minutes to work, thinking of not much else.

The clinic was in the centre of Rickmansworth, a small town some twenty miles northwest of London. The famous *Black Beauty* movie had been shot here many years ago, though the area was now more built up with modern brick housing. While there were still plenty of green rolling hills, it wasn't quite the same as it had been back then, but not many places were anymore. Progress. And Philippa liked her green hills, having spent several years working in the Yorkshire Dales, in the equally famous countryside, the location of James Herriot and *All Creatures Great and Small*. But it was the Rickmansworth clinic she now called home and had done so for the last two years, hoping to become partner one day. She loved the varied work the clinic handled, everything from vaccinations to casualties from a wildlife park close by, though she herself looked after the domestic animals mainly. She swung the front doors open.

"Morning!" called the receptionist, bright and breezy as always.

"Morning, Shruti," Philippa said as she passed by.

"Nice morning again. I hope we're in for a good summer this year."

Still distracted, Philippa mumbled a barely audible reply and carried on walking towards the staff room out the back. She shoved her things in her locker and pulled on her white consulting coat for clinic. Helen, one of the senior partners of the clinic, entered the room just as she was finished getting ready.

"Oh, Philippa, glad I've caught you. I've got to go out on a call later this morning. The park needs a hand with one of the rhinos, and from the sounds of it, it's not good news. Fancy coming out with me? It'll be a change from cats and dogs, and if I have to do what I think I'll have to do, I'll need someone with me."

"Sounds ominous but yes, love to. What time you going over?"

"Should be around eleven. I've checked your schedule already, and it fits fine."

"Great," said Philippa. "Right, then. I'd better get on with my first patient. See you later." She banged her locker shut and left Helen changing into her scrubs for her own clinic patients.

At eleven, they set off towards the wildlife park in Helen's well-equipped van and chatted about the morning's patients, particularly the cat Philippa had encountered yesterday that had got a blade of grass stuck in the back of its throat and was in again today to have it surgically removed before it caused an infection.

"I reckon I must hold the record for the longest blade removed in the country. It was nearly six inches long and concertinaed up in behind her nose and throat cavity!" Philippa said. If she hadn't seen it with her own eyes, she probably wouldn't have believed it.

"Wow, that's incredible," said Helen, deftly shifting gears. "I think my record is only about two inches, though probably just as annoying to the poor thing. It's bad enough when we get a hair stuck that we can't get out, never mind something like grass folded up and stuck." She flicked her indicator to turn into the wildlife park entrance, and the conversation turned from domestic cats to rhinos.

"I can't say I'm looking forward to this. It's never nice euthanising an animal. And a rhino can be a bit tricky for obvious reasons, which is why I've asked you along." Helen pulled into a staff parking space nearest the relevant enclosure and undid her door. "I'll probably have to use a dart but the main reason I asked you to attend is because the drug I will use to put him to sleep with is so potent to humans, that it has to be administered by more than one person in case the one administering it accidentally scratches or injects themselves with it."

Philippa looked shocked, and Helen laughed lightly. “Don’t look so worried. Etorphine actually comes with its own antidote when you order it as well as the safety warning, so there are no mishaps. And I don't plan on catching myself with the needle so, in theory, you shouldn't be needed.”

Philippa watched Helen grab her vet bag from the back of the van, thinking how different Helen's day was compared to her own small domestic animal patients. “Sounds like it would kill an elephant if needed.”

“Certainly would. Probably designed for it. Anyway, here's John,” said Helen, nodding in the direction of a tall, wiry man dressed in a brown lab-type coat who was approaching them. “He looks after the rhinos.” He and Helen shook hands and then Helen turned to her. “ John, this is Philippa,” she said. “Philippa will assist me this morning.”

John offered his hand and greeted her warmly. “Nice to meet you, Philippa. Shame it's under these circumstances.”

“Yes, it is. It’s never a good time,” Philippa replied. She took Helen’s lead and followed them both to the rhino enclosure where her patient lay isolated in her stall.

“Hello, Nandu,” Helen cooed gently to the large animal, keeping a safe distance. “Are you no better today, then? You poor thing.”

The rhino lay quietly, not moving a muscle.

“She's not moved for some hours now,” said John. “Real miserable. I wasn't sure she'd make it through the night.” The sadness in his voice was heart-wrenching.

Helen stepped into the enclosure now, confident she was safe, and began to make her final observations. Finally, she stood and confirmed what they all knew needed to be done.

“Okay,” she said, letting her breath whoosh slowly out from her lungs. “Philippa, I’m going to need your help. John? Do you want a few moments with Nandu while we get things ready?”

John nodded his head ‘yes,’ and both Helen and Philippa stepped out of the enclosure to give him a moment to say goodbye.

“Okay, we’ll not need the dart. The poor thing is too sick to move. I'll get everything I need ready, and when it comes time to administering the drug, that's when I need you on hand with the antidote—

just in case. You'll know if I scratch myself with it because I'll yell like a mad woman, no doubt, so just jab me in the arm like you would a regular injection."

"Let's hope it won't be needed, then, but I'll be right behind you. Ready?"

"Ready."

John left Nandu and the enclosure, gruffly brushing tears from his face with the back of his hand. Philippa stood silently and watched Helen expertly administer the drug. The large, solid animal drifting away peacefully, her eyes closing for the last time. In just a few moments, she was gone.

Later that evening, as Philippa sat on the sofa thinking about the day she'd had, she knew what she needed to do. And just how to do it.

Chapter Twelve

PHILIPPA SAT on her sofa with her wine and nuts, a ritual she did most evenings though it was only usually one glass of wine and a handful of nuts. Tonight though, she'd pushed the boat out somewhat and was on her second, and feeling very comfortable with it. It was while she was sipping her wine, Ed Sheeran quietly singing in the background, that she reflected back on her day, what she'd seen over breakfast and why it had bothered her so much. But she already knew why that was—her father. It was just over a year ago that he'd been arrested for his involvement in an organised dog-fighting ring down in Kent and had been sent down for his part in it as the referee and general dog-fighting coordinator though he hadn't started or funded the enterprise. No, that had been the brainchild of Mac MacAlister, a man you crossed at your peril and a man who had also been sent down. Both men were still detained though they'd both received criminally light sentences—just eleven months each, which was actually at the steeper end of sentencing for their crimes. Most simply got away with a slap on the wrist and a ban from keeping animals. If you're the kind of person who is involved in such a horrific sport in the first place, you're not likely to abide by that as a penalty. And many don't; it's hardly a deterrent. It was a wonder the police hadn't caught up with her father sooner. After all, he'd been active in the sport for many years, for as long as she could remember, really. When she was growing up, most of her friends took up a paper round or car washing as weekend jobs for pocket money, but not Philippa. Her father had had different ideas about how she should spend her spare time. And that involved doing chores for the operation he refereed. While it paid well compared to her friends' small jobs, she'd abhorred it, but of course had been stuck with it. She guessed, looking back, that her father had paid her well to encourage her to keep her mouth shut. And so she had. Cleaning the dogs' filthy crates out and disposing of their dead bodies into the pit they kept behind the big shed was all her responsibility, and she'd simply got on with it. Her mother sympathised, but that was all. She never had been a strong woman herself and told Philippa she should be pleased she had a job at all, never mind one that paid so well. The money always came in handy. Now, thinking back, she wished she'd been stronger herself, said something as the years rolled by, but it's hard to go up against your father.

Then one day, she had discovered what he'd truly been up to, that he had been involved in it all along. Philippa had never been so ashamed in all her life over what he'd done. She'd never plucked up the courage to talk to him about it, nor visit him in prison, and had no desire to, either. Her mother Daphne had stood by him, still loved him, but Philippa just couldn't act as if nothing had happened. She'd been the apple of his eye all through her childhood, though even with his rough tattooed exterior, he would never have harmed a hair on either her or her mother's head. Being involved in such a sport really didn't ring true with the man who had brought her up and cared for her as a devoted father, attending school plays and generally being a great dad but there you go. Sometimes money rules, and it had for both of them. Perhaps she was a bit to blame herself.

She flipped another cashew into her mouth and chewed thoughtfully. It was about the time the trial had started and the story had been back in the news again that she'd decided to change her name to her mother's maiden name of During. She had been Philippa During ever since, severing her ties with the man she'd grown up with. No one at the clinic knew her background in that respect, and that's the way she was going to keep it. So yes, she knew why the recent cases she'd seen in her newsfeed had offended and affected her so much, the light, almost laughable sentences that both the thugs and her father had received for such grotesque animal cruelty. The more she dwelled on what she'd seen and what she'd experienced through her own family, the more determined she became to do something about it and make a difference all by herself. Having spent the morning at the zoo with Helen, she already had the bones of a plan forming, and she'd work on fleshing the rest out later, over the coming days. If she was going to do this, she had to do it right and not get caught and that meant time and patience spent thinking it through, something she had plenty of, patience particularly.

Ed Sheeran came to an end and the room fell silent, the distant sound of traffic just audible on the main street a couple of rows over, a cat outside her house mewing at the wrong door. It was peaceful: no one to think about, no one to consider and no one else to please. The last of the cashews gone, she scrunched the little cellophane packet up and tossed it towards the coffee table where her empty wine glass sat. She wriggled down the sofa until she was laid out fully and closed her eyes to think a while. If the perpetrators of these crimes weren't going to go to prison, then she'd make it her mission to find them and make them suffer in another, far harsher way.

Chapter Thirteen

FIONA GABLE'S phone pinged for what seemed like the millionth time since she'd landed, and she idly reached for her phone and scanned the screen to see what or who it was calling her out this time, she'd certainly stirred up a hornets' nest. But it was neither of those. It was a friend request, of all things, though she didn't recognise the name or the profile picture of the attractive blonde woman.

"Hmm, who are you?" she muttered and clicked on the woman's profile page to find out more. Scrolling down, she saw they had a handful of friends in common, and figuring they'd probably all met somewhere together at some time or she'd changed her name and hairstyle as women continually do, she clicked 'accept' and thought no more about it.

Her new online friend was Jackie Masters, and accepting her request would turn out to be the single biggest mistake of Fiona's life.

Chapter Fourteen

IT WAS time to make contact. Fiona Gable had accepted her friend request and it was time to get to work. After a good night's sleep, mostly brought on by two glasses of wine rather than her usual one, Philippa had slept like the proverbial baby and felt all the better for it. She'd risen, gone for a brisk walk around the nearby park, showered and was sitting, as always on a weekday, in the café, bran muffin and coffee laid out in front of her. It wasn't quite seven am, and even though it was still early, she relished the thinking time to herself along with the knowledge she was about to strike up a conversation with her first victim. Outwardly she was calm and collected, but inside she was nervous, a bag of butterflies. She knew, however, that this wouldn't last long once she got confident chatting with Fiona—like old friends. She just needed to make a start. Clicking the Messenger app, she tapped out the start of a message:

Hello Fiona! Not sure if you remember me, we went to university together, and I thought I'd say hi after your stint in the news! I'd have never have found you otherwise, so that was a piece of luck. Anyway, keen to catch up so drop me a reply when you've got five. Bye.

She clicked the send icon and off it went into cyberspace. She broke a large piece off her muffin and chewed slowly, savouring the maple syrupy taste she enjoyed so much and watched the early risers call in the café for their own coffee. People-watching was one of her favourite activities: she loved to see whose body language said what, particularly to the person they were with. The one who'd woken in a rush and dashed out the door. The one who was oblivious to others around them, nose buried in their phone. The one who really needed some coaching on interacting politely with other human beings, and so on. From the young to the old and everyone in between, she found something in everyone to ponder about. How the old were so wise and how the young were so invincible. So what did that make her at thirty? A familiar buzz coming from her phone brought her attention back to her own table: a message from Fiona.

Hello back! How are you? Good to see you! And thanks for getting in touch. Yes, it's been a bit of an odd couple of days.

You could say that again, she mused to herself, but tapped out quite a different reply.

I can imagine. How are you holding up? Nothing much changes in my world, so yours is far more exciting right at this moment.

Send. She waited.

I have a thick skin, but even so, I didn't expect a shit-storm quite like this. Who would have thought it?

It'll soon blow over no doubt. Hang in there. There will be someone or something else juicier by the end of the week, you mark my words, and they'll be off following the scent like the bloodhounds they are.

Send.

Well, I hope so. My boss isn't too charmed about it. They found out where I work so they've been hanging around trying to interview me. Michael kicked them out of the way, thank goodness. He's my boss.

Talking of men, are you seeing anyone? Maybe even Adam from university?

Send. She added a winking emoji, knowing there was no Adam—well, not that she knew of for definite, but every university had one, didn't it? She was keen to keep the conversation going and find out as much as she could. Maybe it was Michael?

Who, Adam Barnes? Ew! No chance! But no, I was seeing Martin until this all happened and he up and left. Was about to dump him anyway. It had run its course.

Interesting, she thought. Didn't he like her hunting either?

Not a hunter then?

Send. The little bubbles told her she was typing back and she took a mouthful of her warm, milky coffee.

A deadbeat, if truth be told. It had been on the cards a while. I just hadn't got round to doing anything about it. And you?

Still single myself. Nobody on the horizon. Here's an idea! We should grab a wine or two one night then if we're both free agents, see what we can find. What do you think? Catch up in person.

Send.

Sounds great! Look, I've got to get ready for work now, but I'll message you later eh? Then we can arrange something?

Perfect. Speak later then. Enjoy your day.

Send. Sitting back in her seat and sipping coffee, she mused how easy the conversation between two 'old friends' had been, and even though they hadn't made any firm plans, it wouldn't be hard to follow up. And she had the patience of a saint when she needed to. It was the actual saint part that she was lacking.

Chapter Fifteen

LATER THAT SAME DAY, Philippa sat reading at home and her phone pinged again. It was her new 'buddy' Fiona. She smiled as she saw the message preview on the little screen and swiped to read the rest of it in full, knowing from the preview it was going to be good news. She read it out loud to herself, savouring the words as they came out of her own mouth.

Lovely to chat earlier! What are you doing Friday night? Perhaps we could grab a pizza and a couple of wines?

The plan was going better than she could have hoped it would, so far so good. And so easy. She tapped a reply out.

I'll come to you. Be nice for a change of scenery and from my usual venues. Where's good that's local to you rather than going into town?

Send. She waited, almost able to see Fiona thinking about where to meet nearby to her place. Yes, if she had to she'd go into London itself for the night, but she really wanted to be in Fiona's neighbourhood, see where she lived, the general area, get a feel for it. And she'd need to visit it more than once. When Fiona's reply landed, and she read it, she needn't have worried.

If you're sure? There's a smart new Italian place not far from me, and they have live entertainment on a Friday and Saturday night. I'd better book. 7.30 pm okay?

It was perfect, giving her enough time to finish work, get changed and travel south to Croydon. The plan was taking shape.

Perfect. Give me your address and I'll pick you up.

Send.

Wow! If you're sure, great! Chauffeur driven into the bargain!

Fiona added her address, Cedar Road in South Croydon, and Philippa made a mental note of it to look the street view up on Google when they'd done chatting. It was all falling into place quite nicely.

Perfect. Looking forward to Friday evening then. See you just after sevenish.

The first 'appointment' was scheduled, and Philippa opened her laptop to put Cedar Road into Google maps and take her first snoop around. As the page loaded, there it was: a rather large house sat mid-terrace, its white exterior neatly kept, a tiny garden out front, a covered porch and skylights in the roof, always a telltale sign of created space up there. Not bad for a single woman on her own. It probably had four or five bedrooms from what she could see of it, though she wondered how a single woman could afford such a place. Clicking back to the map view, she saw that East Croydon station was spitting distance away from the house, which gave her somewhere to park when it came to it. Entering the two destinations into Google maps, it was just a seven-minute walk, easily do-able. How much better could it get?

She closed her laptop and sat back in her chair deep in thought, the flesh positively adding to the bones of how it would all work, and when. Dinner out was the first hurdle to get over. What she had planned, the bigger plan, would be another day. The only thing left was to organise the two main items she needed for the job. One of those was easy enough; the other would take a bit more creativity. When she got into the clinic tomorrow, she'd place an order for it and have to do so in Helen's name. As senior partner, she'd be the one with authorisation for ordering such a drug. If anyone asked about the order—and she doubted they would—she'd cite recent usage as the reason. She would also have to be the one to intercept the small parcel when it arrived by courier the following morning. She picked the book up she'd been reading before the message had come through and tried to concentrate on the story again, but her mind was swimming with what she was planning, rolling over and over in her mind like waves coming in on a beach. Lacking the concentration to read, she slapped the book shut and went to make a cup of herbal tea before bedtime.

That night, she dreamed of pinging cellphone towers, random *CSI* episodes and old reruns of *Morse* and *Dexter*. There was no wonder, then, that the following morning she stumbled out of bed with enormous bags under her eyes...

Chapter Sixteen

SHE SPENT the rest of her downtime that week with her head buried in her laptop back on the sofa, empty packets of cashews littering the floor. The only reason she bought the small individual packs was to stop her devouring a big pack in one go once it was opened, but the rational reasoning behind it hadn't worked out quite like that. Philippa blamed it on concentration, the mindless slow chewing helping her in her research, her brain ticking over as she added the small morsels of information she was finding out about the life of Fiona and a few of her close friends. Needing as much information and ammunition as she could for her upcoming dinner date, she was conscious it had to be as realistic as possible, and the simple little added titbit of Adam Barnes had been a nice offering. There was quite a spreadsheet running: Fiona's friends' names were listed along with occupations, locations, previous jobs, a couple of birthdays, pictures of their families and outdoor hobbies, email addresses, telephone numbers. All found on Facebook, LinkedIn or other sites from a simple Google search. You name it, there was ready information a-plenty, and Philippa was soaking it up and learning about the life of this complete stranger. In detail.

The fascinating thing was that, with the knowledge of the university Fiona had attended, she could create a visual of the layout. But

Chapter Seventeen

FRIDAY SURGERY COULDN'T ROLL through quickly enough for Philippa, and when the last patient, a dog with an infected claw, had left with its owner, she grabbed her belongings from her locker and hurtled out the back door to her car and home. It had been an action-packed day and a stressful one, and even though tonight could be equally stressful, particularly if she was found out a fake, it had to be easier than ordering a drug with the intent to kill with it and keep the whole transaction a secret. And such a deadly drug that needed special care, both in purchasing and administering it. She really hated lying, but there was no other way. She'd lain awake a couple of nights ago thinking of the best way to procure it, whether to get it from the supplier they used at the clinic or buy it from the dark web. The first option had to be the easiest and probably the safest: the excuse that she was merely replacing clinic stocks after the euthanisation of Nandu. She wasn't familiar with the dark web, so she had no real idea how to go about finding the drug there. You couldn't really Google 'find the dark web' and expect a response—could you? Well, as it turned out, yes, you could, and Philippa had tried it and was surprised that after typing 'find the dark ...' web had been right up there at the top of the search questions. And that meant she wasn't alone with her inquisitiveness: there were a whole bunch of others in there, though probably for far more sinister reasons.

Can you get more sinister than killing someone?

She'd clicked on a couple of links and tentatively had a look around some of the articles on how to access it, but her nerves had got the better of her. Did the FBI, CIA, MI5 and a whole bunch of other national and international security agencies watch these places? Had a flag gone up somewhere with her name on it? Was someone now inside her computer, watching her keystrokes? Was she now live on someone else's computer on the other side of the world, or deep within MI5? The mention of downloading special TOR software to access 'special places' had made her run for the hills, figuratively speaking, and she had closed the browser down very shortly after landing there. She had, however, briefly glimpsed a diagram of what was available had she spent a bit more time and dug a little further. That alone had intrigued and repulsed her at the same time.

So purchasing the toxic liquid had to be through the 'normal channels,' and as long as she had a plausible story if anyone asked, and nobody checked with Helen, she'd get away with it. She hoped. It would arrive at the clinic early on Monday morning, and Philippa planned to intercept the parcel from the courier and take what she needed then. Dinner tonight with Fiona was about finding out where she could infiltrate her life, finding the best point to enter, physically. She would dish out her just deserts for later—in a spade load.

After the short drive home, she parked in front of her house, opened the front door, and headed upstairs to shower and change. While she enjoyed the warm water jets, she thought about what to wear, though it didn't really matter, as long as it all worked with tight blonde curls—a very different look than her usual short auburn locks. The wig was waiting patiently in her bedroom. It had belonged to a friend who had lost her hair from chemotherapy, and she'd been glad to part with it when the ordeal was over, saying she never wanted to see it again. It was a good one, made from real hair, not a nasty nylon one, and it was about to come in very useful as Philippa brought Jackie Masters to life.

With the spreadsheet she'd started with all the details of their 'joint friends,' she'd also had to create the life of Jackie, because Jackie the vet couldn't live and work in Richmond as she did, couldn't have the same background as she did in case something went wrong. Yes, she'd decided to keep the vet story going, after all: that's what she had gone to university for, and where she knew Fiona from. Plus, it was something she could talk about freely, and everyone liked to hear some of her more pleasant war stories—the pooches with odd complaints, the tortoises with housing problems, the mouse that got stuck in its wheel, and so forth. They'd help to ensure a natural conversation with no mistakes, and probably a light-hearted laugh or two.

She dried herself, applied fresh make-up, and dressed quickly. The bedside clock told her she hadn't long left. She sat for a moment to get her crowning glory just right. The wig, once in place, looked like it belonged to 'Jackie,' and, turning her head from side to side, she marvelled at how natural she looked. It actually did suit her.

"Maybe I should go blonde and get a perm," she said to herself.

But it was time to leave if she was going to get there on time, and preening herself was taking valuable minutes. Hoping the neighbours wouldn't see her curls, she draped a silk scarf with a beautiful poppy print loosely over her head and made her way out to the car. She started the engine and drove away quickly. Only when she was a couple of miles from home did she slip the scarf off and get fully into "Jackie" mode, running through the spreadsheet of vital information in her head. She smiled as she remembered the catchphrase from an old TV talent show that had been popular some years ago. Matthew Kelly, the presenter, would ask each of the contestants who they were going to perform as that night. They always said the same phrase, but would insert the name of the star they'd be impersonating.

"Tonight, Matthew, I'm going to be Jackie Masters!" she said to herself in the mirror. And the audience roared.

Chapter Eighteen

OBVIOUSLY, she knew exactly where Fiona lived. She'd given her the address, after all. Jackie pulled up outside the house on Cedar Road. The clean white UPVC windows looked like a recent addition. It looked bigger than it had on her computer, and even though it was nestled in a row of ten or so other houses, all adjoining, it was still larger than other terraced houses she'd come across. The front curtain moved slightly. Fiona had seen her arrive. Just as she was getting out of her car, she heard the house door close, and a woman's voice shout excitedly in her direction.

"Jackie!" Fiona yelled as she made her way over to the car, arms outstretched in preparation to deliver a big hug. Both women wore big smiles, and Jackie returned the gesture with her open arms, ready to wrap around the other woman in greeting. Could it go any better?

"Fiona! Finally!" After a tight hug, Jackie eventually pulled away and looked Fiona up and down admiringly like a grandma would do a growing grandchild, one she hadn't seen in a while.

"You look amazing. You haven't changed a bit! And I love your hair, but then you always did have beautiful thick hair," Jackie said convincingly. Thick hair would always have been thick hair; it didn't suddenly start being so, and it was a safer bet than mentioning a particular colour. Or body shape. Fiona had a lovely curvy figure now, but back in university, it could have been very different. No point in going there and risking it. Fiona touched her sun-kissed locks and thanked her for the compliment.

"I'm famished," Fiona said, "and I'm looking forward to you filling me in on the years we've missed out of touch!" Did Fiona secretly wonder who Jackie was, where she'd come from and how they knew each other? Or was Jackie just imagining it? If Fiona had no clue, she was hiding it well.

"Likewise! It's been too long. Now, hop in, and tell me where I'm headed to. I'm ravenous too!"

"Not far. A lovely local Italian place. They make the best lasagne."

They chatted easily as Jackie drove. At the restaurant, Jackie followed Fiona inside. The place was small, warm and inviting, lit with tea light candles on each table, the smell of cooked garlic on the air; a few bars of Italian singing drifted out from the kitchen area. A young Italian man greeted them and showed them to their table, his gaze lingering on Jackie for a moment longer than was polite. Fiona nudged Jackie as he retreated and whispered, "I think you've pulled already. His tongue is nearly hanging out like a dog's!"

Jackie turned to see the young man just before he quickly looked away. He busied himself folding napkins to save himself from blushing. She smiled inwardly that he'd taken an interest. Whatever you were doing, it always felt good to be appreciated. Back to the job at hand.

"So what's good?"

"Well, I know it sounds boring, but I never deviate from lasagne, garlic bread and, if I've room, good old tiramisu. Cliché, I know, but it's so damn delicious, I can't bring myself to change." As an afterthought she added, "And Chianti. Love the taste and it's a great-looking bottle, too. Did you know it has its own name, the Chianti bottle? It's called a fiasco. The bottom part, the bit covered in straw, gives it the flat base to stand on. The actual bottle itself has a round bottom, much easier from a glass-blowing perspective, and the straw protects the bottle and wine during transport so that they can pack some bottles upright, and some upside down in between the necks of the upright ones. And the wine is the best too!" She sat back and took a breath.

"Wow, who knew that?" Jackie asked. "Are you a wine connoisseur too?"

"Not really. Just like a nice bottle when I can. Probably stems from working at the hotel, chatting to reps when they visit. It's just stuff I pick up along the way."

"So, tell me all about yourself then, Fiona. Do you enjoy your work?"

They looked up as the waiter placed menus in front of each of them.

"Not too much to tell really," said Fiona, opening her menu. "I work as the accountant at a local hotel just out of town, and I've been there since about forever I think. Or it feels like it. It's a bit mundane to tell you the truth but the boss is very accommodating, and we get on well." Fiona couldn't help but smile a little at her own words and Jackie picked up on the double meaning straight away.

"Ha, ha! I saw that little smirk. Is it serious?"

"No. He's just a bit of fun, and that's my bad for showing it. You weren't meant to see that. I'll have to be more careful," she said. She lowered her voice. "He's spoken for, not mine for the taking. Now let's change the subject before someone overhears and puts two and two together."

Jackie took the cue and, both still smiling, they scanned their menus. Fiona ordered lasagne, and Jackie ordered the same. The first rule of getting on with a new acquaintance was to mirror what they do. So Jackie did just that without being obvious about it: pulling a piece of garlic bread off the loaf after Fiona had taken hers, sipping her wine after Fiona sipped hers. The whole evening was comfortable, and the conversation flowed naturally, with no mention of any geeky people either of them might remember from university, or places they might have hung out. Jackie had everything under control, filing all the important details away on the spreadsheet in her mind, and by the time they'd finished their meal, she was ready for the drive back home.

As they waited for their bills, Fiona's phone buzzed with a text message. As she picked it up, Jackie could see the words illuminated on the small screen along with the little green icon, but wasn't close enough to be able to read it.

"Don't mind me," she told Fiona. "Answer it if you want to."

"If you don't mind? I'll just be a moment." Fiona tapped the screen and quickly replied to the text. "Right. That's that sorted. Let's get on our way. You've got a bit of a drive yet."

"That's okay. It's been really great seeing you again, Fiona. Let's not lose contact again, now we've found each other."

The two women hugged and headed for the car in the cooling night air.

After dropping Fiona off, Jackie drove to the train station nearby and sat for a few minutes, just watching and waiting, for nothing in particular. There were hardly any vehicles in the car park late on a Friday night, and she sat in silence, thinking about what she'd learned about Fiona and her life. And the bonus tidbit that her phone didn't have a passcode on it.

"Silly woman," she said, chuckling. She started the engine, pulled out of the empty car park and headed home, smiling the whole quiet way.

Chapter Nineteen

IT HAD BEEN A RESOUNDING SUCCESS. Fiona had been easy to talk to and keep on track to areas Jackie knew about, and staying with 'vet' as her occupation had turned out to be very safe ground—as she'd expected. Before they'd parted company for the night, they'd arranged to keep in touch online and organise another get-together, probably chat over coffee one day soon—though for Jackie, it couldn't come soon enough. Why drag it on much longer? She had to strike while the iron was hot, while the world still remembered what she'd been so notoriously famous for only a few days ago. No, she couldn't wait much longer. *Wouldn't*: she had to act soon. Her plan was to contact Fiona and set up a coffee date with the excuse she needed to talk to her about something somewhat personal that really couldn't wait, and arrange to meet her at her home on Cedar Road late morning. The best day to do that was the quietest, Sunday, today. Dropping by so early on a Sunday meant the streets would be quiet, the station car park would be quiet, and that meant a lot less prying eyes if she was seen entering or leaving.

Digging out her phone, she prepared her message. The plan had rolled around her head for long enough now, and it was time to start, put it in to action.

Hey, can I talk to you today? I need some advice with something, and I think you may be able to help.

Send.

Sounds ominous but yes! You want to meet up?

If we could, I'll drive over to you again, I'm headed that way anyway later today. 10 am be okay for you?

Send.

Yes, then we could go and get a bite afterward perhaps? Great local café around the corner.

Sounds perfect! Thanks. I'll see you later on.

Send.

It was set; there was no going back. Jackie would soon find out the answer to her own question: 'What is an acceptable age to kill your first victim?'

Chapter Twenty

PRESENT DAY

The smell of delicious hot greasy chips from a chip shop nearby filled her nose and reminded her that her stomach was now running on empty. She hadn't expected it to revolt in such a way but at the first sign it showed of doing so, she'd been prepared. Which reminded her: she was still carrying her stomach contents in her bag. Scanning her surroundings for a rubbish bin, she spotted one right outside the chip shop. A thought came to her.

"Why not? Let's have a treat after that," she mumbled, and crossed the road towards the steamed-up windows, the smell of hot chips getting stronger as she approached. Reaching into her shopping bag, she removed the plastic one with its wet contents and dropped it in the bin outside.

"Some tramp is going to get a nasty surprise if they open that one," she mused, and headed inside to wait her turn in the short queue. It was still early lunchtime.

"What can I get you, love?" The man at the counter wore a white coat, batter splashes evident down the front, splodges of grease adding to them. His name tag said "Edward."

"A portion of chips, unwrapped," she ordered. "And I'll grab a can of Coke too, please."

"Coming right up."

She stood and watched as Edward filled a polystyrene tray with hot chips and stuck a wooden fork into a fat chip on top, then placed the tray in front of her on the counter top. She helped herself to salt and vinegar that was secured with a piece of string to stop people wandering off with the two containers.

What was the world coming to when you had to secure a pot of salt? Where exactly would you take it?

"Here's your Coke, love. Enjoy your chips, and your day."

"Thanks, I will. And you," she said, and left to eat her chips outside perched on the low brick wall that ran along the front. As she ate, she glanced at the rubbish bin where she'd just dropped the plastic bag and thought how unfortunate it would be for someone to delve in thinking it might be food. Eating her hot vinegary chips in silence, she came up with a plan to save some poor soul the disgust. She headed back inside to get some more, chewing as she went.

"Can I get another portion wrapped to go, please?"

"Of course you can, love. You extra hungry today?"

"Must be."

Salt and vinegar?"

"Please." She took a long slurp of her Coke as she waited for Edward to wrap the second portion up and hand them over.

"Here you go," he said, handing them over. She took the warm parcel from him and headed out the door back to her spot on the wall where she settled back down to finish her chips. She sat there for a few minutes eating, and sipping from the can of Coke, watching the world go by and wondering what each person had been up to during their morning, suspecting she was the only one among them who had just killed someone. Though she couldn't be positive—how could she know? Still, it amused her. The sugar on top of the hot food filled the void in her empty stomach perfectly and gave her a much-needed boost after the morning's stressful start, and she thought back on what she'd just done.

"Had to be done," she said under her breath, screwing the now-finished paper and chip tray up ready for the bin. Feeling revived, she walked back over to the rubbish bin, tossed her can and wrapper in, and then laid the parcel of hot chips on top. That way, she figured, any tramp that came along looking for food wouldn't have to dig down far, and would almost certainly not get down to the bag of mess she'd deposited earlier. She smiled at her thoughtfulness.

"Best be getting back," she mused, and set off in the direction of her parked car, which she'd left at the train station just up the road. She'd debated whether to drive in closer or not, whether she'd need a quick getaway perhaps, but had decided the wig would be enough disguise. A short bus trip or a walk back to the station would make her less obvious; she'd blend in better. And no one would suspect a killer would take the bus, would they? In any case, the station was only a couple of miles away; the exercise and fresh air would do her good. Besides, she still had one more part of the job to do.

Chapter Twenty-One

THE WALK back to her car had done her good, the fresh air and a belly full of hot chips and sugary Coke spurring her mind on with her mission. Unlocking her car, she slid into the driver's seat and dug her first victim's phone out of her bag. Double-checking that the location settings were still turned to 'off,' she tapped her victim's social accounts one by one and posted the images she'd taken earlier. The photos, even to her, looked pretty grotesque, she had to admit. With each post, she tapped out a short message that read, "Now I'm the trophy. How ironic is that?"

After she'd posted the same message to all Fiona's accounts, she sat back to relish the moment. It didn't take long for the screen to start lighting up as people responded to her very first post, of her very first victim. What do you say exactly when you find a post like that in your newsfeed?

"Great horror make-up, Fiona! Where'd you get that done?" asked one friend.

"Gross!" said another.

"Is that real? asked another.

"That's not funny, Fi. I'm surprised at you!" said another.

"Looks real to me ...oh god I hope it's not ...."

And on the comments went. As more and more friends saw the

image, the conversation started to take a turn for the worse as they realised perhaps it wasn't a fake, that Fiona Gable really was in trouble.

A bit more than trouble, I'd say from that picture.

"I bet this goes viral before the day is out. Heck, it could even make the evening news, then we'd both be famous, though they won't know it's me," she said out loud in the car. "Now, do I ditch the phone or keep it? I'd love to see how this pans out but it's a bit risky." Deep down she knew the answer.

"Just to be extra safe..." She went back into settings and disabled 'find my phone' then she popped the little tray along the side of the phone and took the SIM card out.

"That should take care of things, but just to make doubly sure...." Taking the bottom of her shirt, she wiped the device clean of any prints. Double-checking her surroundings that there was no one around, she opened the car door and dropped the phone onto the tarmac—hard. The screen shattered into a crazy paving pattern instantly, with some sharp shards coming loose. She swung her leg out of the car and dug the heel of her right foot into it, making the whole thing split open. Glancing down at her handiwork, she was satisfied that the pieces that were left were damaged beyond recognition or repair. The phone was useless. Job done. Any pinging towers would be close enough to think the photos had been uploaded from Cedar Road, from Fiona's home, as you'd expect.

Now the whole world would know what might happen when you go big game hunting for sport and a person takes offence—you could end up being someone's trophy yourself.

Getting back into the car, she pressed the ignition button and pulled out of the station car park headed south, towards home. About two miles further down the road, she let the SIM card blow away through her open window. The last of the deadly deed was finally done. While she hadn't spent any time pondering what might happen next, the thought was hovering somewhere in the back of her head. She was almost afraid to go there, to think properly about her future. Had she just ruined it? Perhaps she needed another distraction for the afternoon, or a night out, even, keep her from thinking about it too much, but the overwhelming exhaustion that had started to kick in after the

Chapter Twenty-Two

"So what you doing about it, then? You can't just leave it." Jack was talking to Amanda as she drove them both back from interviewing a witness in a hit and run.

"I don't know. We seem to have reached a bit of a stalemate. I want to get married, and she's happy as we are, doesn't see the need to change anything." Jack twiddled the left side of his moustache, something that annoyed the hell out of Amanda, but she also knew it signified he was deep in thought. She'd yet to see him twiddle both sides at once—could he think that deeply? She smiled at the idea of both hands twiddling away thoughtfully in the coarse hair, his lips twitching a little as he did so.

"What's so funny? What are you smiling at now?"

"Oh, I was just thinking about you, actually, you and your little foibles."

"Eh? I don't have any foibles. Do I?"

Smiling more, Amanda filled him in. "Oh yes, you do. But they could be worse, like picking your nose or something gross." She flicked her indicator to turn right off Purley Way and into McDonald's for lunch, laughing lightly at his screwed-up face.

"So what are they then, these foibles?" He was intrigued.

"Well, your moustache-twiddling for one, when you're deep in thought, and you speak with your mouth full quite often too." She pulled into the drive-through lane and placed her order through the open window. Turning to Jack, who was still thinking about what she'd just said, she asked, "What are you ordering, Jack?"

"Big Mac meal, Diet Coke, please," he yelled from the passenger seat into the intercom, leaning over Amanda as he did so. "And an apple pie," he added in afterthought. Amanda pulled forward to the next window and paid, collected their food and pulled into one of the nearby parking spaces to eat. Unwrapping the paper bag, Amanda sniffed in the enticing aroma of hot burgers and chips.

"I'm starved." She took her burger out of its wrapper and sank her teeth into it, melting cheese and half a slice of pickle dropping onto the napkin on her lap. She picked it up and stuffed it into her mouth before the grease soaked through. Jack took the opportunity.

"Talk about me and my food, can you get any more in while you're at it?"

Amanda was tempted to smile or say something, but after accusing Jack of talking with his mouth full, she wasn't going to be a hypocrite. And her mouth really was full. She shook her head 'no' in reply. When she'd finally chewed the first full mouthful and swallowed it down, she said, "I got too hungry." She grinned. "I'm not usually such a messy eater. Sorry." She took a smaller bite and chewed it, a bit more ladylike and a little less navvy-like. "Haven't even had a biscuit with my coffee this morning, so I'm running on empty." She took a fry and concertinaed it into her mouth, followed straight after by another one.

Jack watched in amazement but didn't say anything further, taking a bite from his own burger and chewing thoughtfully while he watched her. "I reckon time will tell." He went back to the conversation they'd been having before they had pulled in to order lunch. "You two are strong and steady. You'll not let this bother you. And personally, knowing Ruth as much as I do, and knowing how much she loves you, she'll cave." Amanda turned to him and stopped mid-chew. He was smiling knowingly at her, his kind eyes sparkling in mischief then serious and wise like her grandfather's. Their eyes connected and she carried on eating. When her mouth was empty, she said quietly, "You're a wise owl, aren't you? And there's another of your foibles: using surnames rather than first names."

"I didn't call her by her surname. I called her Ruth."

"You did then, but not at work you don't."

"I only do it at work, to colleagues. I'd never call Ruth 'McGregor.' That would be rude. But what's wrong with using surnames at work?"

Amanda shook her head in mild exasperation at him. She knew Ruth would probably cave too, hoped in fact, but not because of pressure: because she wanted to, really, really wanted to. Amanda slipped another fry in between her partly opened lips and nibbled it in. The radio crackled with news of an incident nearby, and they both looked at each other.

"Damn!" Amanda said.

Jack got on the radio and replied back to the controller that they were both on their way. Amanda thrust her half-eaten lunch onto his lap, started the engine and pulled back out onto Purley Way, heading towards an address on Cedar Road.

"That doesn't sound good."

"No, it doesn't."

Less than ten minutes later they pulled up outside the address, the exact house marked easily by the flashing blue and reds of other squad cars. Crime scene tape was already in place around the front of the property, a uniformed man at the front door. Jack was out of the car and up the short front path first, Amanda on his heels.

"Straight down the hall and through to the lounge, sir," said the uniformed officer. Amanda nodded their thanks, and they made their way inside. The house was quite large for a mid-terraced house in this area of London. Houses like this were more commonly known as 'two up and two down,' and many had built extensions on the back to make way for a proper kitchen and inside toilet, though there were probably a few left that still had the loo down the bottom of the garden. This one was different, though, one of the bigger ones, and from the furnishings and the deco, it was obvious the owner had a little money. Jack was immediately quiet and deep in thought, taking in his surroundings, sights as well as smells. Lying on the floor was a young woman. Her throat had been slit. Nobody spoke for a couple of minutes. It was Jack who eventually broke the silence.

"What you thinking then, Lacey?"

"Well, it's obvious her throat has been cut, but where's all the blood? Yes, there's a couple of towels, but they're hardly drenched in it, are they? It doesn't look like she's been moved—no drag marks—and there is blood here, so she was killed here rather than, say, in another room or off the premises. But it's all very tidy too. No sign of a struggle." She stepped over the woman's body and looked out of the window and on to the road out front. "And no forced entry, so she let the perpetrator in voluntarily. Maybe knew them?"

Jack turned to another uniformed officer who had stepped into the room. "Who found her, Sergeant?"

"We got a call from a friend who said she'd seen a picture of her in this state, posted in her social newsfeed. So we came out to check on things, and this is what we found. Reported by Teresa Smith, an old school friend she kept in touch with," he said, consulting his notepad. "The victim's name is Fiona Gable, thirty years old, works as a bookkeeper at a local hotel. Single, though not long out of a relationship according to Ms. Smith—a Martin York. Seems they split up just a few days ago."

Jack took it all in. "Thank you, Sergeant."

"It's odd to have posted the picture online, though. A bit risky, I'd have thought," Amanda said to Jack. "Any sign of her mobile, Sergeant? I would assume it was posted by mobile, but you never know."

"No place obvious, no. The scene is just as we found it—nothing touched, and the crime scene techs are on their way, along with Dr. Mitchell." He was referring to the local pathologist, Faye Mitchell.

"I guess forensics will know more when they've done their thing," she said, scanning the room again. There were photos in frames of what an onlooker would assume were her family in various poses, a few knick-knacks dotted about, but in general, the room was quite sparse other than a few nice furnishings in neutral colours. While it looked stylish, the room didn't strike Amanda as particularly feminine for a woman living on her own. She wandered off through the rest of the property, looking in at each room as she went. When she got to the bathroom and poked her head around the door, she could tell this was where the victim had liked to spend time. The bathroom was decked out with beautiful and expensive-looking white fixtures and fittings, with an array of luxury lotions and potions on gleaming glass shelving. In the far corner, a pile of large white fluffy towels stood on a small wooden bench surface. As Amanda flicked the light switch on with her latex-covered finger, little relaxing swirls drifted from the light fitting, almost like a disco ball from the 80s but far nicer and more soothing.

"Wow," she said to herself as she watched the dots of light float around the wall and ceiling. "Never seen one of those before. How therapeutic." The whole room shouted *luxury*, someone's little paradise, a place they spent time in and spent money on. She switched the light off and headed back to the lounge and Jack. It was when she looked at the body again, laid on the floor, that she realised something.

"Jack? If someone was coming here to commit murder in such a grisly fashion, why would they a) use a towel to soak up the blood and b) not use one from the bathroom? Surely they wouldn't bring their own, would they? Too bulky."

"How do you know these aren't from the bathroom, Lacey?"

"Because that's one of the nicest bathrooms I've ever seen and contains the whitest, fluffiest towels money could buy."

Chapter Twenty-Three

"WELL, I see what you mean about not been killed by her throat being slit, Jack. There's not enough blood on the floor." Dr. Faye Mitchell bent down closer to look at the body in more detail. "Rigor has set in, so she's been here a while, but I'll know more when I've done her core temperature. It's pretty warm in here anyway, and from my first impressions only, I'd say she died sometime earlier today—though don't quote me on that until I can confirm it. The puzzling thing, though, is the lack of blood. I can only assume she died some other way and her throat was slit after the fact. We'll see later." Faye stood up to talk to her team and give instructions. The photographer snapped the scene in short, crisp clicks as other technicians milled around observing.

"Right," said Jack. "In the meantime, I'll leave you in peace and speak to the woman who called it in. If you find a mobile on her, I'd love to know ASAP because we are assuming the photo was posted from her phone but I've no evidence to that as yet. Just let me know if you find it."

"Will do, Jack. I should be here a while, then we'll get her body moved to the mortuary for a more thorough exam. I'll be able to tell you more about how she died then, I suspect, and the toxicology report may show something."

Jack glanced at his wristwatch, an antique from his father or his father before him; he didn't know for sure. "Right, I'll be off then. Speak to you later. I'll be on my mobile."

Faye nodded at him without turning away from the body in front of her. She had noticed the smooth edge of the slit, and it puzzled her. Most slit throats were the handiwork of a very sharp domestic knife blade, but this wound was created by something more akin to a hunting knife, something extremely sharp: it was too neat. She called to Jack as he was going through the lounge door. "Jack, I suspect it's not a regular bladed household knife. It's something far sharper. Let me know if it turns up during your enquiries, would you?"

"Will do," he hollered back, and went back outside to Amanda who was talking to someone on her mobile phone further down the path. He waited for her to hang up before he spoke.

"Where are we up to, Lacey?"

"Door-to-door has started, and I've requested CCTV footage of this street and the surrounding ones, though by looking at the street lamps, there are only a couple evident—if they're even working." She pointed to the two that were visible. "I've got teams going through bins looking for a possible murder weapon, and as the rubbish collection isn't due for a couple of days, there's a fair bit to go through, though we might get lucky. What about you?"

"I'm off to talk to the woman who called after seeing the photo online, then I'll get the computer forensics team to find out more about where the image was posted from. See if we can tell where it was loaded up exactly. I'm still favouring her phone at this point. Most folks don't have a passcode so it would have been pretty easy to snap it and load it from here. And we'll see activity from the cell towers if there was any."

"Slitting a throat and posting the picture like that is a very personal thing to do. I'm wondering what the reason is. There has to be a reason. I can't see this being a home invasion gone wrong. It's too tidy. There's something else behind this."

Jack mumbled 'Perhaps' as he made his way past her and opened his car door to get in. "You'll get a lift back with uniform?" he enquired.

"Yes, will do. See you later." Amanda watched as he fastened his seatbelt over his double-breasted suit jacket, wondering why he didn't take it off. It was a warm, sunny early summer's day, but Jack was a creature of habit. She smiled as she turned to go back inside, an officer lifting the crime scene tape for her to slip under. Back inside, she took another scout around to see if she'd missed anything the first time, maybe something out of place or something the killer may have dropped, even the smallest fragment. But there was nothing of note to her eyes. It seemed like the killer had struck and left, leaving no obvious clues in their wake. Her phone rang.

"Amanda Lacey here."

"Amanda, it's Sergeant Phillip Reynolds, one of the team checking the nearby rubbish bins."

"Yes? Have you found something?"

"No, not exactly, but we have found something a little out of the usual. A bag of vomit in the bin outside the chippy. Should we leave it or bring it in? Only the reason I ask is that if you were puking in the street, you wouldn't bag it, so it seems a little odd to me."

"Yes, I suppose it is, though on the surface I can't see how it might fit in. Bring it in anyway, and I'll give it to the forensic team to take back with the victim. Though I do know there's no DNA in stomach contents, funnily enough: stomach acid destroys it. Don't ask me how I know."

"Eh? Right you are. On my way."

Amanda finished the call and slipped her phone back into her trouser pocket, thinking about why someone would put a bag of vomit into a rubbish bin. Nothing sprang to mind.

Chapter Twenty-Four

THE HOT, steamy bath had felt wonderful, and she felt her shoulders relax as she sat down on the soft sofa in her robe, curling her legs up underneath herself. The clock on the wall in the lounge said she'd been soaking for over an hour. An hour well spent, and it had given her the time to think in peace, something she had initially been afraid of doing. But she felt surprisingly calm, the task complete, and felt no remorse at all. Being on a mission was different than being a stone-cold killer: it was something she *must* do, not something of choice and certainly not for pleasure like the real psychos in the world, the likes of Fred and Rosemary West or Peter Sutcliffe. In the hours since her first kill, she'd not looked at her own newsfeeds or the television or turned on the radio, choosing to find out what was happening only when she'd fully downloaded her actions of the day to herself, in the sanctuary of her hot bath, the enormity of her downright irregular activities settled.

She got up to pour herself a third glass of red, grabbed another small packet of her endless supply of cashews from the kitchen cupboard and took them both back into the lounge. She sat up straight on the sofa, pulled her laptop towards her, rested it on her thighs and went straight to her newsfeed. Surely the police would have been notified by now, and techs in white paper suits would be buzzing around the crime scene like bluebottle flies round rotten eggs. The first post she saw of the incident was from a news channel. The headline read, "Death selfie in own newsfeed." She clicked the link and read the short article, tearing into the individual packet of nuts and popping cashews into her mouth one after the other as she read.

"Well, I guess that's me they are referring to as a killer, though I would say *killer* is a bit harsh. Not a killer per se; more of a missionary." She scrolled further on and read the other comments from her friends who had shared similar articles on the subject of her activities earlier, though of course they wouldn't know it was her. It felt odd to have the secret over them. And what a whopper it was. Talking out loud to herself helped her sort through what she'd done, to process it.

"From the articles, it doesn't look like the police are saying much at the moment, which is good. I wonder how much they know? Guess I'll find out soon enough if they come sniffing at my door. Though why would they?" Picking cashews out of her teeth with her tongue, she took a large mouthful of wine and gently swilled it around the inside of her mouth, holding the liquid in place without swallowing, savouring it there while she thought. She found Fiona's profile page and looked at the posts her friends had tagged her in. Only then did she finally swallow.

While the actual picture was no longer staring out at her, there were plenty of condolence messages and platitudes to each other about being strong and surviving such a terrible time.

"Tell that to the buffalo *she* killed," she muttered. "Who's being strong for *it*?" But her job here was almost over and it had been a fruitful one, though she expected there was much more work to be done yet.

She was about to shut the laptop and wrap up for the night when a picture of a man in Fiona's friend list caught her eye. He was posed beside the carcass of an African leopard, looking pleased with himself, rifle in hand, broad smile stretched across his face like killing this magnificent animal was the most natural thing in the world to have done. The animal's glorious tawny coat was patterned with black rosettes, its head and belly spotted with solid black. It truly was a magnificent beast, though it would have looked even more magnificent prowling in the sunshine in its natural African habitat—alive. She clicked on the man's profile to see more about him, and wasn't surprised when she found dozens of pictures in the same vein. Her heart started to vibrate in her chest, simmering rage building at the discovery of yet another human being with the same vile habit of hunting for pleasure. Moisture gathered on the back of her neck, heat building inside as her pulse quickened, and it was all she could do not to scream her frustration out loud.

"Another selfish prat!" she thought.

She fought to get herself back into calm control by focusing on her breathing, slowly walking up and down the room for a couple of minutes, biting at a perfectly good fingernail while she thought about what to do with her discovery. Then realisation hit. It was too much of an opportunity to pass up. She'd successfully stopped the first one hunting ever again; there was no reason why she couldn't stop this one either. Thinking quickly, she knew what she had to do. But she couldn't operate under the name Jackie Masters again. She had to create another persona, and one that looked quite different from either of her current identities. It was too risky to stay as "Jackie" for any longer: the police were going to be all over Fiona's accounts during the investigation, and she just couldn't risk them putting two and two together. Eventually they would realise hers was a fake account with a mixture of Fiona's real friends and some fake ones behind it. What good luck that one of Fiona's other friends had the same vile hobby. It was time to move on, and quickly.

"Time to delete Jackie and try my luck as someone else," she said out loud, determinedly. Even to herself, she sounded like she was at a blackjack table and thinking of switching games. Drinking back the remains of her fourth glass of wine, she screwed up yet another empty cashew packet and tossed it onto the coffee table. "But I did rather like the name Jackie. Shame, really." She sat pondering, fingers lightly tapping her chin. Everything had to be thought through to the last detail again, and while she already had done so for her first victim, she needed to be doubly sure for the next. With each one, there was more risk of making a mistake. Mistakes could get her caught, and that wasn't an option. She couldn't believe she'd settled on her second victim so soon. After all, it was only a few hours ago she was hunched over and puking into a plastic bag and fleeing a crime scene involving a very dead woman. Whom she'd killed. Her finger paused over Jackie's 'delete account' button for a moment. Once done, it couldn't be undone, so she had to be sure.

Click. The mouse pointer icon stared at her. She confirmed delete with a nervous 'yes.' Jackie Masters and all that went with her online profile was now deleted.

"Right, then. Brunette, here I come," she said with renewed vigour. Pulling up an image site, she picked a woman around her age and size with long straight brown hair and saved a copy of it to her desktop. She created a new profile login and then busied herself setting up another identity using the fake picture. She entered some basic details of occupation, age, and location and then began sending friend requests to several of her new target's friends, many of whom were males. She was banking on them not looking through her past posts too much before they accepted her request because there wasn't a great deal to see. Since friends of friends had worked well last time, it made sense to try this tactic again. Besides, her new persona looked very appealing, hot even. She figured the men would accept her friend request in an instant, and that the women would find her nonthreatening and more natural-looking persona more so and press 'accept' as well. Then she'd be at liberty to get into their lives.

By the end of the evening, her profile was filled out fully and even though she didn't have many 'friends' yet, she had a few, and more importantly the right ones—some friends of her intended prey. She found the original man's profile again, sent her friend request and hoped the picture of 'her' and all of their mutual friends would do the trick.

The sexy Frankie Green was about to make her entrance.

Chapter Twenty-Five

SHE WOKE with the headache of her life. It had all gone according to plan: her first victim was dead, yet Philippa didn't feel right, not as she expected, anyway. Though what exactly would "right" feel like for an unseasoned murderer? And her head was throbbing like an idling motorbike. On it went, and she rubbed her temples to try and ease the pain, squeezing her eyes tightly closed. She'd spent most of the night tossing and turning, going through the events as they had happened: the images of Fiona's house, her body as she lay dying on the floor, the blood-soaked towels, her own upset stomach. All of it. She hadn't enjoyed the feeling of taking a life, but she hadn't thought she'd feel so bad about it afterwards either, not like she did now. And the wine probably hadn't helped.

Lying under her duvet, with the morning sun hidden behind depressing grey clouds, she felt rough, remorseful even, and somewhat depressed—she was in a real funk. Lifting her head off the pillow, it felt like a dead weight, like someone had filled it full of stones while she'd slept. She flopped back down with a loud groan. The clock told her she hadn't got long before she needed to leave, but she couldn't muster the energy to get up and do so. Rolling over onto her side, her back to the clock and the window, she closed her eyes again and let sleep take her back to a welcome place.

More than two hours later, she was awakened by a phone ringing. Thinking it was part of her dream, she ignored it but it persisted, and at last she realised it was her mobile, ringing and vibrating on the bedside cabinet. As she put her arm out to get it, the noise stopped, but the screen said three missed calls—all from work.

"Damn!" she exclaimed. The clock on her phone read nine thirty; she should have been at work well over an hour ago. Sitting up in bed, she prepared to swing her legs out when it all came flooding back to her—just exactly what she'd done. She pressed her hand against her forehead; the volley of pain in her head was extreme. There was a familiar roll in her stomach and she realised she'd probably got a migraine.

"Oh, hell. That hurts,' she said, wincing, and reached for her phone with her other hand. Even if she went in later, she still needed to call the clinic and let them know, and apologise for not being there now. She hit the missed call number. Shruti answered on the fourth ring.

"Shruti, it's me, Philippa."

"Are you okay? You sound terrible."

Philippa made her 'throbbing head' excuses, and after a quick 'Goodbye. I hope you feel better' from Shruti, she hung up and flopped back down, groaning and sighing at the same time, then pulled the duvet up over her head to block the world out.

She felt bad for shirking her responsibilities and taking the day off work. Yes, she had a headache, but that was stress and wine induced, and only she knew why, coupled with what had turned into an anxious night and lack of sleep. . What the hell had she started?

Chapter Twenty-Six

"So what are you saying then, Doc? She was dead before her throat was slit?" Jack asked incredulously. They were all back in the lab, the autopsy complete, Fiona Gable's body lying covered with a sheet on a stainless-steel trolley.

"That's exactly what I'm saying, Jack. The etorphine stopped her heart, which was why there wasn't much blood at the scene. Her throat was definitely cut after the fact."

"So the throat being slit has got to be symbolic to something, then. Otherwise, why bother?" Amanda was deep in thought as she listened to Faye talk through her findings.

"Tell me more about the drug, then," said Jack. "What's it used for?"

"It's primarily used to knock out big animals, like elephants, for instance, and incredibly lethal, as you can imagine, if it's going to do that job properly. You don't need much to kill a human. Did you ever see the American TV show, *Dexter*?"

"Can't say that I have. Why?"

"Well, it was his weapon of choice, though the show didn't portray it as realistically as they might have. He used to stab people in the neck with a syringe full, which really would have killed a herd of elephants, and his victims would lie unconscious for a while. Not in the case of Fiona Gable. A few drops would have been enough to stop her heart permanently. I would say the drug was to incapacitate her while her throat was cut."

"I'm still struggling with why someone would do that. There has to be a particular reason, and not just to kill the victim," Amanda said.

Jack was twiddling the left side of his moustache. "Then we need to find that reason. And we need to keep any mention of this drug away from the press. We also need to find out how the perpetrator got hold of the drug. Who would have access to it, Doc?"

"Vets primarily. And anyone familiar with the dark web, of course. If you know what you're looking for, you can find just about anything online these days. Any ordinary person could be the killer."

"Then we should start with vets, see who uses it and their stock levels, whether anyone has reported any missing." Jack was taking notes in his little book. "I bet there are thousands to go through."

Amanda was searching online with her phone as he spoke. "Only about twenty-five thousand registered in the UK," she announced. "Need to narrow that down somewhat. I'll get a team on it. Let's start with those who deal with large animals first off, near zoos and parks, and work from there."

"Right." Turning back to Faye, Jack asked, "Where was she injected? Did you find the puncture wound?"

"Yes, she was injected here on the back of her right arm," Faye said, demonstrating on her own arm. "The killer would have been behind the victim and plunged the syringe in like so." She demonstrated on Amanda, her back turned to Faye, lifting her own arm and slamming it down, almost touching Amanda's right arm from behind. "The entry angle suggests from up above, and that would seem the most likely way if you were taking someone by surprise. And of course, you'd want to make sure you punctured the skin; the back of the arm is nice and soft."

Thinking, Jack added, "So let's say the victim let her assailant in, walked back towards the lounge and was hit from behind. Then she was taken into the lounge, laid down . . . and that's when her throat was cut?"

"Sounds good to me," said Faye.

"So what about the towels, then? If her heart had stopped, why place towels nearby?"

"There would still be some blood, but I'd say maybe your killer wasn't sure what would happen or was expecting more. Maybe it was their first victim?" Faye was tossing ideas into the air and Amanda caught one.

"I've been wondering why the killer didn't just grab a towel from the bathroom but took a beach towel out of the hall cupboard. Any ideas, Faye?"

"None on that score. Sorry. Does seem odd, though: the bathroom towels would be the most obvious choice location-wise. Maybe the perpetrator has a conscience. Best use the older towels, maybe? I'm guessing, though. I'm not a criminal mind reader, only an evidence reader. You'd have to ask a forensic psychologist for their take on it."

"Anything else, Doc?" asked Jack.

"Nothing. You have it all. Time of death around ten-thirty a.m., heart stopped with etorphine, throat cut after death with a seriously sharp blade, smooth edged, probably a hunting knife, puncture from the injection in the rear of her right arm. Nothing of note in her stomach—only the remains of her breakfast cereal and coffee—and no other evidence found on her body. That's all I can give you. And you've still not found the murder weapon? No knife?"

"No, nothing found. It could be anywhere, though. We may never find it," said Jack, sounding somewhat defeated although it was still early in the investigation.

Amanda thanked her for her findings, and both she and Jack started walking towards the exit door. Jack spoke first.

"Whoever it was had to have planned this. You don't just have lethal drugs on you ready to go unless you set out to kill. And they had to be sure of gaining access to the victim's home, so they probably knew her. I think if we can figure out why her throat was cut, we'll understand a whole lot more. And let's hope this is a one-off."

"I agree," said Amanda. "The computer forensics team hasn't had much luck either, locating where the image was posted from or locating her phone. If the SIM card has been removed and the phone destroyed, that's the end of that. And what about that cryptic message, about Fiona being a trophy? It seems we're one step forward and two steps back, and nothing much to show for it."

Amanda was deep in thought as they made their way back to Jack's car. She looked at her watch. It was 1.30 p.m. "Thought I was hungry. Let's grab a sandwich and head back."

They drove in silence for a while, and then Jack spoke up. "Thinking of the drug the perp used reminds me of lethal injections, like what they use for death row inmates."

"How so?"

"Do you know how a lethal injection works?"

"Can't say I've given it any attention, but I suspect you're going to fill me in with one of your fun facts, am I right?" She caught Jack's smile and joined him. He really was a walking encyclopaedia at times.

"You'd think there was just one injection, right? Wrong: there's three. Sodium thiopental to make them unconscious, then pancuronium bromide goes in to cause muscle paralysis and respiratory arrest, and finally, they shoot potassium chloride in to stop the heart. And what do you know—death. Put them in in the wrong order, though, and all hell breaks loose. It's excruciatingly painful for the person, particularly the potassium chloride part. But that doesn't stop it being the most common way to legally kill those on death row, even if it is botched up regularly. I think I'd rather have a firing squad if I had to choose. Got to be less risky and painless, don't you think?"

"Good to know, Jack. Thanks for that, but I still want some lunch. You hungry?"

"I fancy a Subway. That work for you?"

"Don't care what, so long as it's food. I want to get moving on the vet lead and go back through her friends' statements. There's got to be a clue there. And that cryptic message the killer posted with the photo, about being a trophy, makes me think the victim's love of hunting could be linked to all this. So a hunting knife as the murder weapon would fit."

"Nothing surprises me anymore after nearly thirty years in the job, so some nut job who kills because they don't agree with someone's hobbies is just another check-mark on that list."

"What list is that, Jack?"

"The list of reasons to kill. I guess every perp has their own."

Chapter Twenty-Seven

UNDERSTANDABLY, the story of a woman found with her throat slit in a south London town was on the news. Philippa had been following the story all day, more to see what the police were up to than out of morbid curiosity. She'd scoured newspapers and online news sites, watched the news on TV and even listened to the radio, something she hadn't done in a long time. But in everything she'd read and heard about the attack, there was nothing mentioned about the drug she'd used. Odd, she thought; she'd read enough thrillers to know that toxicology was generally done on a murder victim, though it took time. No, they knew all right. They had to. They just hadn't released that tasty bit of information to the public.

As the newsreader she was watching moved on to another story, Philippa wondered if they had yet put two and two together and come up with vets who used the drug. Particularly vets with patients bigger than regular dogs and cats. But even then, etorphine could be bought on the dark web if you knew where to look. No, she felt sure she was safe: she'd left no evidence at the scene, and had even sat outside the chip shop like anyone else, a normal person, eating an early lunch, without a care in the world. What murderer would hide in plain sight? But the stroke of genius, she thought, was the way she'd posted the image, phone location turned off, sat in a car park at the train station not far from the house and the correct pinging cell phone towers. Any pings caught would be close enough to the house to look like the photos had been posted from there. And of course, she'd disposed of the phone. That would never see the light of day again.

No, all the loose ends had been tied up, and even if they got round to questioning the staff at her clinic, they wouldn't be any further forward. Helen had used the drug on a rhino; that would account for the clinic usage if it came to it, and the order she'd placed herself would have been delivered to the clinic this morning. It had been her intention to intercept it, but with her migraine and oversleeping, she'd failed in that respect. Philippa took a deep breath in and let it out slowly, the air escaping through a perfect 'O' in her lips, satisfied she had nothing to worry about, and that was important.

She stayed on the sofa for most of the day sorting the pieces whizzing around in her head. Finally, at about three o'clock in the afternoon, she'd begun to feel a little better, calmer, less stressed, and the throbbing motorbike in her head had been shut off. The comfort food had helped. Thankfully she had pizza and ice cream readily in the freezer and had made headway through both. In times of need, sometimes you just had to give into what the body craved. She stood and stretched, took her dirty dishes to the kitchen, and, still in her nightdress and dressing gown, went upstairs to change. It was time to stop feeling sorry for herself and get back to being the bright, confident, energetic woman she was normally. Pulling out her running gear, she dressed quickly, crammed a cap on her head and dug around in the drawer for her earphones, hoping there was still plenty of charge in them. Not five minutes later, she was jogging down her road, out towards the green outer fields of Rickmansworth and a hill she loved. It didn't take long for the sweat to rise; her body moved fluidly, her strong legs propelling her forward as her feet pounded the concrete of the path. *Madame Butterfly* in her ears, the music giving her wings of her own. The hours in reflection earlier in the day had done her good, and things were much clearer now. Feeling stronger again, stronger than this morning, she revisited her decision to kill again and it comforted her. She knew Fiona was only the start of things to come. Picking up speed, she pumped her arms as she ran, sprinting in short bursts like she hadn't done in a long while. At last, spent, she slowed to a steady jog, savouring the endorphin rush. Droplets of sweat ran down her face. Killing Fiona had been power inducing, and she knew she'd want that feeling again.

"This is my mission," she said to herself. "Now the hunters become the hunted."

Chapter Twenty-Eight

SEBASTIAN STEVENS ADMIRED himself in the full-length mirror in the plush bedroom of his penthouse apartment, gently rubbing the taut skin of his chiselled stomach, admiring all the hard work he'd put into himself over the years. His year-round tan was just the right shade, allowing him to look like the perfect healthy male specimen that he was. His gaze shifted slightly to a movement behind him. Reflected in the huge gilt mirror was the smooth naked shoulder of a woman. He stood and watched for a moment, taking in her long lithe legs that were partly unclothed by the bed covers, and wetted his lips with his tongue.

Last night had been big. He'd been out with some of the others from work, celebrating with champagne and cocaine, and a couple of ladies had joined in. One of them, a leggy curvaceous brunette with an appetite for a good time, had tagged along back to his suite and was now spread-eagled in his huge bed. At the thought of last night, what they'd done together, how willing she'd been to submit to him and how excited he'd been, he could feel himself getting aroused once more. The woman in his bed was a professional, all right—maybe he'd met his match in that department. He smiled as an idea came to him. She stirred a little more, and as he turned to watch her fully, his hand dropped lower towards his groin and he began to stroke. Here lay an opportunity for the taking.

"I think I've got just about enough time for some action before I have to leave," he said, turning to her, though not expecting a response. Hard and ready, he strode rapidly over to the bed, gripped her by the ankles and roughly flipped her onto her back. Her startled voice fell on his now-deaf ears. He wanted his relief and he wanted it now. He climbed up on top of her, pried her legs apart and forced himself straight in with one hard push. The woman cried out in protest, but after half a dozen "no, no, no's," she was panting with pleasure along with him. Ever the professional and not one to complain. He climaxed rapidly and flopped back down, sated. The assault had lasted all of five minutes.

The woman never said a word, just waited for him to get off her and head for the shower, out of sight. Only then did she move. Like lightning, she shot from the bed, grabbed her few belongings that were resting on a nearby chair and ran for the front door. Opening it quietly, and still completely naked, she hightailed it down the corridor hoping no one would leave their apartments until she was safely inside the lift. She pressed the button to call it. She was in luck—the lift was already near her floor and she stepped inside. Only when the doors had closed and she'd slipped her dress back on did she lean her head back against the wall, close her eyes and try to calm her breathing. What a terrible night she'd had. He'd been so demanding, much rougher than she was used to, and there was no way she was ever going back there again, no matter how much he paid her. Opening her eyes again, she caught sight of how she looked in the mirrored walls of the lift. The dark bruise that covered most of her left eye was going to be even more ugly as the day wore on. It was a good job she hadn't got any more bookings for the rest of the week. She touched the swollen skin around it to see how tender it was.

"Ouch!"

Yes, it was sore, but she'd broken her own golden rule by staying over long after their partying had finished in the private bar, but had she had a choice in the matter? Sure, she'd had her share of coke, everyone had, and he'd looked harmless enough and at the time horny enough, but he'd turned into too much of an animal when they were finally alone. She didn't always want it gentle herself, and as a working girl she always gave the client what they wanted, but he'd taken it to another level and now she'd pay for it. The lift pinged to signal she was now at the ground floor. The doors opened and she stepped out, putting her heels back on as she did so. She needed to get out of the building, as far as possible from the man she'd stayed over with, and home as fast as she could.

Out on the pavement, the cool morning air hit her with a rush and she hailed an approaching nearby taxi. Slipping in and settling herself on the backseat, she gave the driver her address. Her head throbbed violently and she massaged her temples to try and reduce the pain.

"You alright, love?" he enquired gently. "I know it's none of my business, but do you need some help?"

"No!" she cried, a little more loudly than she had intended. Lowering her voice, she spoke again, more calmly this time. "Just take me home, please."

The taxi driver glanced back at her through his rear-view mirror and nodded silently. He'd seen enough young women in a similar state the morning after to know what had probably gone down. Taxi drivers saw, and heard, it all. Within twenty minutes, she was unlocking her own front door. She kicked her shoes off down the hallway and headed straight for a long, hot cleansing shower. It was only when she'd stripped and was about to step into the welcoming hot spray that she caught sight of her own body in the full-length mirror.

"What has that animal done to me?" She stared in disbelief at the array of tiny nicks and cuts that covered the tops of both her thighs and flowed up to her lower stomach. It looked like someone had taken a piece of glass and repeatedly nicked her skin. There were spots of dried blood and dozens of bruises. "I wasn't that out of it to not remember anything about all this happening to me."

There was only one way it could have happened: she'd been drugged.

Chapter Twenty-Nine

THE AIR in Manchester always seemed to be cold and damp, even on an early summer's day like today. The weather woman updating from the TV in his kitchen had forecast a clear day, but an early mist was still lingering miserably in the air. It reminded Sebastian of a scene from a black-and-white horror movie as he walked the few short steps from his car to the front door of his office building. He paused outside for a moment and looked up above the huge bronze doors to the sign that gave the building's name in giant matching bronze letters. Sebast Suites. He smiled. His dad would be proud if he'd still been alive. And talking to him. They'd not parted on the best of terms, and Sebastian just hadn't been able to make him understand his way of doing business, and that being investigated by the fraud squad was something that happened to many business owners. Hell, it was practically par for the course.

When his father had finally passed away after a brief battle with bowel cancer, Sebastian had not been surprised to find out there was nothing in the will for himself—his other two brothers had been given the lot between them. But the money didn't really matter to Sebastian; he was doing just fine, making his own way. He pushed the thoughts of his estranged family from his head, ran the fingers of one hand through his expertly styled dark blond hair and headed inside to the giant marble lobby. He could see himself in the bronze doorframe's reflection as he entered, all six feet of him; he nodded to the security guard and strode purposefully towards the bank of express lifts. As he reached for the button, he heard the light tapping of heels approaching.

"Morning, Sebastian," said a stunning young blonde, all lips and legs, in a voice that was rather too sultry for eight in the morning. Her perfume was a gift to his nose and he breathed it in deeply as he toyed with his dilemma, the dilemma of Georgia, his newish PA. Sebastian liked the thrill of the chase, the hunt, but Georgia didn't quite understand the rules of his little game just yet and had virtually offered herself on a platter for him to take. So far, he'd resisted. The fun for him was most definitely in the game itself. Unless he was paying for it.

He didn't bother to turn around. "Morning, Georgia. Sleep well?" He couldn't resist teasing anyway.

"Mmm, yes thanks," she purred. "And you? Ready to go?" She was playing with him, too.

"Always."

Then he was all business, his tone changing in a flash. "Get me a coffee straight off, would you? And get Jason Whitely on the line when you bring it. He's been after me and I've been avoiding him, so let's make his day."

"Of course."

The lift door opened and they stepped inside. Georgia pushed the button for the top floor and stood quietly beside him. Already, after just a handful of weeks working with Sebastian, she knew when to keep quiet. The other women in the office had given her the heads-up about what he was like, both at work and when he was out to play, though she hadn't experienced any of his playtime. Yet. As long as she did her work well and anticipated his every need, she'd be fine.

At the top floor, the big brass lift doors opened and Sebastian strode out ahead of her, his mobile phone bursting into life as he walked. She watched from two paces behind as his jaw tightened and he barked a reply into it, bringing the brief conversation to a close. She caught the huge glass lobby door with her outstretched right hand before it smashed her in her face as he let it go behind him. Under her breath she cursed him, but that still didn't stop her wanting to chase him. She liked the game too. But her way.

Once inside, he went straight to his office and shut the door. Georgia caught a glimpse of one of the other PAs, Sandra, as she stared after him. "Foul mood?" Sandra mouthed across the dividers at her. Georgia nodded her head and went through to the kitchenette to make his coffee.

Sandra followed her in, and leaned against the cabinets, arms folded lightly across her ample chest, soft wavy auburn curls at her shoulder. "I'll be glad when he's out of here for a few days. Give us all some peace."

Georgia frothed milk and added it to the double shot of coffee in his mug. "And you don't work directly with him," she grumbled. "But I'm looking forward to it too. It'll give me a chance to catch up on my workload, though I expect he'll be on the phone several times a day—and night, too, if I know him." She rolled her eyes. "I've only known him for a few weeks, but I'm pretty sure I have him sussed." She grinned.

"Well, I hope you have Georgia, and you keep well away if you're ever tempted. He can be very persuasive—mark my words."

"Sounds like the voice of personal experience?" She sprinkled chocolate on the top of the milky froth and prepared to leave.

"But it got me nowhere. I suspect that's why I've never made PA to him. Probably fancying his chances with you." Sandra wasn't being mean; the caring note in her voice told Georgia she meant well.

"Catch you later," Georgia said. She picked up Sebastian's coffee and stopped by her desk to call Jason Whitely. When he picked up, she asked him to hold for Sebastian and entered his office. "Jason Whitely is holding on line one and here's your coffee," she said, putting it down in front of him. He picked the mug up and took a large mouthful. Melted chocolate stuck to the creases at both corners of his mouth. She wasn't about to tell him so.

She turned and walked out, closing the door quietly behind her, amused at her own pettiness.

Chapter Thirty

THE WEEK HADN'T BEEN GOING TOO well for Jason Whitely. After several failed attempts to get hold of Sebastian and arrange a face-to-face meeting, he was at his wits' end. And he knew something was up. When he'd first invested in Liberty-Lite along with other franchisees, he'd thought it was going to be his way to financial security, a great business deal. Why else would he have invested? And he'd invested heavily, nearly half a million in fact, scraping the money together from all over, re-mortgaging his house and borrowing off his father. It had been a huge opportunity for him, a deal that would ensure a successful future for him. That had been only twelve months ago, when Sebastian had been nowhere near the picture and a different CEO, [Brian something], was running things. While Jason had known even then that Brian was never going to set the world on fire, the man was as straight as a die and knew what he was doing.

But something had changed, and he had been given his marching orders quite literally overnight. That had meant someone new at the helm, a majority shareholder: Sebastian Stevens. And Jason didn't trust him as far as he could throw him. Apparently, neither did the other franchisees. But as a majority shareholder in Liberty-Lite, Sebastian held the power, and with the others only holding around ten percent each, none of them had much say in things. Now Jason wanted out, to cash in his shares before it was too late, but his agreement stipulated that the majority shareholder had the final say if another investor be found, as to whether or not they could in fact, invest. In other words, if Sebastian didn't like the potential new investor for whatever reason, even if the price was right, he could veto it.

Looking back, with the team as they were then back at the start, it never seemed to Jason that this could ever become an issue. Everything had started out fine. But now Jason smelled a rat, although he didn't know what that rat looked like, or just how big and ugly it might turn out to be. The company had changed direction from the software that he'd been so keen on three years ago, and had since been dabbling in other areas to generate more sales interest. But none of these other areas had panned out, and they'd burned through a huge amount of working capital, leaving the company grossly undercapitalised. Jason wasn't happy, and neither were the others, although they weren't quite as nervous as he was; they couldn't see what was happening right under their noses. And now Jason was good and stuck: no one wanted to buy his shares from him. Anyone could see the company was a dog with fleas, and Jason didn't stand a chance to get back anything close to what he'd paid out, ever again.

He was surprised, therefore, to actually hear Sebastian's voice on the other end of the telephone now.

"Jason! How the devil are you?"

Jason knew he needed to match Sebastian's confident tone. If there was one thing he knew from his dealings with the man, it was that you couldn't show weakness or be submissive. He set out strong with his own agenda.

"Finally, I get to speak to you Sebastian. Anyone would think you've been avoiding me."

"Oh, don't be like that. Busy, busy, busy, that's all. But I'm here for you now, all ears. What can I do for you?"

Jason bit back a snarky retort. *Not yet, not yet*. "I want to talk to you properly, face to face. I've got some concerns and I want to go through them with you in person and as soon as possible. When can we do that?"

"Well, I'm away from Friday for a few days but I'll get Georgia to organise a time with you beforehand. Let's talk over lunch one day this week before I go."

"Right ... okay." Jason was thrown a little off balance. He hadn't been expecting it to have been so easy .

"That's settled, then. Now, is there anything else you want before I flick you back to Georgia?"

"No, that's it."

Before Jason could say goodbye, the line went quiet. Georgia was on the line in a moment.

"Hi Jason, will Thursday lunch work for you? He'd like you to meet him at The Lowry at twelve pm."

"Thanks, Georgia. I'll be there."

"It's all set then," she said brightly, and said her goodbyes.

As she put the telephone down, she nodded to Sebastian, who was lingering by her desk.

"All set."

Chapter Thirty-One

IT WAS ALMOST noon as Jason walked into The Lowry. As he checked in with the maître d', he wasn't surprised to learn that he was the first to arrive; a man like Sebastian loved to make his entrance in his own big way. He sat at the table on his own nursing a glass of water, though the impulse to down a large whiskey before his tablemate's arrival was a strong one. He ran his tongue across his lower lip, the surface dry with anticipation of what was about to come.

At precisely 12.10 pm, he heard Sebastian before he saw him, exuberantly greeting the maître d' by name and patting his shoulder affectionately. He knew many of the staff by name; after all, he ate lunch there several times a week in order to impress whoever he was with. From the corner of his eye, Jason saw him approach his table, then make a beeline off to the left to exchange back-slaps with a man at another table. He sipped at his glass of water and pretended not to be aware of him.

"Jason!" boomed Sebastian at last. Jason felt a meaty paw clap him heartily on the shoulder.

"Sebastian," he said, fighting to keep his voice cordial. He watched as Sebastian took his place at the table, unfolded his napkin onto his lap and then sat back, a fake smile set firmly on his lips , dazzlingly bleached teeth just visible, and looking pleased with himself. A young waiter appeared at his shoulder and Sebastian ordered a large gin and tonic.

"What are you having, Jason?" he enquired.

"I'm fine with water, thanks." Jason smiled at the waiter.

"Suit yourself. Now, what do you want to speak to me about?"

Jason was happy to get straight down to business. He'd assumed they'd order first, but this was fine, too; his stomach was in knots.

"I'll get straight to the point, then." He cleared his throat and carried on, massaging his glass of water, looking for strength in the glass. "I'm not happy about how things are running at Liberty-Lite since you took over as CEO. It's not what I signed up for, and the debts are rising after such a big spend—a spend that you instigated and the rest of us had no say in but are all equally liable for. And since you're not listed as a director of the company, you don't have the same risk, because your shares are owned by the parent company. And that makes me, and the others, feel nervous that you have nothing to lose if it all falls apart. And the numbers say it's headed in that direction." A bead or two of sweat surfaced on his forehead as he finished, and he took a sip of water. He'd said it, politely but to the point. There was no way Sebastian could misunderstand what he'd said.

Sebastian stayed quiet as the waiter delivered his drink, then took a long sip before finally speaking. "So correct me if I'm wrong. What you're saying is you don't think I have the same vested interest in this succeeding, and that you don't trust me? Is that about the crux of it?"

"You have no risk, and you've gone through all the working capital, leaving the company in bad shape. If you were at risk too, I think you might have done things differently, that's all." Jason could feel himself deflating even as he sensed Sebastian was revving up inside.

"You have to spend to accumulate, Jason. You must know that. You haven't got to where you are now by not taking risks, have you?" He didn't wait for an answer and ploughed on. "No, you haven't. And to be fair, I've done this a good few times more than you have, so why don't you leave the CEO side of the operation to the more experienced one?" Sebastian's tone had changed dramatically from the jovial, chummy greeting of only a few minutes ago, and his eyes flashed angrily.

Jason kept his voice level; he wanted to have it out with Sebastian, yes, but not by letting it turn into a public slanging match. "Look, all I'm saying is our agreement is not balanced anymore. When Brian was CEO, he consulted us all equally and joint decisions were made, but now? It's a far cry from any joint decision with the rest, and we feel railroaded as well as worried for our personal financial security. Most of us have had to re-mortgage our homes and the debts that are mounting all carry personal guarantees from us all. All except you."

"Well, I can hardly change that, can I? Maybe it was a better decision to use a company to buy my shares. Maybe you should have sought better advice before getting in with this."

Looking across the table at him, Jason detected his mask of smugness and it annoyed him. "And just how could we have done that, Sebastian? Eh? We don't all have the funds to just do what you did. We had to raise our own money against our homes. The banks needed guarantees if we ever defaulted. Your other company bought your shares, fifty-one percent of Liberty-Lite in fact, and I suspect that will be well protected some way down the tangled set-up keeping you safe. And to be quite honest," Jason continued, getting more and more revved up, "I feel set up." There: he'd said it all. He could feel himself shaking with anger, and hoped it wasn't showing.

"Well, I'm not changing a thing. My agreement is structured properly, and my business acumen is sound. If you don't like it, Jason, I suggest you find an alternative buyer for your shares and present the buyer to the board. As per the agreement."

"You know there's no way on this earth anyone would want to buy the shares with the company in such a mess. How exactly do you propose I do that?" He was beginning to boil inside.

"That, Jason, is not my concern."

He smiled in an almost bored manner, and Jason couldn't stand it any longer. Leaping up from his chair, he leaned over into Sebastian's face and shouted, "You're just scum, Sebastian Stevens. Scum! And I'll have no part of being in business with you. I'll find a way to get out of this—just you watch me." He picked up the remains of his glass of water and threw it in his face, then turned on his heel, leaving Sebastian to mop himself up with his napkin.

A hush had fallen over the restaurant, and as he headed for the exit, he swore he heard a male voice quietly say, "Bravo."

Exiting the lift in the lobby, he made a beeline straight for the bar in the corner and ordered the double whiskey he'd wanted earlier. Now he needed it to calm himself, to think over what to do next. Then he might just have another. Sitting in one of the private booths, the leather seats helping to cool him, he rested his head back and breathed deeply, replaying the whole damn conversation in his head. There he sat for the next two hours, deep in thought, ignoring his telephone, ignoring the rest of the world. If there was one lesson he'd learned from all this, it was that he should never have invested in anything with such a small shareholding and one person holding the majority chunk. He knew there was no way to sell his shares, and the only idea he'd come up with was to sell them back to Sebastian. But he doubted he'd go for it. With the company in such bad shape, Sebastian would stay well away from them, just like any other intelligent prospective buyer. And if he was right with his suspicions, Sebastian wouldn't want to buy more of something that was worthless, no matter how cheaply he was willing to sell his shares. Jason leaned his head back against the leather seat and groaned softly, then signalled the waiter for another whiskey. He was well and truly screwed.

Chapter Thirty-Two

HE'D BEEN EMBARRASSED like that before, though usually by a woman, Sebastian mused as he dabbed himself with his napkin, a waiter hovering at his shoulder trying to assist. He'd seen people looking as he did so, and had laughed it off. Sebastian's reputation travelled well ahead of him. Not all of those looks had been in support of him, though; he knew many of the other diners were probably applauding his adversary, but he didn't much care. He'd gone on to order his lunch regardless, placing a fresh napkin on his lap. He wasn't going to be driven out of the restaurant by someone like Jason, and since his thick skin was as hard as an elephant's, what people thought didn't particularly bother him. And he knew what was about to happen anyway, so there was no point trying to pacify Jason and the rest of the licensees. He'd already started to move the few assets Liberty-Lite held across to the parent company, of which he conveniently owned 100%. The sale of the main licence was the next thing on his agenda. Given that Liberty-Lite then didn't own the license at all, was no longer the licensor, how could it then let each of the men operate their businesses as licensees? Jason and the others would each have a worthless piece of paper and a whole lot of money problems. There would be no license. Sebastian chuckled to himself as he dabbed at a spot of sauce on his lips, knowing full well how it was going to go down, the ruckus and disappointment turning to anger, followed by resentment. Under his breath, he added, "And maybe a spot of conniving, I expect. I'd better watch my back." Though he was chuckling again at the thought of someone getting their own back on him.

Having finished his meal, he stood, placed his napkin on his plate, and headed for the door, ignoring the sensation of dozens of eyes on his back.

By the time Sebastian had reached the office, the wheels had been set in motion. One telephone call was all it had taken to destroy not just Jason's life, but the lives of the other four men involved. By five o'clock tomorrow night, they'd no longer have the right to operate their businesses. If anyone looked at his dealings from the outside, it was a simple business transaction that made sense because Liberty-Lite hadn't made any money for some time and was haemorrhaging cash. If they took a closer look from the inside, though, his methods would probably raise some eyebrows, but were still within the legal boundaries—just.

"Afternoon, Georgia," he said brightly, a cheery smile replacing the tense look that had been in place just an hour or so ago.

While Georgia had the good sense not to mention it, she wondered what had happened at lunch with Jason today. No doubt she'd hear about it soon enough.

Chapter Thirty-Three

JASON WATCHED the conversation on The Daisy Chain, his favourite local community site, while he half-heartedly ate fish and chips straight from the paper on his dining room table—alone. He'd already had his fill, in more than ways than one, both with his meeting at lunchtime with the wanker Sebastian, and now with his dinner. He'd fancied fish and chips after an afternoon of feeling sorry for himself and going overboard with the whiskey. His housekeeper had prepared a wonderful-smelling chicken casserole that was in the oven keeping warm, but he'd wanted comfort food and that's what he'd had. The chicken casserole would see another day. So there he sat, on his own, watching what was going on locally with some of his other friends, picking at chips he now didn't want. He licked the salt and vinegar off his fingers and typed a response to Jordan's comment about the new paper delivery boy and his inability to quite get the morning paper to the right house on time. It was a trivial matter, a first-world problem, but sometimes it was those problems that caused the most irritation. In the grand scheme of recent things that had happened to Jason's world over the last few weeks, it was a minor blip, but he showed support to his friend anyway.

@Belfort, Just sack the paper and read the internet, buddy, it's fresher news anyway. Cheaper too

His reply came back almost immediately.

@Jaybaby, I detect a note of something, my friend. Bad day perhaps?

Jordan had been born with a top-notch silver spoon in his mouth, not even a regular silver spoon and was one of the local elite businessmen. He'd done well for himself with his own company; he'd chosen to stay in sales out on the road himself and appointed someone else as the CEO. Someone he could trust.

"Know your strengths and your weaknesses and make sure you employ someone else to do the things you loathe," had been Jordan's advice once upon a time. The men he dealt with in his sales role got on famously with him and Jordan was a generous man to everyone. Unfortunately, he had the Midas touch in reverse when it came to women. They thought he was a grade one letch and he suffered trying to hold on to a girlfriend for more than a couple of dates. Truth be told, he really was a letch but no matter how many times his male friends had tried to talk to him about it and help direct his ways, he'd always brushed it off as nonsense. And so he was still single. Jason aspired to be just like him in business—his entrepreneurial spirit and technical know-how were legendary. But while Jason was definitely not a letch, he too hadn't been successful in love.

@Belfort, You could say that. Disastrous lunch meeting then drinking whiskey to console. #Shitday

@Jaybaby, Youch. You need some company?

@Belfort, Nah, just feeling sorry for myself. Don't want to spoil anyone else's evening.

@Jaybaby from @McRuth, Bad day means chocolate. Works for me everytime. #familysizedblock

Jason smiled at Ruth's reply: typical woman. Chocolate solved everything.

@McRuth, Unless Cadbury's want to buy me out of a deal, I'll need more than a family block.

@Jaybaby from @Belfort Oh, sounds serious. You sure a manly chat won't help?

@Belfort, Thanks anyway. Fingers crossed for a miracle; otherwise I'll be looking for lodgings before long. #Spareroomanyone

Jason put down the hot chip that he wasn't going to eat and

screwed the paper up with the remains of his supper inside. He couldn't wait for the day to be over.

@Belfort and @McRuth, Early night for me, I reckon. Sweet dreams all.

Then he closed his laptop and took the remains of his evening meal outside to the rubbish bin, turning the oven off as he passed through the kitchen towards the back door. Maybe he'd feel better tomorrow; maybe things wouldn't seem so bad, he thought sleepily.

He couldn't have been more wrong.

Chapter Thirty-Four

JASON WOKE with the mother of all hangovers pounding his temples. As he came round and realised his pain, he was surprised he'd even managed to fall asleep, having lain tossing and turning for what felt like most of the night. When his alarm clock had read 3.15 am, he'd contemplated getting up but had lain there thinking about events from the previous day. Now, with eyes as swollen as a bee sting underneath each one, he winced as he sat up in bed. His mouth felt like the floor of a dusty bird cage. He tried to moisten his lips.

"Hell, what did I drink so much for?" he said out loud, massaging both temples simultaneously. His clock now read 7.30 am, way past his normal get-up time of 6 am.

He did his best in his pained state to dart from his bed to the shower. As he crossed the landing, he caught the smell of fresh coffee wafting up the stairs and even with his hangover, it smelled divine. His housekeeper, Mrs. Meadows, must be brewing herself a cup, not realising he was still in the house. Not that it mattered; she often helped herself to the Vietnamese blend he favoured. He'd bought her some for Christmas, but still, she helped herself when she was here.

A moment later, he was standing under the warm invigorating jets of his power shower, letting the needles do their best for his stiff shoulders while he rubbed shower gel over himself, hoping the strong fragrance would wake him up and wash away the stench of yesterday's whiskey. He headed downstairs for a much-needed coffee. Mrs. Meadows glanced up from her paper at the unexpected intrusion in the kitchen. When she realised who it was, she jumped to her feet and stood looking like a rabbit caught in a headlight. He smiled at her distress.

"Morning, Mrs. Meadows," he said. "Don't look so scared. I've told you before to help yourself to coffee."

She stuttered a little as she tried to speak. "I'm sorry, Jason. I didn't know you were still home. I'll get straight to work!" She stood to take her cup to the sink.

"No, stay and finish your coffee. I'm making one for myself. Do you want a top-up?"

Hesitating, she replied, "Yes, thanks, if you're sure."

Jason moved over to the kitchen counter, filled the tank with water, and added fresh coffee. The machine chugged into action; the strong aroma of coffee refilled the room and he savoured the smell again. He sat down at the kitchen table while he waited.

"Can I make you some breakfast?" Mrs. Meadows asked. "I must say, you look like you had a tough night. Your eyes are quite swollen. Is everything okay?"

"Nothing I can't handle, but thanks for your concern." He thought about it for a moment, and then added, "Well, I hope I can handle it. We'll find out soon enough."

"Well, in times of strife, my old mother used to say eggs on toast and tea sorts most of life's dilemmas out. Would you care for some? I can soon whip up some scrambled eggs, put some food back in your stomach after the drink."

She must have caught a whiff as he'd passed her. He hadn't cleaned his teeth yet.

"Ah, still obvious, is it? Better have some eggs, then, but I'll stick to coffee. I did have some fish and chips last night, though I didn't eat much of it, to be fair."

"Well, you stay sat down and I'll make some breakfast for you. And you can reheat that chicken casserole for your dinner tonight. Can't waste it. It will be quite alright." Her gentle old hand brushed his shoulder as she got to work. She busied herself gathering eggs and cracking them into a bowl, then put two slices of bread in the toaster.

Jason smiled at her motherly dominance. Sometimes, she was just what he needed in his life. At 35 years old and still single, he welcomed her female influence in his life but as a self-proclaimed workaholic, there was little time for a full-on female relationship. Mrs. Meadows was his saviour. He opened the newspaper she had been reading and scanned the headlines, though it was pretty much the same each day. He didn't know why he bothered with it anymore anyway; the up-to-date news was online as he'd said to Jordan last night. Still, kids needed a job to get started with and if no one bought papers, none would need delivering.

Five minutes later, she placed a plate of steaming scrambled eggs on hot buttered toast in front of him and he tucked in, surprised at how hungry he was. Even though his head was filled with worry, he felt a little better once he'd had his fill.

"Thanks for that. Your old mum is right. I feel better already."

"Imagine if you'd had the tea as well!" She winked at him and he got the message.

"Right. I'd better go and get dressed and get going. Problems won't solve themselves sat here," he said, and he smiled at her wise face as he left the room to finish dressing.

An hour later, and he was hard at work, a packed schedule keeping his mind on other things which was probably a good thing. He spent the rest of the day visiting clients, a part of his role he so enjoyed and didn't really class as work he loved it so much. By 4.30 pm, he was headed back to the office when his phone rang. It was his assistant, Jo Jo.

"Jason! Are you nearly back yet? Whereabouts are you?"

"Ten minutes out. Why? What's up?"

"In that case if you're nearly back, I'll wait and we can talk properly rather than while you're driving."

"Come on, Jo Jo. What is it?"

"No, get back here and we'll talk. See you in ten." She hung up.

That had Jason worried; Jo Jo had never hung up on him before, obviously didn't want to be squeezed for the news. That could only mean one thing. Jason's stomach dropped as anxiety enveloped him. When something bad happened at the end of the day, it was usually planned that way, leaving no time for those affected to do anything about it. And since today was Friday, it made it all the worse: he'd have to wait for the weekend to pass before doing anything about it. It was a mean move, and one that he'd experienced before. He pulled into his parking space, gathered his briefcase and entered the building. Jo Jo was there to greet him, and she wasn't looking happy.

"What's he gone and done now? How bad is it?"

She had no choice but to tell him, though she knew he'd be devastated at the news.

"He's sold the main licence, leaving us and the others without any way to operate using his product. Liberty-Lite is now owned by Liberty Invest with no plans to let anyone have access to it. It's over."

Jason stopped moving while he digested what she had said. Jo Jo handed him the brief document she had received that afternoon, and he read it.

"The spiteful ..." Jason screamed at the sky. "You'll not get away with this!"

Jo Jo stepped back fearfully, aware that heads were turning to see what the commotion was about. When Jason had finally stopped yelling, he turned on his heels and stormed from the building, with no clear idea of where he was going. Or what he was going to do.

Chapter Thirty-Five

"WELCOME ABOARD, MR. STEVENS," the hostess cooed, fluttering her eyelashes just enough to be flirty without being overly obvious with it.

Lowering his eyes to read her name badge, which was pinned conveniently over her pert left breast, he smiled warmly and replied, "Good morning, Amber. Nice to meet you," he said, and gave her the once over in a little more detail. Solely for his own pleasure. He was used to women flirting with him, but that wasn't the way he liked it. Not his game; too easy. No, Amber might be a good-looking woman and happy to flirt, but it was the tall dark-haired classy looking woman that stood just behind her that piqued his interest. It seemed she was not impressed with his devilish good looks and charm, nor the wealth that allowed him to travel first class. He glanced her way again to see if she'd meet his blue eyes but she didn't. Sebastian smiled to himself. This flight was going to be such fun, and by the end of the thirteen-hour trip, she'd comply. No one ignored Sebastian Stevens. He was aware Amber was talking to him.

"I'm sorry, Amber," he said, and smiled sweetly. "I was miles away."

"That's okay, Mr. Stevens. I was asking if you'd like a glass of champagne brought to your seat?"

"Perfect. Why not? I'm not on the clock today, or in fact for the next few days."

Amber chimed in again not wanting to miss the opportunity. "Off on holiday?" she enquired.

"Yes, hunting. I won the bid on a couple of white rhino that were up for auction. Hope to get them for my trophy room back home."

Amber's pretty little perfectly made-up face dropped suddenly in alarm though she had the sense not to show her feelings any further. Still, he was the best-looking man on the plane and his hobby wasn't going to stop her having her own fun. She realigned her smile and followed up with, "Enjoy your holiday, Mr. Stevens," then turned and made eye contact with the gentleman behind Sebastian, greeting him warmly.

If Sebastian had noticed her slight recoil, he didn't show it, wouldn't have been bothered anyway. He headed off to his seat. It was the dark-haired hostess that brought him his champagne a few moments later, placing the tall-stemmed flute on his side table with a small bowl of nuts to accompany it. Though Sebastian smiled in thanks, she still hadn't said a word to him other than 'Thank you.' Her name badge informed him she was Valerie, and when she'd left, he silently played with the sound of her name on his tongue. "Va-le-rie, Va-le-rie," he murmured, rolling the 'rie' as he did so. He liked the feel of it.

Chapter Thirty-Six

As his flight touched down in Bulawayo, Sebastian mused to himself that Amber certainly had the hots for him, catching his eye occasionally and doing her best to appear submissive by the way she lowered her eyes at him, and had all but slipped him her number during the flight. Oh, those fluttering eyelashes. It seemed she wasn't that upset with his hobby after all. The thought amused him somewhat. While he wasn't interested in her particularly, he might just make an exception to his own rule and give in to her chase; she had earned it. While not his usual style, there wouldn't be any chance of much woman fun where he was going, and any females in the vicinity certainly wouldn't look like Amber did. When the seatbelt signs were finally turned off, he got up to stretch his tall frame. Even travelling in first class had its limitations but he'd never felt the desire for his own jet, an extravagance he didn't want or need. As the other passengers in his cabin filed off quietly, glad to be at their destination, he hung back a little, pretending to be looking for something in his carry-on bag. And that's when Amber made her last-ditch attempt at Sebastian.

"I'm staying in town if you're not busy tonight and fancy a drink after your long flight," she whispered to his shoulder, pretending she wasn't actually talking to him.

He smiled down at her, showing well-kept white teeth and an interest.

"I have a transfer waiting, unfortunately. How about sometime a bit sooner?" Now it was his turn to be direct. Two could play at that game.

It wasn't quite the response she'd expected from him and took a second or two to decide. "Meet me right outside the main entrance when you've gone through customs. I'll be waiting." Then she slipped away to her station and the other passengers.

"Little minx," he thought, smiling, "but what the hell."

The terminal wasn't much more than a single tin-roofed building with a landing strip in front of it, but there were armed police and security personnel scattered at regular intervals. They all appeared to be young men in oversized uniforms, but still, he wouldn't want to upset one. After a quick passage through passport control and customs, he dropped his bags with his waiting guide and transport, putting them both on hold until he was ready to leave. He'd see their tip was worth the wait. He then made his exit to meet up with Amber. She was standing with her back to him as he approached and he bent down to her right ear with two words. "Where to?"

She turned, smiled flirtatiously, and beckoned him to follow her to a waiting taxi. They both got in, and Amber gave the driver directions to a hotel nearby. They settled back to relax, both knowing why they were going to her hotel room and what was coming next. To be fair, Amber didn't *really* know what was coming to her, though she'd remember her mistake that day for the rest of her life.

Chapter Thirty-Seven

WHILE HIS LITTLE rendezvous with the hostess had been a pleasant one, for him anyway, it had put him behind schedule somewhat and he half wished he hadn't bothered. Still, it was done now and he was finally nearly at his destination. The trip from the airport had been long and tiring—three hours of rough roads and checkpoints with little comfort to rest in properly. But this was Zimbabwe, not Manchester, and luxury first-class travel didn't run all the way through.

As they drove the last few metres towards the lodge complex, he recognised the ten-foot-tall fence running alongside the property, keeping the animals safe from poachers and contained for hunters. There was a certain irony in that, he thought: both sides wanted something from the animals, except one side wanted it for free. Either way, the animal died and by hunting it legitimately, he felt he was doing his bit for the local economy, as well as for sheer enjoyment. The van pulled up outside and he stepped down into the dirt and stretched. It had been a long journey and he was ready for a shower, dinner and bed.

"Welcome, Mr. Stevens, welcome!" the burly lodge manager called out. He jogged over and greeted Sebastian warmly. They shook hands like old friends.

"Good to see you again, Farai. How have you been keeping?'

"Good, good, Mr. Stevens. We thought perhaps you had got lost!"

Farai laughed as if it was the funniest thing he'd heard in a while, throwing his head back dramatically, and Sebastian laughed along with him. His driver would have notified Farai that Sebastian had gone off on a digression, of course, but Farai was enjoying himself. They all knew him so well.

"I never get lost, and I never miss an opportunity when it arises," he said. "And an opportunity arose!"

He threw his head back to match his friend's exuberance. Farai continued to laugh with his guest as he summoned a young man to help to take his luggage for him. "You're in your usual chalet, and I will have a nice cold drink brought over to you shortly. Dinner will be served in approximately one hour." He handed Sebastian his key. "He will take your luggage for you," he said, pointing to the young man. "See you shortly. And try not to be late!"

Sebastian could hear him laughing loudly to himself as he followed the young man, though he did indeed know where he was going. This had been 'his chalet' for the past few years.

Forty-five minutes later, Sebastian walked into the small bar area of the dining room and ordered himself a large whiskey. He took a long slug of it, put his glass down on the bar with a resounding 'Ahhhh,' and turned to see who else was there. Being somewhat of a regular, he knew a few of the others even though they didn't keep in touch in between hunting expeditions. Still, it was always good to see a familiar face, and, spying one now, he took the glass back in hand and walked over to a man he recognised from a couple of years ago. As he got closer, he wracked his brain for the man's name, and held his hand out to shake.

Recognition dawned on the man's face instantly, and he smiled back furiously shaking Sebastian's outstretched hand.

"Robert, isn't it, if I remember correctly?"

"You have a good memory, my friend!" he said in a heavy Texan accent. "Yes, Robert Johns. But your memory is far better than mine, though I know we've spoken before." If the older man was embarrassed for not remembering Sebastian's name, he didn't show it.

"Sebastian, Sebastian Stevens," he said, filling him in. "We met here back in 2013, I recall. You wanted buffalo. Was it your lucky year, or are you back to try again?"

The older man threw his head back and laughed heartily. "No, it was a lucky year that one, and I've been back a couple of times since, though not for another buffalo. Too damn dangerous for me! And I'm taking things a bit easier these days. Getting old. You?"

"Well, I'm in for a slower day tomorrow first off, just playing on the plains, I think, but the following day, I'm up in the chopper. Bought myself a couple of white rhino at auction so I'll try my hand at that. If you feel like coming along, I'm sure there will be room."

"Sure. Are the animals tagged for tracking, do you know, or you just going to fly around and make a noise?"

"They'll be tagged. I want to make sure I get them—I paid enough for them. I'll probably ship them back home." Sebastian sipped on his whiskey as he watched the man decide, his tanned and deeply wrinkled face showing his decision.

"Sounds like fun. I'd love to tag along." Realising the pun, he threw his grey-haired head back again and laughed a deep Texan laugh at his own joke.

Just then, dinner was called and they both followed the handful of other guests to the dining room. Sebastian and Robert seated themselves side by side.

"Sure does smell good!" Robert said to one of the waiters, who was busy setting out trays of food on a big wooden table. It looked and smelled divine. "What's been on the grill tonight?"

"Zebra, sir. Shot yesterday by the gentleman at the end," he said, nodding to a youngish man who Sebastian noted looked as pleased as punch with himself. "Judging by that wonderful vein of fat running through it, it will be succulent indeed. And of course, well prepared by the chef." The waiter smiled.

"I'm sure it will be. Far nicer than antelope in my view," said Robert, picking up serving utensils and placing an array of vegetables on his plate before selecting a steak. Satisfied with his selection, he tucked into the meat first, nodding his appreciation to Sebastian as he chewed. "Wow, that really is good. Better than the steaks we get back home, and as a Texan ranch owner, I've had my share of good ones, I can tell you!" He took another bite. With a mouth half full of meat, he carried on, "Damn, that is good!"

As the others sampled their food, everyone nodded in agreement that it was in fact one of the best steaks they'd had. Quiet came over the table and, apart from the gentle scraping of cutlery on china, the room was silent as the group ate hungrily.

Chapter Thirty-Eight

THE FOLLOWING MORNING, Sebastian awoke just before dawn, showered and went back to the dining room in search of breakfast. Even though they'd all eaten heartily last night, he was famished. He was looking hugely forward to his first full day out hunting, and he needed to keep the fire stoked. Even at five am, the dining room was filling up fast as the other eager hunters emerged and prepared for their day with a big breakfast. Sebastian filled his plate from the buffet with a mixture of fresh fruits, porridge-like Bota, and generous slices of various cold meats, something there was always a plentiful supply of on a hunting trip. What the guests killed and couldn't eat themselves, the locals made use of and welcomed the food into their homes for their families.

"Morning," said a familiar voice.

Sebastian looked up from his breakfast feast and saw Robert at his shoulder. "And good morning to you. Did you sleep well?' he enquired, putting a large slice of fresh orange into his mouth. A little juice dribbled down his chin.

"Like a baby, like a baby!" Robert confirmed. "That's one reason I love coming to this place at my age. The facilities are just great. Sleeping in a damn tent is not my body's idea of comfort, and without sleep, I can be quite cranky, let me tell you. No, I need a good bed for these old bones."

Sebastian smiled at the older man. At the ripe old age of forty-five himself, he could empathise with that, never mind when you're pushing eighty like his friend Robert.

"Well, I'll leave you to your breakfast and go get a plate of my own. Think I'll take it outside and watch the dawn break. No need to rush at my age." And then he was gone, leaving Sebastian to his thoughts about the day ahead. This was the beauty about coming away when he had: there was no one from the office to bother him, and after dropping his bombshell on that greedy Jason on Friday afternoon, he was glad he was out of it until he'd cooled off a little. He thought back to their lunchtime meeting as he ate, and his embarrassment at having a drink thrown in his face. While his skin was tough, it had annoyed him greatly—and in front of people he knew too. Why had the jerk made matters worse for himself by doing that? A waiter speaking to him brought him back to the dining room.

"Coffee, sir?" the young man enquired.

"Please," he said, and watched as the deep brown liquid filled his mug, the aroma filling his nostrils satisfyingly as only hot fresh coffee can. He helped himself to cream, then took a welcome mouthful and swallowed it down, feeling the caffeine filter through his veins almost immediately. He heard Farai before he saw him enter the dining room, and used his napkin to wipe his mouth as he stood to greet the manager. Farai always had a permanent smile on his face.

"Morning, morning, morning, Mr. Stevens! A great day is dawning for you!" he said with enthusiasm. "Your tracker and Albert will be ready to leave from out front in fifteen minutes. Don't be late now, will you?" he finished, laughing cheekily. "And please don't take advantage of anymore opportunities on the way. There is work to be done before it gets too hot!"

With a wink, he disappeared as quickly as he'd arrived, leaving Sebastian to finish his breakfast in peace. Ten minutes later, he was climbing into the Jeep out front with his tracker and Albert, his professional hunter for the day, along with game rifles, an AK-47 for the tracker just in case he needed to kill quickly, ammunition, food supplies and plenty of water.

Albert greeted him like an old friend; they'd hunted together many times in the past. "Good to see you again!" he said brightly, shaking Sebastian's hand heartily.

"And you too, Albert. Are you keeping well?"

"Can't complain. This here is Tanaka," he said, introducing the other man, "your tracker for the duration of your stay, and one of the best, I should add."

The men shook in greeting and Albert informed him they would be heading out east first. "So sit back and relax a while until we get out to where we want to be. Hopefully we'll pick up spoor to track quickly. It's going to be a hot one today, Mr. Stevens, so it's up to you whether we track first then go back to it after the sun cools or carry on. You let us know," he said.

Sebastian nodded and rested his head back as the Jeep pulled out of the lodge complex and they made their way out for the day. After a long flight yesterday, it didn't take Sebastian long to nod off as the warming sun rose further in the sky and they travelled to their first destination of the day.

It was a little over an hour later when the small group finally came to a stop and they prepared to leave on foot. They took a rifle each, and Tanaka took the AK-47. Albert and Sebastian hung back a little to give him some room to look for spoor, evidence that animals had been through recently. Tracks in the dirt were easier to see than other clues, but each small sign signified what or where the animal may be, what direction it had gone in. Tanaka took his time reading the signs until he was happy there was something to follow. Quietly, he raised his arm and signalled the others, being careful not to make any unnecessary noise and spook other animals, which could in turn spook the actual animals they were hunting.

Staying downwind, Albert and Sebastian kept close together, walking slowly through the low scrub bushes, tuning into their surroundings with their eyes and ears, staying alert at all times. Just because they couldn't see an animal nearby didn't mean there weren't any hiding, and the last thing they wanted was to be surprised and attacked as they stumbled across something dangerous. Tanaka had his AK poised at the ready just in case.

Slowly, they crept forward, and after thirty minutes tracking in the dirt, Tanaka stopped up ahead and alerted the others to stand still with a raised hand. Albert whispered to Sebastian that up ahead was a watering spot with an impala nearby, nervously listening, deciding whether to flee or not. "Do you want to take the shot, Mr. Stevens?"

"Yes, of course. Good practice for tomorrow," he whispered back, and they moved forward slowly towards the water. Sebastian engaged a bullet for fire, crouching down behind a fallen tree to take aim. Kneeling in the dry dirt, the hot sun on his shoulders, he was in his element, his passion for hunting racing through his body like a high-speed train. He loved the dominant feeling it gave him. Through the crosshairs, he could see the animal clearly; its slender, angular head and deep golden coat were the perfect picture of nature's beauty. Then he pulled the trigger.

Chapter Thirty-Nine

THE TRIP HAD COME to a close far too quickly. Sebastian rested his head back in his first-class seat, the long journey home back to Manchester in front of him. He loved his hunting trips away, but he always loved returning to his other passion—work. He'd hardly spent any time at all thinking about it while he'd been away, and with only intermittent internet access out in the dry country, it was a good excuse to enjoy what was around him and have some time out.

But his thoughts returned now to his everyday life and catching back up with things, and that meant dealing with the fallout from Jason and his merry men. No doubt they'd been plotting and scheming like vengeful children while he'd been absent, lawyers dragged in and threats made, though it'd do no good. His mind had been set some weeks ago and Jason had brought the date forward with his own greed, for which they were all now paying. No matter; if nothing was going to change on his side, there really wasn't anything else to do. It was done and they were out. He pressed the hostess call button and an attractive woman approached his seat. While she was no Amber, or Valerie for that matter, she was elegant and efficient, with a smile that was natural and friendly.

"What can I help you with, Mr. Stevens?" she asked brightly.

"I'd love a sandwich, chicken if you have it, and a Coke, please," he said, trying his own best smile out on her.

She wasn't taken, it seemed. She replied coolly, "Certainly sir. I'm sure that can be arranged," and then went off to check.

He glanced back at her as she made her way back to the little galley area, her narrow hips the centre of his attention. Another reason he'd be glad to get back to Manchester: he'd missed that aspect of fun and a whole week without was long enough. While he waited for her to return, he pulled up the video that he'd asked Robert to take while they were up in the helicopter hunting the two rhinos and watched it again with the volume turned down low. From the phone's little screen, he could see himself leaning out the side of the big metal bird, rifle in hand and two rhinos running for their lives below. He'd got them both eventually, and he and the other guests had all celebrated that night back at the lodge with copious amounts of whiskey and stories, each hunter trying to outdo the previous one. That was the camaraderie of big game hunting he loved so much: getting the beast you desired and telling the tale of how you did it, the thrill of the chase and the satisfaction of getting your trophy. Or in his case, trophies—plural. No one had managed to outdo him.

As the short clip came to an end, Sebastian had an idea for the angle he was going to use for a speech he was due to give later in the week. The dinner guests were expecting to hear about his business prowess, and in particular, his expertise in raising venture capital, so why not include other forms of raising finance, something that would be particularly useful for the not-for-profit sector? After all, the money from the rhino auction he'd paid so handsomely for was going to conservation and preserving endangered species, and a sizeable donation of $300,000 US was not to be sniffed at. And he could perhaps include the video clip as an example of how he himself had helped the conservation fund. People loved real-life stories, and they'd like that one, he was sure. Besides, the extra publicity was always a good thing and he loved being in the news: it suited him. He smiled at his plan as the hostess returned with his sandwich and Coke.

"Enjoy, Mr. Stevens," she said, handing him a small tray filled with

Chapter Forty

PHILIPPA WAS EATING a bowl of cornflakes at the kitchen table and peering at her laptop screen, reading a news article at the same time. She'd come across the name before, more because of his infamous reputation as a businessman rather than because the world loved him, like they did Branson, for example. It seemed he was a 'Marmite' character: you either liked him or loathed him. And while Philippa hadn't previously had much of an opinion of Sebastian Stevens, after reading this article, she certainly did now. It had been the scathing headline that caught her eye—*Try Killing for Funding.* If that wasn't going to make you stop and read, nothing would. Philippa put her bowl down on the table, afraid she'd spill the remaining contents, and read the whole article again in disbelief. When she was done, she sat back a moment. How disgusting that a man could do something so senseless and suggest others do it for fundraising. She scrolled down the page to the comments section. Even though it was still early, there were plenty of them, all angry, and they were getting more and more heated as the list got longer.

Stevens had obviously hit a nerve with his speech last night, and either his skin was so thick he didn't care who he upset, or he was stupid enough not to know others would be upset. And to show the video just after dinner was in extremely bad taste. The organisers had apologised for not knowing the content of Mr. Stevens' speech beforehand, and would be putting guidelines in place for further guest talks in the future to prevent something like this ever happening again. It had been a PR disaster for them on that front, and the hordes of social media voices had ramped up into frenzy during the night.

She changed sites and looked at her own newsfeed. That, too, had been lit up with comments and opinions as people read the story and jumped on board. And so soon after the last hunter that had been in the news recently, with her throat slashed. It was in her friends' conversations that the comments had been the worst; the news sites moderated comments before they were posted, but not here, not between friends. Many suggested what they'd like to do with his rifle for money if they ever had the opportunity. If anyone had been in support of Sebastian Stevens, they were keeping their heads well down.

She glanced at the clock on her screen and headed upstairs for a shower. Standing under the warm jets, she shampooed her hair and thought about her mission. Of course, now she'd have to kill Sebastian. She'd gotten away with Fiona's death so far, which had been a blessing, but there was clearly a lot more work to be done. It wouldn't be quite so simple to insert herself into the life of a man like Sebastian. A simple friend request would never work; this would need a lot more research and planning. And soon, before the fire went out of the situation. She needed to make a statement through him, to send a message to others involved in this barbaric sport, and raise awareness of the need for it to be stopped. With so many people angry at him, the police would have a tough job weeding out the serious threats. Besides, a man like Sebastian would have his fair share of enemies anyway, so no one would be looking at a woman called Philippa.

Nevertheless, she had to act quickly, hatch her plan and make it work. When she got home from the clinic tonight, she'd work on finding a way into his life—then work on destroying it.

Chapter Forty-One

SHE'D BARELY SLEPT all night. Thoughts had kept rolling around in her head as she tried to think of plausible ideas on how to get into the creep's life. While she knew she could get into his digital life fairly easily via other means, it was his physical life she was after, though she drew the line at getting physical with him. She shuddered at the thought of such an arrogant and obnoxious man sweating and grunting on top of her—she couldn't go that far—but she was willing to do other less intimate things, whatever those might turn out to be.

She lifted her head off the pillow to check the bedside clock. It read 4.31 am, way too early to get up, but she was never going to go back to sleep, if ever she'd even been there at all. Might as well put the time to good use, she thought, and climbed out of bed. She padded downstairs to make a mug of tea, then grabbed her laptop and took them both back to the comfort of her still-warm bed, propping all her pillows up behind her. No need to get up properly yet, but there was still work to be done.

"Right. What else can we find out about you? What's the golden key to the door of Sebastian going to look like? What form will it be in?" She tapped the keys and started a Google search of him again, but this time, she looked at mentions of him from ten pages back rather than the more recent or newsworthy. She'd already looked through those and found nothing of any real use. "There's got to be a gremlin or two on you somewhere, a passion I can take advantage of perhaps." Philippa browsed and read, sipping her tea and trying to digest as she learned, looking for clues and a possible answer to her little problem. There were pictures of him at events; she noted with interest that every single one of the women he was photographed with had long, dark hair. "Good to know," she thought.

Searching further, she located his offices. She deduced from various interviews that he lived in the trendy, affluent, upmarket side of Manchester—Blackfriars, near Spinningfields. No surprises there—where else would Mr. Bachelor of the year live? Not that she'd be applying to be his bride anytime soon. She entered Blackfriars into Google, and wasn't surprised with what she found. A top-end apartment area for the extremely wealthy who liked to stay close to the town rather than out somewhere in the greener parts of upmarket Altrincham, Bowdon and the rest of Cheshire. The luxurious apartments came with a price tag of around £1.5 million, a lap pool, high-end gym and spa on site; no need to slum it with the general public someplace else. She could imagine him popping down for his workout. Men of his age and ilk generally kept in shape. It was the older guys who spread around the middle as they got older and cared less.

With her new knowledge of where he spent most of his time during the day and when he spent time at home, she'd put a plan together before the day was out and start the ball in motion. Time was at a premium. She had to be quick. The first thing she needed to do was get up to Manchester and take a look at his life in person, see exactly where he lived and worked and where the opportunities to infiltrate were, because there would be some.

She glanced at her clock. It was 6.15 am. She became thoughtful again. "What the hell. I'll have to go today," she said to the empty room, throwing the covers back and clambering over the bed. "I'll call in sick on the way." She showered, dressed quickly and left for the station.

Forty minutes later, balancing a hot coffee and a raspberry muffin in one hand and her bag in the other, she stood waiting on the platform to head into Euston and then catch a train north to Manchester

Piccadilly. At least the morning sun was shining, making her feel a bit better about what she was going to have to do again—though not the actual deed itself, not today. Today was all about gathering intel, finding the weak spot in his sad life and doing something with it for the greater good. The rumble of the approaching train brought her attention back to the present and she concentrated on getting close to the automatic doors for a speedy entry and hopefully a seat. When the train finally stopped, a mass of people stepped forward at the same time and while she didn't want to push and shove her way in, she wasn't going to be left standing either. The doors opened and she found herself in pole position for a seat directly opposite. She quickly claimed it as her own, taking care not to make eye contact with anyone as she did so. Needs must on a commuter train around London. It was a free-for-all. Today was no different.

People sat either side of her and more stood with their backsides positioned haphazardly just at her head height. The doors beeped closed, shortly followed by the train lurching forward. They were off, and she let a breath out as she tried to rearrange her coffee, breakfast and bag without any mishaps. The coffee tasted good, the caffeine welcome after a sleepless night, and she broke the crunchy top off her muffin and chewed thoughtfully. It wasn't a long journey into London, only thirty minutes or so, and she used the time to think. Hopefully she'd be able to spread out a bit more on the next train heading north, and even though she fancied a nap for the two hours ahead, she couldn't afford the time. Instead, she'd have to be content with travelling like a sardine in a tin with everyone else. Someone's swinging bag caught her on the arm and she looked up. A man mouthed his apology, and she looked away nonplussed. The next thirty minutes couldn't go fast enough.

Chapter Forty-Two

PHILIPPA STOOD LOOKING up at Sebast Suites. The tower dominated the skyline, the water from the nearby river reflecting, twinkling, but definitely not inviting on the glass-covered exterior. Inside the building, many of the richest companies had office space and enjoyed the luxurious river views and the no doubt sumptuous interior. But Philippa wasn't there to enjoy either of those. She took a seat on a bench nearby to watch people coming and going. The huge gilt doors were too gaudy for her taste, but that didn't matter: she'd never be working there. She made herself comfortable to sit and watch. Women in tight pencil skirts and blouses pretended they were on a *Suits* set, heels as high as Donna's and faces just as beautiful; the men looked much the same as Harvey. What these people must spend on their wardrobes each month was probably more than she paid for her mortgage. And that was her choice, doing the job she loved. She was not one for being cooped up in a high-rise typing all day.

She'd only been watching for half an hour or so when she spotted him in the lobby through the giant glass windows that ran along the bottom of the whole building. His tall commanding figure in a deep navy-blue suit and white shirt had her mesmerised momentarily as she watched him approach the front doors and step outside into the sunshine. It seemed she wasn't the only one watching, though. Heads both male and female turned to see as he passed, and if Sebastian noticed, he didn't show it. That surprised her a little; but his lack of arrogance now might be because of his recent publicity, she thought. Maybe people were watching him not for his good looks and physique but for how he'd so famously screwed up.

He strolled down the walkway towards a row of trendy shops and coffee houses and she stood to follow from a distance, taking care to stay well back. Not that he'd notice her, not yet. But he wasn't going far, it seemed. He slipped inside a café a moment later. Philippa stayed outside, not wanting to go in with him, but she could see he wasn't alone. She decided to go back and sit just outside Sebast Suites and wait there for his return.

"I wonder why he'd meet someone in there rather than his office?" she wondered. "It's literally only around the corner. Perhaps he wanted to get out of the building." The thought puzzled her, but as she was just getting to know him and hadn't got much else to go on, she didn't have the answer. Maybe he always did that. Taking her seat again, she prepared for a long wait. Then she got one of life's little surprises. Coming out of the main entrance, looking stylish in her own pencil skirt, was a woman she recognised, a woman from university, a woman she'd drifted apart from some years ago, a woman called Georgia. She looked stunning, stylish and beautiful, and she was headed right towards Philippa, although she hadn't seen her as yet. Philippa wondered what to do: should she make herself known or avoid a collision course? As a believer in fate and making things happen, she went with the first option. Georgia turning up at that precise moment was surely a message, an opportunity, and she wasn't about to ignore it. She stood and waited for the woman to get closer.

"Georgia?" My goodness, it *is* you!" she said, beaming. The woman stopped, confusion written across her beautiful face.

"I don't believe it! Philippa? So it is!"

The two women embraced and giggled as though the years hadn't gone by and they were still attending lectures or studying for exams.

"Hello, Georgia," she said, pulling back from their embrace to look Georgia up and down and admire how she looked. "You look stunning! Though you always were the glamorous one of the two of us."

"Nonsense, Philippa. You have the brains as well as the beauty, the whole package. What are you doing here?"

"I'm just here on a spot of business, really, and thought I'd take a look around. It's a trendy, cool place now, isn't it? They've done a great job with the whole area."

"Yes, and it's a lovely place to work, and you know I do like lovely things." The two of them laughed lightly. Georgia had always been the dainty one of the two of them, while Philippa had been much less so. Georgia looked at her watch. "Have you got time for a coffee? It would be lovely to hear what you've been up to and my boss isn't due back for another forty-five minutes. So if we're quick ...?"

"I'd love to. You lead the way. But I'm buying!"

The two women headed towards a café in the opposite direction to where Sebastian had gone. Once inside, they sat down in a quiet booth and ordered. Philippa jumped straight in with questions. If Georgia had been sent as a signal to help, she needed to make good use of their few minutes together.

"So tell me what you're doing now. You obviously work in the Sebast Suites. Who for? Some oil tycoon or fashion house perhaps," she said excitedly.

Georgia laughed lightly. "I wish it was with someone so exciting but no, just a local businessman, though he is rather gorgeous. I've only been there a couple of months so still pretty new and getting used to him." As an afterthought, she added, "And I wouldn't mind getting used to him a bit more!" Georgia winked at Philippa.

"Some things don't change! Have you been there with him yet? I bet you have already. Tell!"

"I wish, but sadly no. In the short time I've been there, he hasn't made any sort of move on me. I'm rather disappointed if the truth be told. And I wish he would. With his reputation with the ladies, I'm beginning to think I'm ugly."

"Not likely, Georgia. Have you looked in the mirror recently? You're stunning."

"Thanks, but he's made it clear he's not interested in alone time with me. I've been flirting with him, quite outrageously, actually, but nada, nothing. Doomed before we've begun."

"And who is this gorgeous creature you've got the hots for? What's he called?"

"Sebastian, Sebastian Stevens. You've probably heard his name recently. He's been in the news a bit."

Philippa couldn't believe her ears. Georgia worked with Sebastian Stevens. Philippa gathered her thoughts quickly. trying not to show her surprise or good luck. "Wow, yes, I think I heard his name recently. A bit of trouble, if I remember rightly?" *Stay cool, Philippa.*

"You could say that. Since that whole hunting thing, the office has gone bananas with calls and messages from people expressing their disgust. Even a couple of serious threats, would you believe. I'll be glad when it's all blown over."

Philippa took the opportunity and waded in. "Tell me more. How's he handling it all?"

"He's not. We all are—the other staff. We're fielding things, though he's been in a real nasty mood since it all came out. Imagine what he'd be like if he were privy to most of it. He'd have a heart attack for sure."

"So where is he now, since you're here with me?"

"Oh, he's got a meeting just down the way. Didn't want to meet in the office. Not sure what it's about but he's been pretty cagey about it. Concocting something, I expect."

"Does he live in the building too? I expect there's a penthouse at the top."

"No, he had a place on Blackfriars, overlooking the river, I believe. Never been lucky enough to be invited. Why'd you ask?"

"Oh, no reason. I just figured he might have a place close by, being a rich sexy businessman and all."

They both laughed like two teenage girls drinking Coke floats. Georgia glanced at her pretty watch again.

"Look, I've got to go, but it's been lovely seeing you."

"Yes, it has. We shouldn't leave it so long next time. Why don't I send you a friend request in the meantime? I'm sure I'll be back in Manchester pretty soon. We could have drinks and dinner?"

"Great! Let's do that now, and definitely put me down for a good old night out. I'll show you the sights."

As they both stood and walked towards the door, they promised to stay in touch online in the meantime. Philippa kissed Georgia on the cheek.

"It's been lovely. You go, and I'll see you soon," she said. She watched Georgia walk back towards her building, noting a few stares as she passed. She was still one beautiful woman. And she could be the ticket into Sebastian's life. Or death.

Chapter Forty-Three

WHAT A STROKE OF LUCK. Not only seeing Georgia, but finding out she actually worked for Sebastian into the bargain. The gods had lined up for her for sure. She couldn't have planned it any better. Now she needed to make the most of the opportunity, the relationship, and exploit it where she could.

After Georgia had gone back inside, she'd stayed waiting in the shadows for Sebastian to return from his meeting, being careful not to be seen by her again if she popped back out for some reason. He hadn't been long behind his PA, and Philippa had studied his face as he approached the building, a man with something on his mind for sure, and she could guess what it was. She'd hung around outside for a few more minutes when he'd gone in, then ventured up to his floor but didn't attempt to go into the reception area. If she'd been spotted again, it would look too suspicious. There wasn't much she could achieve after that, but she felt content anyway that she'd seen his place of work and the man himself. Knowing that all the pictures of him online seemed to be with dark-haired women, she wasn't surprised that Georgia hadn't got anywhere in her quest to sleep with him: the beautiful blonde simply wasn't his type.

Searching the images online had paid dividends. His snazzy Aston Martin, pictured in a few of the photos, had conveniently showed the registration plate and that meant getting his actual address in Spinningfields was not going to be a problem at all. She took the lift back downstairs to the lobby and out into the warm sunshine of the early summer's day, then headed out on foot, towards the post office to put another piece of the puzzle together. The teller had been most helpful with the address, and once she had what she needed she set off again. Thoughts of how best to get into his physical life ran through her mind as she walked and she realised she hadn't got nearly enough intel on the man to do so yet. She stopped at a bench and dug her phone out of her bag. If she was going to use Georgia's help, she may as well start now. And that meant keeping in touch with Georgia. Pulling up the Messenger app, she tapped her message:

Fancy meeting you today! What a lovely surprise! I'll message you later to chat more. Enjoy your afternoon. Bye!

Send.

A few seconds later, Georgia sent a smiling emoji as a reply.

But she had work to do before she could head back home so she headed for a taxi rank up ahead and slipped inside the back of a waiting car.

"Blackfriars Street, please," she told the driver, and settled back for the short drive, watching the sites of trendy Manchester as he manoeuvred them through lunchtime traffic. Her stomach rumbled; she'd have to grab something once she'd seen inside his building and was safely on her way back down south.

"Here you go, Miss," said the cabbie, turning onto his street. "What number do you want?"

"I'm not sure, actually. Deansgate end, and I'll figure it out from there." She knew exactly where she needed but wanted to approach the building from a little further away than directly outside.

"Right you are," he said, and pulled over outside an Italian restaurant close by. As she opened her door, the smell of warm buttery garlic and herbs assaulted her nose and reminded her stomach it needed refuelling before too much longer. She paid the driver and stepped out into the street. As he pulled away, she took in her surroundings and headed to the address the post office had given her, the only building that bore his style of luxury. It would have been obvious, really, where he lived on the street. She checked her piece of paper with the apartment number on it and stopped outside, looking through the glass doors to the inside of her second lobby of the day.

"Here it is," she said under her breath, and tried the door, which, to her surprise, opened easily. A woman in a maid uniform pushing a small cleaning trolley startled her from the left side as she entered.

"Good morning," the woman said. She had an Eastern European accent, though from which exact country Philippa had no idea. The name printed on the lanyard hanging around her neck read 'Daniela,' and Philippa suspected she was originally from somewhere in the Czech Republic, possibly a generation or so ago.

"Hello. Good morning." She stammered slightly at being caught out by the young woman who she now knew to be Daniela.

"Are you looking for someone? Can I be assistance?' She was smiling and looked friendly enough, so Philippa took her chance.

"I'm actually here to see Sebastian, but I've just realised I don't know what his apartment number is, but no bother. I will give him a call," she lied. She pulled her phone out as if she was about to do so.

"Ah, Sebastian. No, don't bother him. He's up on the top floor, of course, but he's not at home. I'm sorry. Can you come back later?"

"Oh dear." Philippa feigned disappointment. "I must have got mixed up. Now I'll be in bother."

"He'll be in his office at this hour. Do you know where that is? I can tell you if you don't. It's not far."

"That's okay, thanks. I know where it is. He must have said his office rather than his home. Silly me. I bet he left here hours ago."

"Yes. He leaves early, around seven am. I know because I clean his apartment first each day, which pleases me to start early. I can then get back for my little one when I have finished everyone else." She smiled at the thought of her child. "Oh, listen at me. Sorry, you're not interested in all that. Forgive me. I don't have many people to talk to all day," the woman said, smiling and wafting her hand at herself dismissingly.

"No need to apologise. I understand. It's me that's in the wrong place at the right time. I'm the silly one!" Philippa said, laughing lightly at her 'mistake.' The other woman smiled along with her.

"Well, since you're here, is there something I can leave for Mr. Sebastian perhaps?"

"No, but thanks. I'll head over to his office now and put my mistake straight. You've been helpful. Thank you," she said, and turned to open the big glass door again.

"You're welcome," the woman said after her as Philippa headed back out onto the street, not daring to look back in case the woman was watching her. Bumping into the woman had been helpful in more ways than one. She now knew what time he left for work each day as well as who did his cleaning daily. She wondered if Daniela's lanyard contained a master swipe card to get into all the apartments. If she cleaned each of them every day, she was never going to have separate physical keys for each individual apartment, not in this day and age. Or maybe there were keypads on the doors requiring codes? Until she could gain access to the interior for herself, she'd have to assume it was swipe card access. A plan formed in her brain. Could it be that simple? Could that be it? All she had to do was get that swipe card and a uniform like Daniela's and turn up early one morning. She let the idea percolate.

The smell of cooked garlic hit her again as she got closer to the restaurant. "What the heck. May as well eat here," she decided, and made her way to one of the small outdoor tables that was partially hidden by a tall pot plant on the pavement. She sat down. From her vantage point, she could clearly see the entrance to the building she'd just been in and watched with interest as a van cruised to a standstill right outside the door. Daniela reappeared, got inside, and the van drove off.

"How convenient," she mused. The van was emblazoned with the words "Maids of Honour, Domestic Solutions." Another piece of the plan had just fallen into place. Today was obviously her very, very lucky day. As the waiter approached her table, she ordered a glass of red wine and a chef's special pizza, figuring she deserved every last bit of it.

Chapter Forty-Four

SHE WAS EXHAUSTED by the time she'd got back home. Investigating someone quietly was not something she was used to doing and all the travelling, the lack of sleep the previous night and the hanging around watching and waiting had taken its toll on her, mentally as well as physically. Turning her key in the front door, she welcomed kicking her shoes off as she stepped inside, the coolness of the hallway floor instant therapy to her throbbing feet. She splayed and wiggled her toes and groaned with pleasure before shutting the door behind her and padding towards the lounge, where she slung her bag on the floor and collapsed on the sofa.

"I'm knackered," she declared to the wall. Blowing a heavy sigh out through her mouth, she sat for a minute or two, head back, eyes closed. The room was deathly quiet; not a sound could be heard. Just the way she liked it. Sometimes she found the quiet too loud, with nothing and no one to break it, but on a day such as this, it was perfect. Her phone buzzed with an incoming notification and she opened one eye, deciding whether to see who it was or ignore it. Her inquisitiveness got the better of her and she sat back up to grab her bag and retrieve her phone. Philippa smiled. It was a message from Georgia.

Lovely to see you today. Such a surprise! We've so much to catch up on and you mentioned you would be back up soon, so let me know when and we can go out for dinner. My treat!

Philippa smiled: such a spot of good luck seeing her old friend had been, and so useful in her mission. She tapped her message back and hit reply.

I know, how lovely! And I must say you still look as gorgeous as ever! And yes to dinner, though we will argue about the bill at the time. How was your gorgeous boss this afternoon? In for a penny, in for a pound, she thought. May as well start the conversation in the required direction.

Oh, you know, still sexy as all hell but a grumpy bugger. I'll forgive him, though, if he relents and takes me up on my offer! Whoever he met with for coffee riled him up a bit and he was in a foul mood all afternoon.

Philippa wondered if his meeting had been anything to do with his speech and video debacle from the other night. *Anything to do with his speech, do you think, or has that died down a bit?*

She waited while Georgia replied, the little dots on the screen telling her she was busily tapping a reply back.

I suspect it was, though I know he really pissed a licensee off just before he went off on his little trip. Pulled the license from him and left him high and dry. Sure knows how to make an enemy or two at the moment.

Philippa looked at her response thoughtfully before tapping a message back. *Seems he has a bit of a mess to clear up all round. Maybe you should offer him a massage to calm him down.* She picked a blushing emoji, added it on the end and hit reply. The three little dots came back and she waited.

Need to be a brunette for that, I reckon, and according to the gossip at work, he likes the submissive types in the bedroom and that's not me. I might look girl next door but I like to be in control, remember?

Philippa smiled at that, remembering back to a time at university when Georgia had dressed up as a dominatrix for a fancy-dress party and had had no end of offers, one of which she'd taken up. Scared the poor bloke half to death apparently.

My god, I remember that! I remember the poor bloke you left with, too. Did he ever recover from his ordeal, do you think?

He could have used the safe word ... But yes, he was fine. Took him a couple of days though. I wonder whatever happened to him? He left that year to go on to some training placement. Actually quite liked him.

So are you going to dye your hair and be a good girl in your quest for the hunk, or move on to someone else who would welcome the gorgeous Georgia? Has boss man got a girlfriend, do you know?

Definitely single, and doesn't mind paying for what he wants, apparently. And no, I suit blonde much better. Probably not the brightest thing to do anyway. Imagine work the next day!

I wonder which escort agency he uses. How interesting!

There was a pause at Georgia's end. Then, *That's a funny thing to wonder about.*

Ah, just intrigues me, that's all. Ever been inside a brothel?

Can't say that I have, no, but I should imagine they're a bit yuk! Why, have you?

No, me neither. But I can see why some men use them, particularly the wealthier ones. Like ordering off a pizza menu. If you're paying, you order exactly what you want, toppings and all, and if they don't supply it, you go elsewhere.

Georgia replied with a handful of laughing emojis.

Never thought of it like that. I must ask him!

As your vet, I would strongly advise against that! Philippa replied with her own laughing emoji.

It was fun chatting with Georgia on her phone and Philippa felt a little bit guilty that she was using her good nature to get intel on the man she worked for, but she was on a mission now, and any snippet of information could prove useful to her down the line. But it was also getting late and she needed food.

Anyway, it's been lovely chatting, and let's do keep in touch. If you do get it on with your hunk, spill! I need to have a shower and get something to eat. Speak soon?

You bet! If it goes off, I'll let you know. Georgia ended with another emoji, one with a halo around its head.

Philippa laughed to herself and sent a couple of kisses back with *Night, night*, then sat back in her chair to think for a moment.

"Needs must Philippa, needs must."

She headed upstairs and turned the shower on. She slipped out of

Chapter Forty-Five

SHE SLEPT SOUNDLY THAT NIGHT, tired out from her lack of sleep from the night before and the resemblance of a workable plan progressing nicely in the back of her mind like coffee percolating slowly on the stove. As she broke through to wakefulness, she stretched and glanced at her clock. It was still early. Her alarm was not due to go off for another thirty minutes and she dug deeper into her duvet to adjust more to the dawning morning light. Thoughts of what she'd learned yesterday drifted into her mind and made themselves at home, the much-needed sleep helping her gain clarity on what was about to happen. There were a couple of steps she needed to get in place today, someone she needed to get help from without raising any alarm bells, as well as getting her equipment in order. At this stage, she couldn't tell just when she was going to pay Sebastian a visit. That would depend on him to some extent, but if he was feeling stressed, and she knew he was, he might be more inclined to need his submissive fix sooner rather than later. Could that be the way to go? The scenario also had its drawbacks, but then so did being a cleaner.

With the weak sunshine peeking through the cracks in her curtains, she swung her legs out of bed, reaching to turn the alarm off before it pierced the quiet, and padded her way downstairs to the kitchen. Once there, she brewed tea, filled a bowl with cornflakes and sat watching the world wake up through the kitchen window. She picked her phone up and prepared a message:

Pete, fancy a drink after work tonight? I'm buying.

Not expecting him to be up and online just yet, she carried on with her cereal. She was surprised to hear her phone chirp almost immediately.

If you're buying, I'm coming! Where and when?

He made her smile; he had always been a cute kid when they'd lived as close friends and neighbours down the same street some years ago. Their age difference had never been a problem; Pete had been grateful for the friendship. When his mother had died at the hands of his father when he had only been thirteen, he'd ended up in a series of foster homes, but Philippa had always kept in contact with him, like a big sister, trying to look out for him where she could. She'd thought of taking him in herself, but university and then her career had prevented her. She was not willing to give her life up totally for a young lad down the road. And so he'd ended up in the system, then done a spell in juvie for petty crimes, his way of dealing and rebelling at how life had treated him. Now, at twenty years old, he'd straightened himself out, got a proper job, and put his talents to good use. He was a bright young man, and as long as he stayed with the right crowd and didn't get lured back into his old life, he'd make a go of himself. She tapped back a response:

Meet you outside your office, say 6 pm? We can grab a burger if you like. Not had one since forever ago. Need a greasy-melted-cheese-with-ketchup fix. And a beer. Had too much lettuce and salad of recent.

Perfect. Sounds good. See you later.

Great. Now all she needed to do was drop her questions into their seemingly innocent conversation about spyware and she'd have what she needed to get the plan moving. Until she could access Sebastian's computer, she wasn't going to get far, and Pete was going to prove invaluable. She chewed cornflakes thoughtfully, mulling over her two plans, then stopped as an unwelcome thought came to her. If she somehow managed to get Daniela's lanyard, she needed to make sure she could actually gain access to his apartment *and* that he would be there. As she hadn't got access to much of his life yet and hadn't the time to stake his routine out for a couple more weeks, she had no way of knowing what his life held, or his diary for that matter; Georgia would be suspicious if she asked her outright. How exactly could she find out without looking suspicious?

Stealing the key card had its drawbacks too: Daniela would simply get another key pass from her employer, and could very well end up walking in on her as she was bang in the middle of the deed. That then posed a problem with what to do with her, a witness, and as Philippa had no beef with her, it would be a senseless death.

And she wasn't sure she could do that.

No, it was too risky, and because of that, she discarded the idea of playing maid for the morning.

That left one other feasible option: she was going to have to be hooker for the evening.

As long as she could get access to Sebastian's keystrokes and monitor what he did online, it wouldn't be too hard. She could gain access easily. Once she was at the building at the designated time, he'd let her in readily and she'd play the part well—up to a point. And if the doorbell chimed from another waiting escort while she was inside with him, it would simply be ignored. She'd never heard of hookers having their own sets of keys and doubted his next hooker would be any different.

The next bit of her plan was to finalise her supplies and costume. She drank down the last mouthful of warm tea and headed upstairs to get ready for work, thinking about what to wear as a submissive for the event to come.

Chapter Forty-Six

SHE LEFT her car in the station car park and rode the train into London to meet Pete. No sense trying to navigate the traffic or find a parking space around Green Park at rush hour. It was coming up to six as she exited the tube station and headed towards his office, and she could see him loitering in the distance, leaning up against the wall, one foot bent up behind him to balance himself. He waved as he saw her approach and she waved back.

Pete had always been generous with his affection towards her and welcomed her with wide-open arms that quickly turned into a bear hug.

"Oooh, it's so good to see you as always," he cooed, keeping a firm hold on her then pulling back slightly.

"And you too, though if I can't breathe I'm not going to be much good as a burger partner tonight," she said, laughing back with affection.

"I've missed you a bit, that's all." He took a step back and looked her up and down. "And you look great, by the way. Have you been working out?"

"No, not really, but I'll take the compliment anyway. Just working hard."

"So, where we headed first, then? Food, beer or a bar with both?

I'm famished!"

"Let's go for bar with both. Where's new around here?"

"Nothing much that I know of, but what about a walk to Soho? Always something new popping up there. Let's be adventurous." Pete winked at Philippa as he turned in the direction of London's trendy Soho area. Philippa fell into step beside him. There was a comfortable minute or two of silence before Pete asked her a question.

"Was there something in particular that you wanted to see me for or just to catch up?" His naturally acute perceptive skills had heightened during his time in juvie and had helped him avoid trouble on several occasions. Now he found his skill useful in many aspects of his life—like sussing someone out that had an ulterior motive, or wasn't being totally honest about something.

"Nothing gets past your radar, does it?" said Philippa brightly. "You've got me. I do have something on my mind."

Turning his head and smiling at Philippa as they walked, he said, "Just one of my many skills. Now tell me what I can help you with."

Philippa had been prepared for this and had, she hoped, the perfect scenario ready. She also hoped he wouldn't see straight through her story.

"It's not for me I need your help. It's for a friend. She's convinced her husband is having an affair and wants to snoop a little, but not with a private detective. With spyware.

"I see. Go on."

"He's been visiting escort sites, she thinks, and wants to set him up to serve him right, but in order to do that, she needs access ..."

"To his computer." He finished the sentence for her. "And let me guess, she needs to clone his keystrokes and point to a fake page of her own to set the trap."

Philippa turned towards him and caught his eye. She blushed a little at being caught out. While she knew he could sort the keystroke cloning part out, she hadn't thought about the fake web page. The idea pleased her, though, and she went with it.

"Exactly. She wants to turn up instead of the escort he thinks he's booked, and Voilà ! He's nabbed. And in a whole load of do-do. She's convinced he's been doing it for some time. Now she wants the proof."

"Can you get me the laptop he uses?"

"Definitely not, unfortunately."

"No problem. It would just have been a bit easier. There's always more than one way to solve a problem."

"There's another way to help her?" Philippa was playing her part well, though she didn't like lying to her friend.

"Sure is. Just need to know the name of the site he frequents, and then create a fake email from them and send it using BLAT or something similar. Or if you don't know the site, find out where else he shops or what services he uses, then pose as one of them instead. It's to the same end. When he clicks on the embedded link, the spy software will download itself onto his hard drive and voila! to coin your phrase. You will have access. He won't know a thing about it."

She was shocked, if truth be told. "It's that simple? Really?"

Pete laughed at her naivety. "Why do you think all those spam emails you get from god knows who trying to get you to click on links are worth their time? Anyone can create a fake email newsletter or branded email just by cutting and pasting a logo. And with a little know-how for the email address, the average Joe wouldn't know the real one from the fake one. That's what they are banking on."

"And when the spyware is downloaded, what happens next?"

"The person who sent it can see a duplicate of their intended's screen, exactly what they are looking at. Then, when he makes his booking, you can pounce again."

"Eh? What with?"

"You have, or should I say she has, a choice. Either let him book his chosen woman and your friend turns up in her place, or send a cancellation email with 'our' apologies and suggest another lady, this time the page of your friend. Obviously, her face will be hidden slightly. That's a bit more work, and in my view a bit more risky, but both plans have their faults."

"What about the other plan? Less risky, do you think?"

"From what I can see, the only real risk is if the real escort gets there before your friend. That could be interesting!"

"Can't we somehow cancel the other woman, give my friend a fighting chance of catching him out?"

Pete was quiet for a moment while he thought it through. "If the site uses a Messenger app or emails its ladies with the booking details, we could perhaps get into that and change the time slightly, making her, say, fifteen minutes later for example? That way, he'd be having kittens at his wife turning up, she could have it out with him, then the real escort shows. Bang! Fireworks in the hallway." Pete grinned.

"You're enjoying this, aren't you?" she said. "Is this even legal?"

"Of course not, but anyone can do it. Just ask your favourite search engine how to do anything and it's all there. And of course, there's the dark web, but that's another story."

"Sounds like we don't need the dark web—the regular one has it all! What's the name of the software that will be downloaded? Is this something I can do instead of you doing it?"

"Hey! Who said anything about me doing it?" He stopped walking and turned to Philippa. "I'm not doing it, but I'll tell you how to do it, though I'll always deny any involvement if asked. I've worked too hard to keep clean."

Philippa had the good sense to be embarrassed at suggesting he tarnish his good work. "Sorry, Pete, I didn't think," she said abashedly. "My bad."

Pete let a breath out and calmly said, "I know. Don't worry. I don't mind telling you the how, but the doing is all up to you two. Just don't get caught yourself. People get pissed off at being spied on."

"Got it. So what's the software called?"

"Met something or other. I'll just double-check first. There may be a better one since I last used it. I'll email you details on how to create the fake email, from my personal account, one you can't trace back, of course." He turned and smiled at her again. "Got to be careful in all that you do, and I suggest when you've done with what you need, you delete all evidence you had anything to do with the scam. Take your laptop to be cleaned maybe. Let your friend be the one to actually do it, not you." He stopped walking and turned towards her, a serious look on his face. "I'm deadly serious on that part, Philippa. Keep out of it. Just pass the knowledge on. End of story."

Philippa was beginning to feel a little serious about it all. Of course, she didn't want to get her 'friend' into trouble, but she hadn't thought

Chapter Forty-Seven

AND SO THAT night after work, Philippa got busy on her computer, but not before giving Georgia a call. There was just one piece of the puzzle that Georgia could help with, even though she didn't know she was doing so.

"So, how's it going with Mr. Handsome? Any gossip on that front?"

"Sadly, none. I think I'll just give up. And he's got a date for the night, some fundraiser, so no doubt they'll be pictured together in the tabloids tomorrow. We'll see her then." She sounded somewhat subdued, almost petulant, and Philippa smiled wistfully into her phone.

"Poor thing! She won't be as gorgeous as you, whoever she is," she replied, trying to cheer her friend up. "What's the occasion, anyhow?" Philippa could see an opportunity surfacing. She had intended to find out if Sebastian was a member of a racquet club or what his favourite wine shop was, so he would open an email from them—only one that she'd created, a Trojan one.

"It's for autism spectrum disorder. There's a silent auction, which is ironic after the last auction he was involved in landed him in the mire, but his PR company have suggested this little affair will get him back in the good books with the public."

"How's that?"

"He's offered himself up as one of the prizes: a night on the town with the great Sebastian Stevens, no less. It will be interesting if it goes to plan. If no one bids, he's going to be damn grumpy!"

"Will you be bidding, Georgia, get the ball rolling?"

"Not on my wage, though I know that there has been some marketing budget set aside to bid to save the embarrassment if no one else is really interested. He'll never know, and we can all rest a bit easier. That's the plan, anyway."

Philippa couldn't believe she was hearing it. Could this be a better opportunity than the Trojan email and replacement hooker?

"What time does it start and where is it?"

Georgia laughed, "You're not going to bid, are you?"

"Of course not. He's all yours, babe. And anyway, I'm in London remember—I'd never get there on time even if I was in the slightest interested in him. Which I'm not."

"Auction starts at nine, at The Lowry, his usual haunt."

"Well, I wish him luck," Philippa said, and moved away from the subject of him so as not to arouse suspicion. "What are the other prizes on offer for the cause. Anything more in my price bracket?" She was just making conversation now, no ulterior motive.

"The usual. A handful of paintings by local starving artists, some quality guitar time with a famous musician, the man himself and a few minor experience days like ballooning. Hopefully they hit their collection target. It's a great cause."

"Yes," said Philippa thoughtfully. "I hope so too. I've got some research work to do, so I'd better say good night. Let me know how it goes, if your marketing department have to buy their own boss for a date. What a giggle!"

Georgia giggled back in reply as they said their goodbyes, then Philippa spread out on the sofa with her legs outstretched and her laptop on her thighs. She laid her head back to work through this new opportunity that had come to light, to think some of the finer points through. Would it work? Was it a better plan or should she stick with the current one?

After ten minutes of tossing both scenarios around in her head and working through what could possibly go wrong, she decided to empty her thoughts out on paper and make a list. Seeing the pros and cons might make the answer obvious. She took her pad and split the first page into two columns.

"Let's start with the original plan first," she said out loud. As her thoughts came to her, she put them under one of the headings. One by one, the risks and advantages went down until, after nearly ten minutes, she couldn't think of any more. Then she did the same for the possible new plan.

Thoughtful, she said, "I bet they'd accept phone bids, I don't have to be present." She scribbled her answers down with that in mind.

"No one would know who I was, what I looked like, nothing." She chewed the end of her pen. "But the PR company may want to photograph us on our date. That would cause a problem. Then if he died that night... Too obvious." She chewed the pen again then swung her legs off the sofa in one decisive move. She stood and headed into the kitchen, poured herself a glass of wine and grabbed a packet of cashews. By the time she'd returned, her mind was set.

"Stick with the original, Philippa. Great heists don't deviate from their plans and neither should you, though there are a couple of snippets you can use from your newly acquired knowledge." She tossed a handful of nuts into her mouth and pulled her laptop closer. The thought of bidding for her killer had its own appeal, particularly as that was how he'd come to be in her sights in the first place, bidding for two white rhinos. She had no intention of ever being caught. If she could pull off what Pete had suggested, no one would be any the wiser.

She got to work creating the fake email. Rather than try and work out which escort site he used, she now had a much simpler way in—the hotel from the fundraiser tonight. She thoughtfully typed the message that would get his attention and added the all-important bogus link, hyperlinking it to the Trojan file she had already sourced with Pete's help. The vital cog in this wheel, the life-changing email message, was coming from the hotel, supposedly thanking Sebastian for being an auction prize at the fundraising event, and if he clicked on the link, he could browse the many photos that were taken of him at the event. Someone as arrogant and self-centred as Sebastian was would be sure to take a look. As the Trojan file did its thing in the background,

Chapter Forty-Eight

THE FUNDRAISER HAD BEEN a giant pain in his ass but he'd said he would be there, and being one of the auction prizes, he'd really no choice in the matter. He'd sat through a nauseatingly boring dinner conversation with a bunch of sycophantic young entrepreneurs and several of their girlfriends who all looked like the same stereotypical bachelorette reality television wannabes. Each had straight long blonde hair, dark false eyelashes, a spray tan and pouty lips, and one in particular had made no bones about her flirty behaviour towards him, her leg brushing his under the table at every opportunity. Women frequently threw themselves at him and while it was a novelty occasionally, generally he tired of it. There was no fun if there was no chase and he liked to chase, to dominate, to be in control—of everything, including the bedroom. It had been dull personified.

Sebastian sat back on the white leather sofa in his apartment and sipped whiskey from a thick cut-crystal glass, thinking back to earlier in the evening when he'd picked his plus-one up for the event. She was cute, dark, and extremely malleable, and he'd purchased her before solely because she looked good on his arm, and was more his type. A professional at what she did, she was his date of choice at such events since he didn't need to worry about staying with her for the night, nor her saying the wrong thing to the wrong people. She'd been instructed to keep her trap shut, smile sweetly and generally look stunning, and on that she had delivered. But she didn't do the full submissive thing, and as he sipped his whiskey, he thought yet again about how she'd look naked. And on his bed.

He reached over to the coffee table for his laptop and opened the web page of the agency he used for her, clicked on her profile and studied her a little more. She really was quite stunning. Shame she didn't list more on her menu, things to his taste and needs. In the dock below the page, his email counter showed six so he clicked to see who the emails were all from, scanning the subject line for something to catch his interest. There was one from the hotel, which he opened. The message thanked him for his participation during the evening, and invited him to browse some of the superb photos that had been taken at the gala event. He clicked the link to the photo gallery, but when it didn't go anywhere, he assumed, wrongly, that the link was broken. He'd see them later anyway. The PR people from the office would have taken the appropriate ones.

Little did he know what was happening deep inside his computer: the Trojan program was quietly accessing his hard drive, his keystrokes and all that he did on his computer, inserting itself—and its hidden mistress—into his life. Giving up on reading email, he clicked back to study the woman on the screen, the one capturing his attention. She did something for him, but not nearly enough, and as a familiar stirring pulled him, he opened another browser tab and entered in the site address he got the most pleasure from. While it was late now, that didn't stop him from booking someone for another night and thinking about just what he was going to do to her. The time spent waiting, anticipating, was equally as exciting as the time he actually spent with his chosen one.

He smiled as he scanned the women, the posed, sultry images; many of them had visited him at his apartment or at various hotel suites around Manchester in the past. He paid them well, over the odds in fact. He saw this as an investment, and a way to keep their mouths closed if he got carried away.

One young woman in particular stood out to him, her innocent looks appealing to his desires. She was someone he hadn't seen before.

"Chloe" had the requisite long dark brown hair and young looks. She also had an exceptionally pleasing body to go with it, making her the whole sweet little package. He checked what she offered and, liking what was listed, clicked 'book.' It was obvious what these girls did for a living, but of course everything was in code on the website so as not to break laws, though if you knew what you were looking for, it was an easy code to break. He smiled to himself as he stared at the young, innocent-looking face looking back at him. He wondered how she'd fare with his requests the following night. Would she be back for more on another occasion? If he paid her well enough, he hoped she would.

"She'd better be good. The last one couldn't get out of here quick enough, and while I'm paying for all night, I mean, *all* night," he warned the image on the screen.

He closed his laptop down and headed to his bedroom, where he stripped, showered and then climbed into bed with his mind full of Chloe and his specific special fantasies.

Chapter Forty-Nine

LYING on her own bed just north of London, Philippa watched in amazement at how she was able to follow the prick's activity so easily. While she had hoped he'd take the bait, she hadn't expected him to do so quite so soon. She had been reading when her laptop screen had stirred into life. Chloe looked young, though that could be a soft-focus lens for the photo, to entice those who liked a younger body. Still, recreating Chloe's look wouldn't be too hard, and if she kept her eyes averted in true submissive style, he probably wouldn't even notice the replacement at his door. Once he invited her in and she was following dutifully behind him, she'd show him who the submissive one was, and it wasn't going to be innocent little 'Chloe.'

Now she needed to gather the few items needed to pull it off and get back up to Manchester to be in position and ready, and that meant an afternoon away from the clinic and a cheap hotel room to get herself prepared. She hoped escorts arrived bang on the dot, and figured they wouldn't voluntarily be there a moment longer than was needed or paid for. Clients, especially control freaks like Sebastian Stevens, probably expected and appreciated punctuality. Well, *she'd* have to be a few minutes early to gain crucial entry, and as Chloe was booked for 8 pm, there was precious little time to waste. She jumped

Chapter Fifty

THE MORNING at work flew by with the usual small-animal crises: toenails to be clipped, 'flu vaccinations to be had and a poor old cat with a nasty abscess on its back leg from an infection after a fight. It was work she loved doing, and today in particular, she was glad of the routine and being able to concentrate on the job at hand rather than the evening to come.

And she needed to be at work for another reason—to get the drug. Being off sick that one day had spoiled her interception plans and the drug was now safely in the dispensary. And she needed it. Without being able to subdue her victims so easily, she wouldn't be able to complete the task fully, just wouldn't be strong enough to overpower them, and Sebastian was a big man. She'd found a moment to retrieve the small vial and it was now safely in her locker.

Philippa hated lying but had needed the afternoon off for her plan to work. A sick grandmother was a plausible lie to tell. Everyone had one of those, didn't they?

"I'm off shortly, Helen. Thanks again for letting me get off this afternoon. Gran will appreciate me being with her for a couple of days. At least I can help out until she gets back on her feet." Philippa hated lying, but needs must. Her gran had died several years back but, for her cover, had suddenly come back to life.

"No problem. I hope she's feeling better soon. Just let me know in good time if you think you'll need Wednesday too, so I can organise cover for your clinic." Helen had always accommodated the rest of the team's needs, and it was one of the reasons she had a steady practice with a low turnover of staff. No one ever took advantage, and was always grateful when a need arose. No one more so than Philippa.

"Thanks. I will, but I'm pretty sure one of the cousins will be covering. I'm just doing the two days." Searching in her handbag for a lost fictitious item she added, "Damn, I must have left it in the other room." She excused herself and made her way back inside, to the dispensary, the location of her all-important drug of choice. If it was noticed that the drug vial was missing, she already had her excuse ready to go, but hoped it wouldn't be spotted before she got back with another successfully intercepted replacement next week. She knew by not following protocol for such a drug, using the excuse of 'I dropped it and disposed of it' wouldn't sit well, and could land her in a spot of trouble, but it was less trouble than she could be in for other matters. She'd just have to take the risk. It wasn't a well-used drug at the clinic, so the chances of it being needed in the next few days were pretty remote. Still, always good to have a premade excuse for the missing vial should anyone quiz her.

She slipped the vial into her handbag quickly. She'd take better care of its transportation once she was safely in her car outside. She then slipped out of the staff entrance, saying goodbye to no one else. Once she was safely in the confines of her car, she took the little vial out and wrapped it in her handkerchief, then slipped it into a small box she'd already placed in the glove compartment. With it safely wrapped up, she started the engine and headed towards the station and another trip north.

Everything else she needed was packed safely in the boot of her car, including her other weapon of choice, the knife she'd used on Fiona's neck, all wrapped up equally securely. She'd had the good sense to soak it in bleach after that first kill, mainly to clean it and get rid of any DNA present from the blood, and had stashed it under a loose floorboard in the little back bedroom of her house. Even though no one had ever questioned her about the woman's death—and why would they?—she still felt the need to hide it, just in case. Who knew where the police were at with their investigation, whether they had someone in mind for the crime, under surveillance even, and she wasn't going to take the chance on someone with a warrant coming knocking on her door.

Now, however, she needed it again, so it was hidden in her boot, under the spare wheel, wrapped up in a long thin box like a gift for someone, complete with a big red bow. She'd smiled with wry amusement as she'd wrapped it up in birthday paper; the bow was a nice touch, and it would make it look a lot less conspicuous if it was ever discovered. The only thing she still had to get was her wig, and she planned to pick that up from a small specialty shop on the outskirts of Manchester. She'd winced at the price of it, but if she was going to be convincing, she couldn't turn up in a cheap nylon one. Someone like Sebastian would notice in an instant and she couldn't risk being turned away for any reason.

A few minutes later, she was parked in the station car park. She removed her tools from the boot and placed everything in her trolley bag. After a quick look around that no one had seen anything, she locked her car with a confirming 'beep' and set off in the direction of the platform. By late afternoon, she'd be picking up her new disguise and heading to her hotel to put all the pieces of her plan together. She hoped Sebastian liked the outfit she'd chosen for him, a rather virginal cream dress. Teamed with her new long, dark hair and the right look on her lightly made-up face, she'd be submission on steroids. He was going to get the shock of his life when he led her inside: the young submissive woman he'd purchased for the evening was anything but.

However, needs must, she told herself again. She had to kill another killer.

Chapter Fifty-One

THE JOURNEY back up north had been an uneventful one. She kept herself to herself, looking like any other single woman off to see her ailing grandma. She'd shared a table seat with a gent who hadn't taken his head out of his laptop all the way up and had barely acknowledged her when she asked if he'd mind her things while she went to get a coffee.

After an hour, the trained pulled into Piccadilly Station and she alighted briskly with everyone else. The platform was always cold and draughty in Manchester, whatever the weather, and today was no exception. She pulled her jacket around herself a little tighter and began to tow her trolley bag along the concrete. She was grateful of the fresh air filling her nostrils and made her way towards the taxi rank. Her first job before going to her hotel was to pick up the wig she'd had put aside and she gave the driver the address of the specialty shop as she climbed into the back seat. She closed her eyes to the early rush hour traffic as they made their way to her destination. It wasn't long before he pulled up outside.

"Please wait, I'll only be a minute," she said, then headed inside to pick up her order. She paid in cash, then exited the shop, turning her face slightly aside from the security cameras, and slid back into the rear seat.

"Portland Street, please. Just drop me at the lower end, if you would. I could do with some air."

"Right you are," the driver replied, and they headed off in the direction of her hotel for the night, not that he'd know that. She didn't want people knowing her business, and she knew she needed to take precautions. Leave something out or make a stupid mistake and the consequences could be dire. While she wasn't a pro at doing this kind of thing, of course, she was learning to think of all possible eventualities, including paying with cash wherever she went. Her next major concern was not actually checking into her hotel, but leaving it dressed as Chloe later and avoiding the CCTV cameras in both the hotel and the surrounding area.

The taxi pulled up at the curb a little way off from her hotel.

"Thanks very much," she said, and gave the driver cash. She waited until he'd driven off out of sight before she ventured to her chosen hotel and checked in, paying for the room in advance, and of course, in cash. She signed her name as Chloe Baxter, and that's who she'd be until Sebastian Stevens had been punished.

Chapter Fifty-Two

THE ROOM SMELLED of stale cigarettes and cheap air freshener, and she idly wondered what the top cover on the bed contained by way of other people's DNA. The 70s-style green swirly-patterned carpet was worn in places, the dated furniture scratched, the table top covered with hot mug circles, the shiny finish long gone. All in all, it was a dump, though the lobby itself hadn't been too bad; that's the part that management obviously focused on. Good for the website photographs.

She took her jacket off and hung it in the wardrobe, then unpacked her outfit for later, setting her wig on the corner of the old wing chair. She laid her other items out and ran thorough her plan once again, tossing around various scenarios and rehearsing in her head how she should react to each of them. Her main concern was getting into Sebastian's apartment before Chloe, his true escort for the evening, arrived, but not early enough to put the plan in jeopardy and be spotted acting suspiciously. She took her chance among previous guests' DNA, sat down on the bed cover and rummaged in her toiletry bag for the two miniatures she had brought with her for strength—she had been correct in assuming that her room would have no minibar. Whiskey and vodka weren't really her thing—she was more a wine girl—but as she unscrewed the top off the whiskey bottle, she was glad she'd brought them. Her nerves were jangling, and she hoped the hot fiery liquid would help settle them as it burned its way down her throat. She winced, screwing her face up in disgust, though the warmth it provided was welcome.

She had just two hours until 'show time' so she headed to the tiny bathroom, thinking a soak in the bath would help calm her. The water at least was fast and hot, and steam was soon rising from the stained tub. She added the contents of the mini shampoo bottle for bubbles. In the absence of a working extractor fan, the little room was immediately filled with steam. She tested the water temperature with her fingertips, turned both taps off and climbed in, sliding down until her shoulders were covered. It felt wonderful; it was a shame she wasn't someplace nicer. She needed to relax a little before the main event of the evening. Allowing herself the luxury of closing her eyes for a minute or two, not for the first time that day, she wondered where this would all lead, what was in the near future for her. Relaxation was soon replaced with fear as her thoughts turned in a different direction. Would she get away with murder? How many would she have to kill to fulfil her mission? How and why would she eventually stop? So many questions, and none of them with answers. The thoughts terrified her and she opened her eyes in a flash like she was wakening from a nightmare, alarm written all over her face, her breathing rough. She shook her head to remove the negative thoughts and sat bolt upright, bubbles clinging to her shoulders, water splashing over the sides on to the floor.

"You can't afford those thoughts, Philippa! Get a grip!" she scolded herself, and reached for the tiny individually wrapped soap bar to wash. "Focus, or you'll mess up. Now get ready, and get it done. You can dwell on things later if you have to, but now is not the time!" She sounded hard on herself, harsh to her own ears, but the voice was right. She washed quickly, then climbed out of the bath and let the water go, the loud gurgling sound grating on her nerves as the last of the water went down the wastepipe and out into the ancient drains of Manchester.

The once-fluffy white towel did the necessary and she tied it around herself while she expertly applied a light covering of make-up, complete with pale pink lips. From her research on being a submissive, she knew that hot red lips were not expected; that was more for a dominatrix, and Sebastian would be looking for, and expecting, something much more innocent, more virginal. She let the towel fall onto the floor and stepped into the cream dress: oh yes, this was going to be perfect. A little rose water behind her ears, kitten heels on her feet, baby-pink toenails ... She admired the look she had created. Even without the long brown wig on, she looked perfect for her mission. Almost elf-like.

"And tonight, I'm going to be Chloe," she said to her reflection, smiling broadly.

Not wanting to leave the hotel completely dressed as the woman she was impersonating, she carefully placed her wig in the silk scarf she had brought and added it to her bag, the wrapping paper and bow of the 'gift' for him just visible in the bottom. Tucked securely in an inside pocket of the same bag was the syringe of liquid.

She stared at the woman in the mirror, her mood changing to serious. She was ready. She gathered her kit, picked up her room key, and left.

"Taxi, Miss?" the doorman asked as she stepped outside into the evening.

"Please," was all she said until, for the third time today, she slipped into the back seat of a cab. The only address she gave the driver was the street and a number well below the one she actually wanted, and that's just where he dropped her some ten minutes later. She paid in cash again. and once the cab was well out of sight, she checked her watch and slipped down a nearby side street, finding privacy in a dingy, dark doorway. Avoiding the remains of desperate lovers' activity that lay scattered on the ground, she put her brown wig on and double-checked herself in her little compact mirror.

"Hello again, Chloe."

She smiled at herself in an effort to relieve some of the tension she felt inside, then pulled on pale latex gloves. She took the syringe from the safety of the inside bag pocket and slipped it inside her sleeve, balancing it ready in her hand.

Everything was set now, and she strode purposefully out of the doorway and towards the main entrance of Sebastian Stevens' home.

Chapter Fifty-Three

SHE PRESSED the bronze buzzer with a latex-covered knuckle.

"What is it with him and bronze?" she wondered absently while she waited for his voice, careful to keep her eyes lowered and her face turned away from any possible nearby cameras.

"Come on up. Level seven," came Sebastian's voice. Nothing more. She could have been anyone. The lift was already at the ground floor and her knuckle pressed the number 7. The heavy metal doors pinged open and 'Chloe' stepped out, still taking care to keep her head low, not looking too confident: he could well have been watching from somewhere. There was only one door visible on level seven. There was a foot holding it open, and her heart pounded in her chest as she got nearer. Then a male form filled it completely. 'Chloe' took comfort in the little plastic syringe hiding in her right hand and sleeve as she briefly glanced at him. He spoke first, as she intended him to do.

"You're a little early."

"Sorry, Mr. Stevens. It won't happen again." Never raising her head for eye contact, she heard him laugh a little at her response, delighted in her meekness. He held the door open for her to step inside.

"Oh, after you Mr. Stevens. You're in charge." Still no eye contact.

"That I am, Chloe, that I am. I think we're going to get along just fine tonight." That chuckle again. It turned her stomach. He led the way into his vast apartment with 'Chloe' a step behind. The door clunked shut behind them.

Now she had to move fast: this was her chance, while his back was towards her and before she had to commit to anything more perverse, like what he was expecting her to do. The plastic syringe felt immensely heavy as it slid all the way out into her palm. She flicked the cap off. In one rapid movement, she raised her arm to full height and then brought it down fast and hard, slamming the needle into his flesh. It caught him in the back of the shoulder, his widest part, and she pressed the plunger, silently delivering the syringe's deadly contents.

He flinched at the sharp stab. "What are ..." But his words trailed off as the poison quickly took effect. Down he went, and down he stayed. It was over in a matter of seconds. 'Chloe' bent down and looked at him properly from a slight distance. He'd slumped down the hallway wall and crumpled in a heap, his legs buckled under him. She watched as the second hand of her watch circled around, and on its third pass, she stepped towards him and felt his neck for a pulse.

Sebastian Stevens was gone: the first part of her plan was a success so far.

As she was rising back up, a loud sing-song tone assaulted her ears. She shot her hand to her mouth: the doorbell. And now a rap on the door, and a woman's voice. The real 'Chloe' was only a few feet away. How had she gained entry? Someone must have let in her through the main lobby entrance, just like Daniela had let her in just a few days ago. Holding her breath, she stood motionless, hoping the woman would get the hint and leave soon. There was another knock, firmer this time. Oh god... What if the other woman had Sebastian's mobile number, just in case of a change in plan? Energy filled her veins as she sprang noiselessly from her spot and scanned the surfaces in the main room for his mobile. She had to turn the volume off, and quickly. It wouldn't do if 'Chloe' could hear it ringing from her spot on the other side of the door. At last she spotted it.

"There you are, you trouble causer," she hissed. She tiptoed to a glass coffee table, grabbed the mobile and turned it to silent, just as it started to vibrate. The doorbell rang again followed by another sharp rap. Philippa stood frozen to the spot. She waited patiently for five full minutes more, then finally heard the woman's footsteps receding down the hall. The phone vibrated one last time with a text that went unanswered.

It was time to activate the next part of her plan—the bit she abhorred.

She stripped off the cream-coloured dress and laid it across the back of the sofa, keeping her wig in place but tying the long locks back with her silk scarf. She played with the corners of it as she spoke quietly, almost soothingly, to herself.

"Always loved this scarf. So pretty with the big red poppy on it, don't you think?" She moved back over to Sebastian and knelt beside him. Running her fingers through his thick dirty-blond hair, she said warmly, "You really are quite good-looking close up. Lovely blue eyes. I can see why women throw themselves at you." She carried on, cocking her head to the left as she spoke to him kindly. "Georgia—you remember the gorgeous Georgia, don't you? Your secretary PA lady? Well, I know her too as it turns out. How funny is that? Yes, I do. We went to university together, and she told me she wanted to go out with you, but you just weren't interested in her, were you? Did you know she had the hots for you? Now she'll never have the chance. You put paid to that with your stupid evil hobby."

As she talked to him, she manoeuvred him into an easier position than the crumpled state he'd landed in, which was no mean feat given his size. Slightly out of breath as she repositioned his dead weight, she carried on chatting to him like they were old friends about to sit down for supper together.

"That's not why I'm here, though. I wouldn't be going to all this trouble because you've ignored her. Oh no. There is a much bigger reason, and it involves your other hobby, not the hooker one. Can you guess what it is?" She stood over him, panting slightly. Satisfied he was where she needed him to be, she excused herself.

"Won't be a minute. Just need some towels. I expect you have a sports cupboard somewhere, for beach towels maybe?" Blowing him a quick kiss, she left the room to explore. She returned a moment later, collecting the little gift-wrapped parcel out of her bag as she passed by.

"I'm impressed at your orderliness. Nothing out of place

anywhere," she said as she laid a couple of the beach towels around his head and neck. "I don't want to spoil your bath towels. That's why I'm using these. It could get a bit messy and I can see you wouldn't like mess. Thought that would be best. I hope you appreciate the thought," she said, smiling. Satisfied with her towel arrangement, she sat back on her heels and looked at him. The towels made him look like something from a pantomime. She drew in a deep breath: time to focus on what she was now about to do. Her stomach rolled slightly.

"Oh no, not again," she whispered, but it was going to be futile. Darting up from her spot, she rushed to the kitchen and hung over the sink, fighting it back, willing herself not to vomit. Leaving evidence like her stomach contents was out of the question. When the sickening feeling finally left her, she checked under the sink for spare rubbish bin liners and peeled two off the roll. She put one inside the other, ready for what now seemed the inevitable. Tucking them under her arm, she headed back to Sebastian, her face as deadly serious about the upcoming task as that of any seasoned psychopathic serial killer. Her tone was now direct and serious, the banter gone.

"I'm going to show the world what happens to people like you. Have you figured out the offending hobby yet?" she taunted him, waiting for an answer that would never come. "No? Well let me give you a hint. You take a trophy from it. Yes, that's right: your hunting. It's despicable, and that's why I'm going to take a trophy from *you*. Your. Own. Dead. Head. And I'm going to parade it online, just like you did, except you're not going to like it. But your haters will. And there are plenty of those."

Squatting behind him and pulling his head up by his blond locks, she struck quickly in one swift cut. Blood oozed out of the gash onto the towels and the sight of it worked rapidly on her stomach. She grabbed the rubbish bin liners and retched violently into the bag, again and again and again. When she was finally empty and the spasms had stopped, Philippa tied the bag up, ready to dispose of later.

"Damn stomach. No matter. Perhaps I'll get used to it."

There was more clearing up to be done.

Chapter Fifty-Four

SHE DRESSED QUICKLY. One last scout round, and she was ready to leave. Then it hit her. What about the Trojan on his laptop? Could it be traced back to her if anyone inspected it? Of course, there would be an investigation: just like Fiona Gable, Sebastian Stevens had quite obviously been murdered. You couldn't do what she'd just done to yourself. Why hadn't she asked Pete about whether the damn Trojan could be traced? She could have kicked herself, but there was no point in getting angry about it now: she needed to figure out what to do. The sleek silver machine glared at her from its spot on the glass dining room table and she knew she had to take it with her.

She shut the laptop down, then slipped the whole thing into her bag along with his phone and everything else. It was getting late, and it was time to go, but there was still one important aspect of the mission to complete: post the image of her trophy for the world and his friends to see. But she wanted to be out the building before she did that, though still close by: pinging cellphone towers were an important part of this plan. The investigators would know his phone had been used after his death and they'd be able to trace the location to a point nearby though not the exact location. It was a point she couldn't afford to overlook. She would post the photos later from a nearby doorway, but right now she had one more job to do.

"Smile for the camera!" Lifting his head by his hair, she took three photos of the very dead Sebastian, then tapped the icon to his social media accounts. Unable to resist, she took a quick look at his recent activity and was quite surprised to see there hadn't been much in the last few days, not since the auction video debacle at any rate.

"Got a little burnt, did we? Well, I wonder what your 'friends' will say when they see this little offering from you. My kind of trophy, and if I say so myself, you do take a lovely photograph—very photogenic. I can see why the ladies swoon at your feet. I just hope Georgia isn't too upset." She slipped her feet into her shoes. "But I think she'll get over it." She slipped Sebastian's phone into the side pocket for easy retrieval once she was outside, and took a last look at her victim.

"Toodle pip," she called over her shoulder as she closed the door softly behind her.

Chapter Fifty-Five

LEAVING the building dressed nicely in her cream linen dress, silk scarf tied in her hair, and stylish though rather full bag balanced on her shoulder, she marvelled at the ease of it all. The only thing she hadn't planned on was her upset stomach again, the contents of which still needed to be disposed of.

It surprised her that she'd reacted that way again, and while the first kill had understandably taken its toll, she had sincerely hoped it wouldn't be the same this time round. She couldn't afford another day in bed, nor the time off work.

To get away from the building safely, she slipped down the same quiet side street from earlier and into the same smelly, darkened doorway. She held her breath as she removed the bag of vomit and set it down, then slipped her scarf and wig off, putting the wig back into her bag. Maybe a rat would find the vomit bag later, or a street cleaner in the morning. Either way, it was a long way from being connected back to her. She tied the silk scarf elegantly around her neck, the beautiful red poppy print fully central, and fluffed up her own short auburn hair. With a final application of bright orange lipstick, she was all set to enter the night again—not as the submissive Chloe, but as the strong woman she knew so well, as Philippa.

But there was just one last piece of the puzzle to do before she left.

She pulled the phone out, tapped the photo icon, and selected the recent images she'd shot. Picking one, she selected "upload to Facebook," typed "Who's the trophy now?" and hit post. Mere seconds later she saw her handiwork in full Technicolor on Sebastian's profile. She grinned, turned the phone off, removed the SIM card and played with it between her fingers as she walked away.

Rather than exit the side street the same way as she'd entered, she kept on walking down to the other end and turning left, feeling comfortable, confident, and in control, humming something tuneless as she went. Sebastian had paid for 'Chloe' in advance, the terms of the transaction, and Philippa hoped the agency wouldn't stiff the woman and leave her out of the cut, but there was no way to ever know. Funny the things that go through your mind after you've just committed a murder. She meandered through the back streets towards where she figured she'd find a taxi rank and slipped onto the backseat of the first one in the queue, her fourth cab of the day.

"Where to?" the driver asked in heavily accented English. From his voice, he sounded East European and she idly wondered if he was related to Daniela, though why would he be? There were literally millions of Eastern Europeans now living in the UK.

"Where can a girl get a drink safely around here? Where do you recommend?"

"I know just the place! Be there in ten," he said, and set off. Philippa fastened her seatbelt and opened her window, letting the phone and then the SIM card drift from her fingers as the taxi as it made its way towards town and her destination. The air was cooling rapidly and, shivering, she wound the window back up again. Her head on the back headrest, she let out a slow heavy sigh. The night's activities were catching up with her and she wished she's told the driver to go straight to the hotel. But she needed to re-line her stomach with food. The taxi slowed and pulled into the curb.

"Here you go," he said, pointing to a small trendy bar on the other side of the street. Outside, there were pavement tables filled mainly with small groups of women, laughing and giggling with their friends, most of whom were sporting long streaked hair and big sunglasses perched on their heads.

"Thanks," she said, and gave him a £20 note, which was enough to cover the ride and include a tip. Once she was out of the taxi, she waited until he'd driven out of sight, back around the corner, and set off in the opposite direction than the intended bar. The air was almost cold now, and with no jacket and an empty stomach, she shivered. Covering her tracks took energy and planning, but now she was driven by the simple need for food. She walked to the end of the street in search of something to eat.

The evening's activities rattled around her head as she walked almost robotically towards a fish and chip shop looming in the distance. The cold night air had a faint tinge of hot fat and vinegar and the closer she got, the more she wanted what was on offer. She could see the main door was wide open. The queue of seven or eight people was a good sign, and she joined them in waiting her turn. A couple of minutes later, she was tucking hungrily into a parcel of hot greasy chips drenched in salt and vinegar, the little wooden fork working hard up and down between her mouth and food on the table in front of her.

Conscious she was eating too fast, she gathered her food and stepped outside again, back into the cooling night, the hot food giving her some warmth now, and stopped at a vacant space on an old bench. She perched there by herself, watching Manchester by night. She bit back a smile as she took another soothing mouthful of hot, greasy fried potato. "This could be a new habit of mine: kill and chips!"

Chapter Fifty-Six

JORDAN WAS CLIMBING out of his pride and joy, a navy-blue F-Type Jaguar, a two-seater sports car that he loved almost as much as he loved himself. Almost. He was a polarising character; most men he came into contact with loved him and his extremely generous ways, though women found him one big slime-ball and gave him a wide berth. He was oblivious to either fact. Jordan was a flashy man, but good-spirited with it, and he did a great deal of good in the local community with afterschool clubs and events. For some reason he couldn't fathom, he'd never found the right woman to settle down and share his life with; they never stayed around for long. And so he'd almost become a self-made bachelor and short of going on *The Bachelor* to find a bride, he'd resigned himself to his own company. And the company of his friends.

Scrolling through his newsfeed as he walked up to his house, he smiled at some of his friends' posts, sharing typical 'lad' pranks and videos, funny memes and comments. Didn't they do any work all day? By the time he had reached the front door of his red brick detached, he'd spotted the post that would stay burned in his mind for the rest of his life. Sebastian Stevens, long-time friend and confidant, was posed in a grotesque style, fresh blood seeping from a neck wound, eyes firmly closed, his skin the colour of pallid cheese. Jordan stood motionless by his front door, frozen to the spot, the colour draining from his own face, just like his friends had. His hand shot to his mouth as bile surfaced from an empty stomach and he heaved the foul-tasting liquid on to the lawn beside him. When the spasm receded, he dared himself to look again, and note the time it had been posted. It had been just seven minutes ago. With trembling fingers, he searched for Sebastian's number and pressed the call button, knowing it would simply ring out until it went to his recorded message. There was no point in leaving a message; he knew his friend was gone.

The next call he placed was to the police. With a trembling voice to match his fingers, he gave the operator the details he knew: Sebastian's address in Manchester, his work contact details and his own contact details. He'd no idea where his friend lay but at least now they had two places to start looking for him. He got himself inside and made a beeline for the sofa where he sat down heavily, the air sucked out of his sails. A decanter of brandy and matching crystal glasses sat on a small table. With heavy legs he moved towards it and poured himself a hefty glass. He knocked it back in a couple of gulps, wincing as the amber fluid burned its way down his throat and hit his empty stomach. In a strange way, the smarting felt good and he poured himself a chaser, though not as large, taking it back to the sofa to sip on. And think. Who would do such a thing, and why? Two questions were burning to be answered, but Jordan had no clue where to begin.

Chapter Fifty-Seven

"LOOKS like we've got one of our own," Rick said into his phone. "Just like the same thing they had down in Croydon—the victim's picture posted online, throat slit."

Duncan, Rick's partner at the Greater Manchester Police, rolled over in bed to listen and grunted into his phone, "Damn. We need that like a hole in the head on top of everything else we've got going on. Tell me more." He flicked the bedside lamp on. It was past 11 pm, and his wife stirred grumpily at the intrusion.

"The victim is Sebastian Stevens, the same Sebastian Stevens that was in the news for all the wrong reasons only a few days ago. He's the hunting fundraiser guy that showed that kill video at a dinner and grossed everyone out. And while he's a bit of a prick, he's now very dead. Someone got him at his home address on Blackfriars Street, one of those nice penthouse-type places. Shall I pick you up or meet you there?" Rick gave him the address on Blackfriars.

"Meet you there. I'm on my way." The phone line disconnected and Duncan swung his legs out of the bed. He dressed in jeans and his normal hoody, grabbed a jacket off the back of his chair and headed out.

It wasn't hard to see which building it was as he approached. The flashing blues lit up the whole street. The distinctive mortuary van was already parked up, so that meant the doctor on call was probably already inside. Rick parked his BMW and slipped out onto the street as Duncan locked his own car. They met in the middle of the tarmac and walked towards the building together.

"Who's the doctor on call? Any idea?"

"No idea. Guess we'll soon see," said Rick. Let's hope it's not 'Stanley Stanley.' It's too late in the day for his cantankerous moods. We should be still tucked up in our beds."

Duncan grunted in agreement. Dr. Stanley Winstanley was not a well-liked man. He was, in fact, a real pain in the ass for the majority of his waking hours. Thinking about what Rick had just said, he added, "And who in their right mind would call their kid Stanley when your surname is Winstanley? That's just cruel. I bet he had a crap childhood. Bullied, I'd bet. Probably why he's so damn grumpy all the time now. Never got over it."

It was Rick's turn to grunt. They ducked under the crime scene tape that cordoned off the front entrance to the building and foyer beyond, and strode up to a couple of uniforms stationed at the door. Both Rick and Duncan flashed their IDs and opened the main door.

"Top floor," added one of the uniforms helpfully as they went inside. "Only seven flights up the stairs." Both detectives grimaced at the thought of hiking all the way in the absence of a usable lift. It was being dusted for prints; the black powder was evident around the floor buttons.

"Finding a usable print on a lift button has got to be like finding two hens teeth, hasn't it?" Duncan grumbled.

Rick ignored his partner's observation but did note his wheezing.

"You need to keep your fitness up Duncan. You sound like an old man climbing these stairs. Not good for you."

"I'd rather be a bit wheezy than pound the pavements like you do for jollies. Plus I like the odd pint."

"And you can have both, you know—fitness and a bevvy occasionally. They aren't exclusive to one another," retorted Rick, and sprinted the rest of the way up showing off.

At the top floor, they greeted the uniform on the door and stepped into Sebastian Stevens' suite. Duncan whistled through his teeth as they emerged into the main living area, which had a spectacular view out over the city through the floor-to-ceiling glass windows. Duncan walked past Sebastian's body and stood looking out at the night. The city was lit up like a Christmas tree.

"Wowza! What a cracker of a view."

Rick waited for a moment for his partner to finish being in awe and then cleared his throat. "Now that you've got that out of the way ....."

"Alright buddy, I'm on to it."

"Evening," thundered a familiar voice behind them.

Both men turned in the direction of a short, rotund balding man. As usual, Stanley Stanley was wearing a white paper crime scene suit that made him look like a giant golf ball, his head a speck of dirt on the top. Stanley had lost the battle of the bulge a long time ago.

"Evening, Stanley," said Rick. "Just arrived ourselves so can't tell you much more than you probably already know. Sounds the same as the woman from Croydon a couple of weeks ago—throat slashed and posted on his own newsfeed for his friends to see. In fact, it was a friend that phoned it in." Rick flicked through to the last page of his notebook where he'd written the name. "Yes, here it is. Jordan Jenkins."

Stanley Stanley looked nonplussed and made his way over to the prostrate body. He knelt awkwardly down at Sebastian's shoulders and peered closely at the gash in his neck, breathing heavily as he took in the detail.

Rick wondered if he'd make it back to a standing position unaided and hoped the older man wouldn't need to lean on him as he clambered back up. Duncan watched from nearby, smiling to himself, knowing exactly what Rick was thinking; they'd both been there before.

"Hunting style of knife, I'd say at this stage. Have you found the weapon yet?"

"No, not yet," said Rick evenly, biting back the retort that they'd only just got here. "Doesn't seem to be much blood, do you think?"

"Leave the thinking to me, son. It's more my area than yours."

"I'll leave you to it then," said Rick curtly. "Let me know the time of death when you've estimated it. I'll be here a while yet." He made his way off to look around the apartment in more detail, muttering to Duncan as he passed, "Sanctimonious old git. Isn't it about time he retired?"

Duncan replied with a faint, knowing smile. "Come on, let's get this processed until his lordship has something for us. You want to interview the friend by phone or shall I?"

"I'll speak to the friend. Probably have him go into Croydon tomorrow to fill out a full statement, but I'll get what he knows down now."

"Uniforms will do the neighbours. I wonder how the killer gained access. Maybe he knew them?" He looked around the big lounge area. There was no obvious sign of a struggle and since the victim was laid out on the floor close to the hall, he surmised the perpetrator might not have gone into the lounge at all. And then there was the lack of blood. In his experience, that meant not everything was quite as it seemed. The loose facts dropped into Rick's head in random deposits; nothing made any sense yet. But they would. Rick Black was one of the best young detectives in the GMP, and that's why he was on the fast-track program. With two victims, they now had a possible serial killer and it was going to be his job to make sure he or she was caught and put away for good.

He turned back to Duncan. "Come on. Let's get this show on the road then."

Chapter Fifty-Eight

RICK HATED WATCHING POST-MORTEMS. And Duncan knew it, and sometimes fed on it, just for fun. Like now. They both stood in the cold, clinical room filled with steel trolleys and sinks, the pungent smell of cleaning fluid drifting up their nostrils. Duncan watched as Rick's colour gradually left his already pale face. Was he going to fall over again or manage to hold it together? Rick caught his eye and steadied himself nonchalantly with a hand on the tiled wall, like it was the most natural thing to do. Duncan smiled his way and Rick did his best to return one though it looked more like a grimace. He was desperately suffering.

Stanley Stanley was babbling on about an old case a couple of decades ago where a victim's throat had been cut and the similarities between the two cases, but neither man was really paying attention. He'd get back on point eventually and they'd re-engage. Dressed head to foot in surgical scrubs today, Stanley Stanley looked like a giant pale green marrowfat pea in white Crocs. His voice finally took on a different tone and the men knew to tune back in to present day-discussions. Duncan cleared his throat to speak.

"So he was dead before his throat was cut, then. How did he actually die?"

Stanley Stanley pointed to the puncture wound on his shoulder.

"He was injected here and it's my guess that whatever is in his system —and I won't know until later today exactly what that was—it probably incapacitated him and ultimately killed him. He was a tall, fit man; he'd have been a challenge for anyone to apprehend. Then, for whatever reason, the throat was cut, and with an extremely sharp, smooth blade. Not something out of the kitchen drawer, I wouldn't think. The average household's knives wouldn't be sharp enough to make a quick clean cut like this."

Rick turned away as Stanley Stanley ran his gloved finger along the incision, opening it a little.

"No, you're looking for a blade of about six inches long with a pointy tip," Stanley Stanley said, almost lovingly. "And deadly sharp."

"Anything else?" Rick had found his voice, for a moment at any rate.

"Not a lot, I'm afraid. The killer was very thorough and didn't leave anything behind. I expect he wore gloves and maybe coveralls. Not a hair to be found on the body, either, though I'd be surprised if you didn't find any in the apartment. He had a bit of a reputation with the ladies by all accounts, but you'll know more about that than me when you get digging."

"Do you think the knife could have been a hunting style of knife, then?" asked Rick.

"Quite possibly. Hunters would keep their knives sharp, more so than your average thug on the street looking for trouble. No," he said, scratching his stubbly chin in thought, "I'd say someone knowledgeable on hunting and knowledgeable about looking after their gear."

"That fits with the other victim, the woman, the one from further down south," said Duncan. "I rang Croydon station this morning and spoke to the detective handling the case, DS Amanda Lacey. I'm betting the drug is ..." Duncan checked back in his notebook for the name, "etorphine, I believe. Could knock out an elephant, apparently."

Stanley Stanley scratched some more and added, "Well, that would do the job, alright. Probably a bit of overkill, if you'll pardon the pun. Nothing surprises me anymore so I won't even wonder how someone could get hold of such a drug." He turned back to Sebastian's body and pointed to his shoulder. "The puncture wound being where it is probably meant that he was taken by surprise while his back was turned. The confined space would have been ideal to strike, and that stuff is active in seconds. Damn lethal, as you can see." He waved his arm over Sebastian's lifeless form. "I'll confirm whether it's the same drug later when I know for sure."

"Well, if it is, this could get interesting, because the perp obviously has an axe to grind about something. At least we can check for a link between the two victims, though hunting seems the obvious line currently. The DS, a woman called Amanda Lacey, is headed up here today, so she should be in early afternoon. We'll confer then."

Rick had returned to a more normal colour and ventured away from the tiled wall that was supporting him, keen to get back to more common ground and away from dead bodies. "Right then, coffee I think, Duncan, then we'll go over what we know again so we're ready for our visitor later. Let's hope she can throw a bit more light on things. I'll go over the statements of the other residents. Did you manage to get the CCTV footage from the building and surrounding areas?"

"Still waiting on the building footage, and there's nothing of any value on the street cams but we'll go through them again, perhaps. There were a couple of women enter the building at around the time of death, but it's hard to make a visual from the footage. Their faces aren't visible. I'm hoping the building footage will be better. A couple of the neighbours were also out and about but no one was acting obviously suspiciously. All looked like they knew where they were going; no one was loitering."

Rick made his move towards the door and thanked Stanley Stanley, who nodded in reply, barely looking up from his own area of expertise.

"It would take some guts for a woman to knock him out," Rick continued, "or someone who knew exactly what they were doing and could be sure of when to do it. Sebastian Stevens is a big, strong-looking man, and catching him by surprise in the hall would only give a minute window if the jab was what knocked him down."

"Can't rule anyone out at the moment but I'd be keen to find those that were nearby inside. And Amanda said they hadn't had any luck with cameras at their end because it was down a quiet suburban street, in the victim's home as well. A camera-free zone." Duncan grabbed the door and held it open for Rick. "It doesn't help when your victim isn't a well-liked man either. Could be a whole list of enemies, though the hunting knife angle seems the most obvious. We know for a fact the guy hunts."

"He did, but he won't be anymore."

Chapter Fifty-Nine

RUTH HEADED over to Amanda's, a takeaway from Wong's in her hand, a bottle of white in the other. While they both abstained from drinking during the week normally, self-imposed rules were there for the breaking when the need arose. And the need had arisen. When Amanda wasn't working on a taxing case, it was easy, but throw a murder into the mix, and a glass or two of wine was a decent crutch on which to balance the crap of her day. And who liked drinking alone? The bag of Amanda's favourite, sweet and sour pork, was heavy in her hand, the pleasant smell of tasty food wafting invitingly into her nostrils as she unlocked the front door and went inside.

"Hi hun, I'm home! And I've been out gathering and came across dinner! Hope you're hungry," she called.

"Be down in a minute," Amanda called back. "And yes, famished."

Ruth could hear water running in the bathroom and helped herself to wine glasses and plates in the kitchen. A moment later a damp-looking Amanda stood in the doorway wearing track pants that never saw the track. She was rubbing the side of her wet head with a towel. Her short blonde hair was at all angles.

"Hey," was all she said. They never needed much more than that after a long day, except a hug.

"Hey back. I've brought wine, too," Ruth said, handing her a glass.

"I know it's technically a school night, but I thought you'd appreciate a glass, so sit down and I'll serve up. Got your favourite." Amanda stepped forward from her spot in the doorway and landed a light kiss on the back of Ruth's neck as she got to work filling two plates.

"What did I ever do to deserve a woman like you? You spoil me rotten and I really appreciate it, you know. Thank you."

"As you do me, too, when I'm working hard. It works both ways. Here, eat it before it goes cold," she said, passing a plate to her. Amanda took it and sat down at the kitchen table. Taking her first mouthful, she groaned in pleasure.

"That. Is. So. Good!"

Ruth waited a moment before tucking in herself, watching as Amanda chewed ravenously on crispy pork balls now covered in sticky sauce. "I met Dad for coffee today. He still seems so lost on his own."

Amanda stopped chewing and waited. Ruth wasn't one for talking much about her family, but since her stepmother had passed, she'd been making more of an effort to get to know her father better. After all, she hadn't known him growing up and had only found out about him as a teenager. As a young woman used to looking out for herself, she'd paid him little attention, but that was changing.

"That's only to be expected, hun," she said. "They were together a long time. A death takes a lot to get over, particularly one that wasn't expected, like your mum's."

"I know, but it got me thinking. You know, about us. We're solid as a rock, I know, but anything could intervene and destroy it. Your job can be dangerous. I could get hit by a bus tomorrow. And we'd each have not much left. Like Dad. And he's rattling around in that big house on his own. That can't be helping."

Amanda watched while Ruth finally took a forkful of food and chewed slowly. Her features were all deflated somehow. Ruth rarely showed her emotions. Amanda spoke first.

"We should invite him round for dinner one night after work, or go round there and take him something nice."

"Yes, and we can do that, but he'll still be on his own when we leave. He'll still be lonely that night. And he's not keen on selling up, either. He says the house and gardens remind him of her too much."

Tears started to fill Ruth's eyes as she struggled to stop the emotional spillover. She was normally so controlled.

Amanda was at her side kneeling on the floor in an instant. "Hey, this isn't like you. What's brought this on?"

"I've been thinking a lot about us. I know you want more, but the truth is, I'm scared." Tears dripped off Ruth's jawline into her lap, salty blobs dampening her jeans in small patches.

"Come here." Amanda wrapped her arms around Ruth and pulled her close, Ruth's wet cheeks brushing against her own. "Shh. Let's not worry about that now. I'm not going anywhere either way. And time always heals, and it will eventually be okay again for your dad. It just takes time." Amanda rubbed her back soothingly as the tears started to subside. "And in the meantime, we need to look out for him and include him more than ever. And so do his boys. Maybe give them both a call tomorrow and fill them in. They probably aren't as aware of how he's feeling as you are, being that bit further away." She handed Ruth a serviette to dry her face with.

"Thanks," she said, sniffing. "And sorry... I'm not sure where that all came from. Maybe I'm getting soft."

"Hey, no need for apologies. We're friends remember?" She paused for a moment, then continued. "Well, a bit more than friends, actually. And you've always been soft." Amanda beamed her best smile and Ruth couldn't help but return it. "Now, eat your pork balls. They're getting cold. And if you don't want them, then I'm having them."

"Oh no you don't, Amanda Lacey. Keep your hands off!"

"That's better. Now pass the fried rice and let's lighten the mood a little, eh? And later, we'll plan some days out where we can take your dad—if he doesn't mind being in the company of a couple of women."

Ruth doubted he'd mind their combined company at all. And as for herself, she was finding she wanted more of it. A lot more.

Chapter Sixty

"WE'LL PULL in and get coffee at Watford Gap services. Let's get out of London first," Amanda said with authority. "You can wait until then, can't you?"

Jack was useless at making his own coffee, even with a pod machine in the station, and had almost given up trying to learn the simple action of water, pod, button, milk, stir. Nine times out of ten he got a cup of hot milk, without the coffee. And now he was looking petulant. Amanda groaned at him in desperation. Watford Gap services wasn't exactly around the corner. She grabbed a paper cup, slammed a pod in the machine and pressed the button for him. The familiar steam-engine sound erupted and thick brown coffee gently poured into the cup, the smell always a welcome one at any time of the day.

Amanda spoke affectionately but with an exasperated edge. "Now I'm going to have to have one!" She handed the first cup to Jack, who smiled like a young boy who'd just got his own way and knew it.

"No sense in making us both wait," he said. "We can take these with us, so cheer up, Amanda. It's only delayed us by two more minutes, not really enough to get all huffy and puffy about."

She knew Jack was right, but there was so much going on in her head it was a struggle to cope with it. Not getting enough sleep wasn't helping either; she was dog tired but had no hope of getting a good night in with a murderer on her patch and upset in her personal life. Ruth's tears last night had come out of the blue, and Amanda thought back to her touching comments.

Solid as a rock. They were.

She tipped a sugar into her paper cup and stirred it.

"Since when do you take sugar?" Jack asked as they headed out to the car.

"I don't, but I'm running on fumes at the moment," she said curtly.

"I'll drive," said Jack. "No point you doing it if you're tired. First stop, Watford Gap. We'll grab a bite there and be in Manchester centre for about two o'clock if the M1 isn't too bad." Jack flicked the indicator and pulled out of the yard at Croydon, headed north. After a few seconds of quiet, he piped up. "Here's a fun fact for you. Did you know Watford Gap is the oldest service station in Britain? It opened when the motorway did in 1959 and because it was open at all hours, it was a common meeting point for bands in the early hours of the morning, travelling after their gigs." He turned towards her and saw her watching him so he carried on. "They'd meet for a bit of supper and hot chocolate. Hendrix, The Beatles, Pink Floyd and a bunch of other rock bands were regulars when the restaurant opened a few months later. Then it went downhill in the 70s and was refurbished again some years ago. Probably time for another, really. The food got so bad in the 70s, there was even a song written about it—can't remember who sang it now—but Watford Gap had become synonymous with crappy food. A bit like British Rail had with their god-awful sandwiches." At his own mention of bands, he turned a CD on low. ELO's "Mr. Blue Sky" played quietly in the background.

"Good to know, Jack. You're full of useful info, aren't you?" she teased gently. "And I'll add a little more: it's nowhere near Watford, and it marks the north–south divide of the country."

"Well, everyone knows that. That's not news, unlike my rock band connection, so no points to you in this pop quiz" He was smiling.

"Just drive, would you?"

"Yes m'lady!" He saluted in mock-Thunderbirds style.

"Changing the subject, have you ever come across the two detectives we're going up there to see? I only spoke to Duncan."

"No, never come across either of them but someone, and I can't just remember who, said that Rick Black is on a fast-track program, one of them that should make him Inspector within two years. Must be bright enough."

"Here's hoping. And here's hoping the two murders will give us something useful to work with because we haven't got much to go with on the perp at the moment. No missing drug at the vets that use it, no sightings of anyone coming or going, and no real enemies, though the hunting debacle could have rousted someone. The reference to being a trophy is the only thing that links it to hunting, and the extra-sharp blade our victim's throat was slit with. The picture was loaded by her own phone and that's gone, probably forever. So, here's hoping they have a bit more."

Amanda nodded her head in agreement, and let her mind pick over the facts they did have. The gentle rumble of the engine soothed her tired head. "Mr. Blue Sky" changed to "Scarborough Fair." and after twenty minutes of listening to Jack talk about nothing in particular, she was sound asleep.

Chapter Sixty-One

AMANDA FELT the car come to a standstill and opened one bleary eye. The familiar sight of a red coffee chain store logo and people milling about told her they were at Watford Gap already, and she looked over at Jack somewhat sheepishly. Slithering back up her seat where she slumped down she said, "Oh, sorry, Jack! I must have fallen asleep."

"And that's why you're a detective, DS Lacey—your ability to figure these things out." He was smiling as he added, "You're obviously tired out so don't apologise. No big deal. I won't tell. Didn't know my company was that riveting though." He opened the driver's door, then turned back to her. "You coming for a bite to eat?"

Amanda didn't need asking twice and opened her own door. The sound of nearby motorway traffic assaulted her ears, and she followed Jack inside the building and headed for the food court. As they waited in line to be served, Jack began to reminisce again.

"I've not been up to Manchester in a long time. Used to live up north for a while, not far from Old Trafford actually. MUFC country."

"I never knew you supported the Red Devils."

"I don't, really, don't support any football team, but I used to go to the odd game with my granddad sometimes, though it was a bit different back then. Have you ever been to the grounds?"

"No, never had a reason to."

"Well, if we have time later, we might drive over and grab some fish and chips from Lou Macari's. He used to play for MUFC, among other teams, and opened a chippy when he retired. They're legendary, though it will only be open if there's a match on. I'd have to check. Not much else down there to be open for but worth battling the crowds for a piece of hot fish in crispy batter."

Amanda smiled as he carried on talking. She'd worked with Jack for long enough to love him like a father, and she affectionately linked her arm through his and squeezed it gently. They knew each other so well, had been through a lot together both with work and their personal lives. He'd been a shoulder to cry on and someone talk to when she'd eventually come out, though even now, she wasn't exactly telling the world. It was nobody's business but hers, but Jack had understood and had been the support she'd needed as word at work got around. And the jokes and innuendos had begun.

And Amanda had been there for Jack, too, when his Janine had died. She looked across at him now, smiled fondly at his deep-wrinkled face. He was unaware she was watching him, somewhere deep in thought and oblivious to her caring gaze. She knew he thought of her as the daughter he had never had. When the day came for Jack to finally retire, Amanda knew it would be a sad one. And it was not that far away, either.

"Let's hope there's a game on then," she said, and squeezed him again.

They ordered sandwiches and drinks and made their way through the busy food court to a cluttered but empty table nearby. Jack watched as Amanda pilled dirty plates and mugs into a pile and shifted them to the edge, wiping the top clean with a serviette.

"You always do play mother, don't you?" He placed the tray of food down and she took the contents off before sliding the tray down the side of the table.

"Somebody's got to look after you. If I hadn't been here now you'd have a big greasy burger rather than a healthier option. Stop griping."

They both sat down and tucked into the rather average sandwiches and lukewarm coffee.

"Things haven't got much better then, food-wise, I mean." Jack grimaced, a blob of mayonnaise dropping onto his napkin in front of him. "You had any more thoughts on getting hitched yet?"

"No, not really, though maybe subconsciously, which is adding to my lack of sleep. Hardly time to think about it when I'm awake." Changing the subject, she asked, "Do you think Manchester will let us interview those close to the victim?"

"Who knows. Not our case strictly, or jurisdiction. Depends on the boys in charge. Why?"

"Well, since they are two blokes, I thought I might ask if I could interview some of the women. There's bound to be some. Stevens was a player, after all. Perhaps play the 'woman-to-woman' angle."

"Be good if you could, though don't get your hopes up." Jack wiped his mouth with his serviette, smearing the mayo blob from earlier across his lower lip.

Amanda pointed to her own lower lip, motioning that he needed to wipe his again.

"Gone?"

"Yes, all gone. You're good to go. Finish your sandwich and let's take our coffee's and get going. I'll drive this time."

"Oh no you won't," Jack retorted. "I don't want you dropping off again and killing us both. I'm driving."

"Yes, Dad," she said, and saluted. Still chewing, they put their rubbish into the bin by the exit and headed back to the car. As Jack pulled back onto the motorway, Amanda's phone buzzed.

"DS Lacey."

"DS Lacey, it's DS Rick Black here, GMP. You still en route?"

"Yes, just left Watford Gap. What can I do for you?"

"I'm off to chat to the victim's PA later and I thought you might want to come along? Woman to woman? Might get a better result. She's extremely distressed, apparently, so I just thought it might be best."

Amanda smiled into the phone. *Perfect!* "Good idea, Rick. Happy to. I'll text you when we hit Manchester, shall I? We can go together." Rick agreed and Amanda hung up. Turning to Jack, she grinned. "Great minds think alike, eh? He wondered if I wanted to sit in on the interview with the PA, a woman. Do my woman-to-woman routine. Bloody good idea, Rick, even though I say so myself."

Jack turned and beamed at his partner. "Sounds like these boys are a good sort. You know how some are a bit over-protective of their cases, and if you want info, go get it yourself and all."

"It makes sense to share and be decent about it," Amanda agreed. "Perhaps more women would still be alive today if the Yorkshire Ripper had been caught earlier. Nine sodding times they interviewed the killer, nine times by five different forces. Can you believe that? And none of them picked it up." They both fell silent. Policing had changed in recent years because of cases like that one. When Peter Sutcliffe, aka the Ripper, had finally been arrested, convicted and imprisoned, the nation had breathed a collective sigh of relief.

At length, Jack piped up again. "It will be good to see what HOLMES2 spits out."

Thinking, he added, "Here's another fun fact for you, Lacey. Did you know that the original HOLMES database was actually named after Sherlock Holmes?"

"I didn't. I thought it was an acronym for Home Office Large Major Enquiry System."

"Well, yes, it is, but the stories were the motivation for the name first, then the acronym fitted it. It got upgraded back in 2000."

"Well, it will be good to see what spits out now with the two victims and what leads they are following up here in Manchester."

"I guess we'll soon find out. It's not far now."

Jack and Amanda slipped into the healthy peacefulness that close friends and colleagues can share without the need to fill the silence, each preoccupied with their own thoughts. It was almost 2 pm when they finally parked up by the police station working the case in Manchester.

"Let's get moving then, Lacey," said Jack, "and see if we can't get those fish and chips later if there's time to spare."

Amanda knew Jack's focus was on the victims themselves, of course, but secretly she knew he hoped for another chance to reminisce.

Chapter Sixty-Two

"I THOUGHT the GMP was at Bootle Street, in the city centre," Amanda said as Jack opened his car door to get out.

"No, they left there about three years back. There's a local public booth in the Town Hall building now, not much else. You ever go in Bootle Street?"

"Just the once. It was like the TV set for *Life on Mars*, dingy and decrepit, if I remember correctly. They probably filmed *Whitechapel* in there too. Now that was an ugly set if ever I saw one. Gave me the creeps watching that every time someone went to the loo. Those corridors were too creepy. Ugh." She shuddered. They both started walking towards a brick building in the distance.

"So why are we here, then, and not the Town Hall?"

"Because it's only a public counter in there. The rest of the work is done from here," he said, pointing to a new modern building. "This," he said, waving his arm, "is Longsight police station. Built in 1998—another useless fact for you."

"So what will they do with the old place then?"

"I hear Gary Neville and Ryan Giggs, two ex-players, bought it. They're planning on building a five-star hotel and apartments, though the locals are objecting, so who knows if it will go ahead." He held the front door open and Amanda slipped inside ahead of him. They made themselves known to an officer at the front desk, then sat to wait for Detectives Black and Dukes. It was only a moment before Amanda spotted the two men approaching them. One of them, a rather good-looking man, had a beaming smile that went from one ear round to the next, and Amanda couldn't quite keep her eyes off it. Had she ever seen a smile so wide? With tight dark curls on top and short sideburns, he looked like a young Buddy Holly, though a little taller; she estimated a whopping six feet, four inches. But the resemblance was uncanny. His dark hair certainly suited his surname of Black, too, and she watched as he made a beeline for her, his hand held out in front of him, ready to shake.

"Glad you could both make it. I'm DS Rick Black, and this is DS Duncan Dukes. I believe you've already spoken?"

Duncan was at his side, arm extended, and everyone took turns shaking hands.

The formalities complete, Black steered everyone back towards the back offices and through to a meeting room just off the main incident room. The visual board was displayed front and centre, covered with photos and possible lines of enquiry about Sebastian Stevens' gruesome killing. Black ran through the case so far—what they knew and what they were still waiting for. He confirmed that it the same drug had been used to kill both Stevens and Fiona Gable. And, like Fiona Gable, Sebastian Stevens had been dead before his throat had been slashed. There was no mistake: they were dealing with the same person.

Black concluded by saying, "I'm going to interview his PA shortly. She had access to his work life and a good portion of his personal life, though she hadn't been working for him that long. Amanda, I think it might be helpful if you come along, in case she's more comfortable divulging to another woman."

"Perfect. Yes."

"By all accounts, our victim had quite a personal life and quite a reputation with the ladies, both organic dates and transactional. Let's just say he had some particular tastes that he paid handsomely for. And that brings us back to the two women who were in the lobby that night. We think one was an escort, although she only stayed for a few minutes. But the other we have no idea about. Her head was low the whole time, and if she is our perp, she was in the building for around forty minutes, ample time to do the job. Unfortunately, when she left the building, she headed down the quiet back streets and we lost her on camera.

"Computer forensics are working on Stevens' office hardware, but his personal laptop is missing, and that could hold the key. Who knows."

Jack turned to Duncan. "How are you doing with the origin of the drug? Have you canvassed the vets who use it up here, or any of the suppliers?"

"Still going through the list but nothing concrete so far. Should know more by the end of the day. Nothing at your end?" Duncan looked at Jack and Amanda, though he already knew the answer: they'd have said something if they'd got a result to share.

"No, but we do have a couple of places that have used the drug recently. They are both near wildlife parks or zoos. And both have legitimate back-up stories. Still, neither has been ruled out at this stage."

"Right. I'll take Amanda with me," said Rick. "Duncan, why don't you show Jack the CCTV footage? There may be something for fresh eyes to find."

"Will do, and we might drop over to his apartment again."

His chair scraped on the tiled floor as he stood, signalling that the briefing was drawing to a close. The others stood in unison.

"Let's get going, then, and meet back here later. Are you both staying over?"

Jack took that one. "Probably not, but open at this stage."

Rick showed them back out and into the main incident room.

"Is there a game on tonight, do you know, at Old Trafford?" Jack asked.

"A fan, are you?"

"I was thinking more of the fish and chips, actually," he said, smiling.

Chapter Sixty-Three

THE THING that struck Amanda about Georgia first off was her absolute beauty. She was a stunning woman, and Amanda immediately wondered if she and her boss had had a fling or two. Two beautiful people working together—it seemed a natural conclusion. They were sat in the boardroom at Sebast Suites, steaming mugs of peppermint tea set out in front of each of them, as Rick gently took Georgia over recent events again, Sebastian's enemies and his hobbies, his sexual relationships. Georgia was still clearly distressed at the loss of her boss, the red rims of her eyes a telltale sign she'd cried hard, and recently. Her nose was as pink as if she'd had a heavy cold and used a few too many rough tissues.

"He had his fair share of enemies, I know, and after that video hit the press, he did get some hate mail but nothing serious, nothing worthy of calling the police for. Just general hateful comments. I deleted them, the emails he got, but you may still be able to trace them." She sounded hopeful. She was trying her best to help. She wiped the end of her nose again with her tissue, making the pinkness a tiny bit brighter.

"What about his working relationships? What's been happening there of note?" Rick had a gentle manner as he questioned her, though Amanda suspected that had she been a suspect rather than the victim's colleague, he'd be showing quite a different side of himself. But his approach was working with Georgia. She seemed reasonably relaxed.

Georgia thought for a moment, silent, and looked at the floor for direction before she finally spoke.

"There has been a bit of an upset with a working relationship recently. I know the man involved wasn't happy with Sebastian, not at all, though Sebastian wasn't too bothered. He had a hard skin most of the time."

"Who was that?"

Amanda studied Georgia and her body language while Rick wrote in his notebook. Georgia was now feeling somewhat uncomfortable, and it was starting to show. Amanda took the opportunity to speak. Leaning closer to Georgia, she added gently, "Anything, no matter how small, could be useful. This man—it sounds like we should have a chat with him. What is his name, Georgia?"

Amanda's voice had the desired effect. Georgia relaxed visibly and spoke up more confidently now. "He's Jason Whitely, one of the franchisees whom Sebastian was working with. I believe there was a big disagreement a few days before all this happened, and Jason was livid. From the little I know of the situation, he lost a lot of money to Sebastian. He sent some threatening emails. He was extremely angry and upset. You don't think he had anything to do with it, do you?" Georgia looked genuinely concerned. "He is such a nice man! I can't believe he'd have anything to do with it." Her voice rose an octave in distress.

"We'll take a look," said Amanda evenly. "We are investigating all leads at the moment so it may come to nothing."

Georgia's eyes returned to their normal size as the alarm in them slowly dissipated.

"We'll need his contact details from you," Rick said. "What about anyone else?"

Georgia gave him a short list of names of people who had had recently argued with Sebastian or sent him heated emails.

"Let's talk about what you know of his personal life, if we can," Rick said, changing tack. "We know he dated regularly though didn't have a regular partner, and that he also had certain. . ." he paused for effect, ". . . tastes." Do you know which sites or agencies he frequented?"

Georgia blushed and re-examined the floor again, as though looking for strength. Amanda nodded to Rick and he took the hint. He stood. "Excuse me a moment, please. I need to make a call." Extracting his phone from his pocket, he left the room, leaving Amanda to take over.

"Please, Georgia," she said, "anything, no matter how small, could help find Sebastian's killer. What was his favourite agency?"

A fresh tear slid down Georgia's cheek and she dabbed it with her already wet tissue. "There was one, well, a couple actually. I think he regularly fell out with them, the agencies, I mean. Some girls didn't provide exactly what he'd requested and things could get heated between the agency and Sebastian. I often smoothed the waters for him."

"I'll need the names of the agencies, and the women, if you know who they were."

Georgia nodded. "I'll write them down for you in a minute. I'll have to look a couple of them up." Thinking again, she added, "I think he had a booking the night he was killed. I'm pretty sure I saw something." Realisation set in again and her hand flew to her mouth. "You don't think it could have been one of the women?"

"As Detective Black said earlier, we're looking at all angles. Can you think of anyone or anything else that has maybe been a little out of the ordinary recently? Maybe someone from the past popping up, someone in the building acting suspiciously, or hanging around his usual haunts? I believe he liked to have lunch in The Lowry regularly—maybe he'd mentioned something or someone?"

Georgia was once again quiet in thought. She shook her head 'no.'

Rick re-entered the room quietly and apologised for his absence. Amanda moved her head from side to side ever so slightly, just enough for Rick to get the message.

"Well, you've been extremely helpful, Georgia. Thanks for your time. If you could get us the names before we leave, that would be great," Amanda said, smiling. "And here's my card, just in case you think of anything else. And like I say, no matter how small, it could be useful."

Georgia managed a slight smile in return and got up to leave the room and get the names. While she was gone, Rick filled Amanda in on what Duncan had found out with the CCTV camera footage. Jack had apparently spotted a woman later that night on other footage who looked to be dressed identically to the woman seen leaving the building, though her hair was different. She was wearing the same dress and the same distinctive scarf with what looked to be a large red poppy printed on it. He opened his tablet and showed Amanda the footage. He paused the video; the woman's form filled the screen, though her face was still not visible.

"Looks like it could have been a disguise after all, not a long-haired woman at all," he concluded. "So now we have something a bit more concrete to follow up on. They are trying to trace all her movements that night via the cameras, see where she ended up or get a clear image of her face, but it seems the woman we're looking for has short hair, not long like the person who entered the building that night."

Georgia entered the room again as Rick was finishing his last sentence. She carried with her a list of names, all typed out neatly on a single sheet of paper, and placed it on the table in front of Rick. She peered at the tablet screen.

"Is that someone of interest?" she asked. "A shame it's so blurry. It could be anyone. Nice scarf, though."

"Thank you, Georgia," Rick said neutrally, avoiding the question. "You've been very helpful."

"Anything to help out. I hope you catch the person that did this, and soon. I know Sebastian wasn't liked by all but he didn't deserve to die either. Let me show you both out."

As the three of them walked back to the lift, Rick spoke to Amanda in a hushed voice.

"And it looks like we might have a lead on one of the two vet clinics."

His conversation wasn't hushed enough. Georgia's ears pricked up. Something clicked inside her head.

Chapter Sixty-Four

IT HAD BEEN a stressful day and Georgia felt like she was existing in a complete daze. First the realisation that her boss, no matter how awkward he could be, had been murdered, then dealing with the fallout from that as well as the police knocking about and looking into his life, from all angles. She was worn out both mentally and physically and there was no sign of the pressure letting up anytime soon.

She grabbed her bag and headed for the lift, feeling the need suddenly for some fresh air. She hoped the two detectives were gone from the vicinity completely because she just couldn't be bothered to talk to anyone else right now, never mind the authorities. The lift pinged its arrival and she stepped inside, keeping her head down until she alighted at the lobby. A cool breeze blew in from the open front doors, making her lift her head. The lobby seemed unusually bright, the marble and brass gleaming in the afternoon sunshine, but the way the building was positioned, it sometimes caught the stiff breeze that blew. In winter it was never welcome, but on a sunny day with so much stress on her shoulders, it most definitely was.

Georgia headed for the coffee shop just around the corner, the one where she'd met up with Philippa. Was it really only a few days ago? A booth at the back was free and she slid along the leather into the corner and rested her back across it, half on the wall, half on the leather backing. She was sorely tempted to swing her legs up in front of her and catch forty winks, but as she let her eyes close for a moment, a voice interrupted her.

"What can I get you?" She slowly raised her eyelids. It was a hovering waitress with her hair all piled up in a doughnut-shaped bun on the top of her head. For a moment, she said nothing, but stared at the neatly tucked hairdo.

"Are you okay?" asked the waitress.

"Do you serve alcohol in here?" Georgia asked.

"We do. We have wine and beer."

"In that case, I'll have a lite beer, in a tall glass please. Do you have Sol?

"One Sol coming up," said the waitress, and she slipped away, leaving Georgia to close her eyes again.

When she heard the glass being put down in front of her, she kept her eyes firmly shut, thinking back to recent events and the bits that had clunked into place a short time ago. Thoughts of coffee had gone out of the window when she'd entered the booth, but thoughts of Philippa and their recent 'chance' meeting hadn't. Had she planned to enter Georgia's life again, or had that really been a coincidence? Had the detective said their person of interest had short hair and not a long wig as they might have first thought? Then there was the mention of a vet clinic to follow up on. The three things glowed in her mind like flashing red lights at a railway crossing. *On, off, on, off.* Was there another explanation? If so, why hadn't Philippa been back in touch herself? She was bound to have heard the reports of Sebastian's death on the news and online, yet nothing. Georgia found that odd, now she thought more about it. Rummaging in her bag, she found the card the female detective had given her and stared at it for a moment, then tapped it thoughtfully on the table in front of her, the sharp edge of the card hitting the glass table top crisply. Tapping the card with one hand, she picked up her beer with the other and took a long gulp, the cool bitter liquid massaging her parched throat and filling her with renewed energy. One long gulp quickly turned into an empty glass and she topped it up from the remainder in the bottle, which she sipped slowly until it was all gone. Staring at the remaining creamy foam that

Chapter Sixty-Five

THE NEXT DAY was filled with much of the same: questions from all angles about all areas of Sebastian's life and death from all kinds of people, some official, some plain nosey, and she'd had enough. The end of the day couldn't have come soon enough, and Georgia and her colleagues were glad to finally leave that evening.

"Who's for a quick drink before home? Anyone?" asked Sandra, one of the other PAs, flicking back her lovely bouncy curls. Georgia was tempted, but waited for a response from the others before committing herself. It seemed everyone wanted to get as far away from the place as soon as possible, and who could blame them? Sandra was thin on acceptances.

"Might get a burger just after ....?" Sandra used her sing-song voice, not wanting to drink on her own.

Might as well, thought Georgia. She had nothing else better to do and she was up for a glass of wine. "Count me in. I could kill for a chilled glass of Pinot Grigio right now, and then some."

"Excellent!" Sandra cheered. "Can I tempt anyone else?" There were plenty of head-shakes as they filed into the lift; no one else seemed keen. Sandra turned to Georgia. "Looks like you and me, kiddo. Where do you fancy?"

"Don't care. The closest probably, then on from there. After this crappy week, I might really push the boat out and get smashed. Couldn't tell you when I last did that."

"My kind of girl!" Sandra high-fived Georgia, a huge grin stretching across her face. "Stick with me, then. We'll have a great night, and I know just where to start!"

As the lift stopped in the lobby and everyone piled out, Georgia hung back with Sandra a little and they walked together out of the building for the weekend. The early evening temperature was just right, a mixture of summer sun and a light breeze. The sun's rays reflected off the many glass-covered buildings, making some too dazzling to look at for long. Sandra steered them into a nearby bar and they took seats on tan leather stools at the bar. A small bowl of dry roasted nuts was placed in front of each of them, and the waiter appeared to take their order.

"Glass of Pinot Grigio for me, please," Georgia said. "I don't really care which one. Whatever you have opened is fine."

"And I'll have the same, for now." Sandra smiled at the cute young man and watched as his cheeks turned a pale pink. When he'd left to pour their drinks, Sandra leaned in and said, "Too cute and probably too young, but that doesn't stop me looking."

"I don't know how you've even got the energy after the week we've just had. I'm exhausted. And not sleeping either." Two cold glasses of Pinot Grigio arrived and Georgia took a sip of hers immediately, closing her eyes as the cold liquid slipped down her throat. She watched Sandra do the same.

"Damn, that's good! So, why aren't you sleeping if you're so tired? Are you worrying about something?" She flicked a couple of nuts into her mouth and chewed hungrily.

Georgia picked her glass back up and took a much larger mouthful, draining about a quarter of her glass. Sandra noticed but said nothing, waiting for Georgia to answer in her own time.

"I've not stopped thinking about Sebastian's murder," Georgia said at length. "Like we all haven't, I should add. But you see, I can't help wondering if I know who might be responsible. For his death and maybe that other woman."

Sandra's glass stopped halfway to her lips as she registered what Georgia had just implied. "Holy freakin' moly. Really?"

Georgia nodded sadly.

"What are you going to do?"

"Well, that's just it. I'm really not sure because I could have it all wrong. And that would be disastrous for the person. It could ruin their life."

"Well, look at it this way. If they are responsible, they have ruined two lives already as well as the lives of their loved ones, and if they've done it twice, they could well do it again. And again."

"Do you think I should say something, then, let the police work through what I think? I mean, I don't have a shred of evidence, just gut feeling and coincidence."

"I do. Imagine how you'll feel if someone else turns up like Sebastian did, and you could have perhaps stopped it. You'd never forgive yourself, would you? And you'd have that on your shoulders for the rest of your life. I say, do yourself a favour and tell them what you know, let them look into it."

Georgia sat staring into her drink, looking miserable and tired. "I hear what you're saying and I've tossed it around so much that I'm sick of thinking about it anymore." She paused and took a sip of wine. "I'm going to do my own bit of digging first and then depending what I find out, I'll tell them this weekend if it still points to one person. Deal?"

Sandra raised her glass and lightly tapped Georgia's. "Deal, but make sure you do!"

"Can we change the subject now, away from death and investigations?"

"I'll drink to that," said Sandra, and clinked her glass again.

Later that night, when Georgia got home, she started scanning through Philippa During's online profile, her old posts and pictures. Yes, she was a vet; yes, she lived in Rickmansworth; yes, she did have short auburn hair. But there was something else that caught her attention in one of the past images. Something Georgia had seen only too recently.

Chapter Sixty-Six

@Jaybaby "I guess you've heard about Sebastian?"

@Belfort "Yes, I have. Couldn't have happened to a nicer guy." #thief

@Jaybaby "Seems a bit rough, old boy. He was a good friend of mine." #Steadyon

@Belfort "I know. Sorry, but I've just lost a chunk of money to the man through his greed. Wouldn't wish that on anyone though." #notsorry

@Jaybaby "What happened. May I help somehow?"

@Belfort "Not here, mate. I'll message you privately. Any sign of who did it, do you know?"

@Jaybaby "Not that I'm aware of, but it's GM Police, not the Met. @McRuth, you any idea?" #Amanda

Chapter Sixty-Seven

RUTH WAS DOING a crossword puzzle at her kitchen table when she saw the ping come through. She picked up her phone and tapped on the site to see what Jason was tagging her in. Reading through the conversation so far, she knew instantly what it was—the death of Sebastian Stevens. She typed out her reply:

@Belfort Not sure myself. Amanda is working the case with the GMP detectives. Not here to ask. #checklater

@McRuth Would welcome the intel, though I guess it will be on the news if they had made an arrest.

@Belfort Sorry Jordan, I know he was your friend. Terrible way to go. Have the GMP interviewed you?

@McRuth They have indeed, but couldn't tell them much. Just saw his newsfeed and called it in.

@Belfort from @Jaybaby Has the image been taken down yet so no one else has to see it?

@Jaybaby No, and it's been pasted all over the news and web so it's still very much out there. #Horrific

@Belfort Any news on the funeral? Not that I'll be going but gives closure to friends like you.

@Jaybaby Apparently not until his body can be released. Could be some time. #murderinvestigation

@Belfort Sorry to hear that. If you want to chat over a pint, sing out, alright?

@Jaybaby Thanks, appreciate it. Likewise re earlier comment.

@Belfort from @McRuth Same goes from me Jordan. Just let me know.

@Jaybaby @McRuth Thanks to you both. #greatfriends

Ruth signed out and picked her crossword back up again. She was stuck on three across: garden tool, three letters ending in 'e.' As she stared at the page, her thoughts drifted back to her stepmum, who'd died tragically. Her passion had been her own garden, a garden that had got her in trouble when she'd gone somewhat overboard with her shovel one day and ended up killing and burying the landscaper. While Ruth didn't condone what she'd done, she'd kept the secret safe, not even telling Amanda or her father. How could she? The landscaper still lay in a grave in the back garden, though her stepmother was unaware that she had figured that snippet out. By the time she had, it had been far too late.

"Hoe," she said to the paper and filled in the gaps, completing the day's puzzle. She checked the kitchen clock. Today's crossword was not a personal best, time-wise; maybe tomorrow's puzzle would be better. The back door opened and Amanda walked in.

"Perfect timing," Ruth said, standing and wrapping her partner in a bear hug, kissing her cheek into the bargain. "Want some hot chocolate or something else? Have you eaten?"

"Hi, hun. Yes, I've eaten but I'll join you in hot chocolate." Kicking her shoes off, she sank onto a chair and blew out a heavy breath, closing her eyes and stretching her legs out in front of her. Ruth busied herself with hot milk and glanced across at Amanda, at the short blonde hair framing the face of the woman she so loved.

"Tough day, eh? Shall I run you a bath, put some Radox in?"

Amanda groaned in pleasure, eyes still closed.

"I'll take that as a yes, then. We'll drink our chocolate first. But can I ask you a work question before you unwind?"

"Shoot." She still hadn't opened her eyes.

"How's the sick selfie case going? Only Jordan was asking. Sebastian was his friend, as you know. Are you any further forward? Any arrests imminent?"

"You know I can't discuss open cases, Ruth," Amanda said, sitting up and opening her eyes again, "but between you and me, we've nothing positive as yet, but that's all I can say, so don't go telling Jordan anything. Truth is, we have diddly to go on at the moment."

"I know. I'm sorry. Just wanted to help him out. Must have been pretty traumatic to see that."

"It's not often we don't get to the bottom of things, and I'm confident we will with this too."

Ruth passed her a steaming mug of hot chocolate and Amanda took a sip. "Mmmmm, can't beat it! Even in summer it's still good and comforting," she said, and sipped some more.

"I'll just go and turn the taps on while you drink," Ruth said, and left Amanda sat on her own, thinking about what they did know about the cases—a blurry picture of a short-haired woman and possibly a vet connection. It wasn't a lot to go on. They needed to catch a break, and soon.

Chapter Sixty-Eight

ANOTHER STIFF GLASS of wine later and Georgia was pretty certain she was onto something, though she desperately wished she wasn't. It all pointed to the same person, a person who had come back into her life, supposedly by chance, a few days ago. Had it all been a ploy? Was that why she'd been waiting outside the offices, waiting to 'bump' into Georgia, complete with a fake story? Now she felt used and stupid. Worse, she had probably been at least partly responsible for Sebastian's death. Without her feeding his personal information to Philippa, he might still have been alive. Instead, he was lying in a cold fridge in a mortuary in a dank hospital basement instead of enjoying drinks with his friends. Or girlfriends.

Georgia tapped the card in her fingers and picked up her phone, then set it down again. A voice in her head told her to dig a little deeper before she did anything else, something she might regret if she indeed had it all wrong. She opened her Messenger app and tapped out a message to Philippa, as if nothing was on her mind.

Hey, what you up to?

The reply came back quickly.

Hey Georgia! Nothing much. You?

No, had the week from hell so far, what with Sebastian's death. Think I'll get hammered.

Send.

Wow, yes. I heard about that. Terrible! You holding up?

The replies were coming naturally, no thinking-time delays. Maybe she was barking up the wrong tree after all?

Yes. So many questions, though, from the police and whatnot. Ready for my bed tonight, let me tell you.

Send.

Yes, poor love. Well, you look after yourself, eh? Get some rest. And we'll speak soon?

Thanks. I'm going to head up to bed now, read for a while, clear my head.

Send.

Sounds good. I'll let you go then.

Philippa signed off with a smiling emoji. Georgia stared at it. Was she way off with her suspicions after all?

Georgia sat back on the sofa, her thoughts whirling. Her friend sounded as normal as normal could be. Had she got it all wrong? Surely there was more than one scarf with a big poppy on it, and surely other vets had short hair? And anyway, what exactly did a murderer sound like—Hannibal Lecter? The only thing left to do was to sleep on it, to make a decision tomorrow rather than do anything rash now. Sometimes, things looked a little clearer after time had passed.

With a heavy sigh, she trudged upstairs to read for a while. When she finally drifted off to sleep sometime later, the dreams that came were not pleasant ones: Sebastian laughing, blood dripping from the corner of his mouth as he laughed harder and harder, his face contorting as he crumpled to the floor. A woman with a knife just behind him, talking to her with words she couldn't hear. A bright red poppy on a scarf wrapped around a woman's severed head, eyes dead. Georgia tossed and turned to shake free of the dream, sweat gathering on her forehead and chest soaking her nightdress as the droplets turned into a wet river. When the dream finally broke, she surfaced back into the safety of her bedroom wide awake, panting hard.

"Just a dream," she said to herself, her voice shaking. "Just a dream."

Chapter Sixty-Nine

IT HAD BEEN QUITE the bonus finding out one of Fiona Gable's friends was a hunter too, and there was no way she could let it go. Of course, poor dear, departed Fiona had other hunters among her friends, but as Philippa had scrolled through and looked at what this particular man had posted, she realised he must have been away hunting at the same time as Fiona had been. Had they both been at the same place? Had they swapped war stories around a campfire over whiskey? Had they compared kills, reliving the experience over dinner? The thoughts grossed her out—the two gloating pigs sharing a meal together and talking about the one that got away, probably overstretched somewhat for the purpose of a better story. Or maybe there hadn't been a need to; maybe the day's hunt had been action-packed enough that there had been no need to add gory details. She stopped at the photo of him posed arrogantly beside a dead leopard. She could practically see the target forming on his head already. No longer would that graceful animal roam the African plains or sleep comfortably draped over a branch. No, he'd taken all that away from it. So now it was her turn to take something from him.

She'd sent him a friend request, and he'd accepted it almost immediately with a short note back saying how nice it was to see her again.

Pft! It amazed Philippa just how shallow the man appeared to be, and despite not knowing a thing about him save for his deplorable hobby, she hated him already. But the picture she'd used had worked and that was the main thing. Able to see into much of his life now, she'd watch from the sidelines for a few days while she decided what to do about him—or rather when to do it. She stared at his profile picture like she was trying to read his mind, understand his thoughts, what went on in his head. Cocking her own head to the right, she said "For a complete prick, you're damn handsome. That dark hair of yours actually makes you look a little exotic. Where do you originate from, I wonder? I mean, originally, your roots? I guess I'll just have to guess for now, and I'm guessing maybe somewhere in the Middle East. Remind me to ask you when we finally do meet—just to quell my own curiosity you understand." For now, though, her plan was to look and listen and flirt with this rather tiresome but handsome sleaze-ball.

Scrolling through his profile, she clicked 'like' on a couple of his posts and left a nondescript comment on another, just enough for him to see she was out there, interacting with him, playing with him. Knowing he was married with children, she played it safe for now, but her direct messages to him would become quite different. With no one to see those apart from Aaron and herself, she could be as flirty as she needed to be. Or he wanted her to be.

Aaron Galbraith was now enemy number one, and her new fake profile of Frankie Green was going to see he got his comeuppance.

Aaron checked his newsfeed while his beautiful wife Stephanie took a long, well-deserved soak in the bath upstairs, taking advantage of some quiet, alone time. They'd been married for ten years and had two wonderful young twin sons, Josh, and Jasper, who were sound asleep in their bedroom. At the tender age of seven, they were like two peas in a pod, not only identical to each other, but mini-versions of both parents combined. With Stephanie's dark, sultry looks and almond eyes and Aaron's dark hair and deep hazel eyes, there was no mistaking whose children they were when they were all out together. They looked like the perfect magazine shot family, needing only a small dog to complete the look. And no doubt they'd get one one day.

With everyone safely sleeping or soaking, Aaron took the opportunity to chat to Frankie, a woman who'd popped into his online life a couple of weeks ago when she'd sent a friend request. While she looked vaguely familiar, and gorgeous, her name didn't register with him at all, though she was friends with some of his other friends. He just couldn't place where he knew her from; he hadn't bothered to ask, not wanting to offend. Women changed their hair all the time, so she could well have been cropped and blonde before the long shiny hair she sported in her pictures now. And since she was such a stunner to look at, and quite a flirt as it had turned out, he'd left it at that. And he liked the mystery.

He smiled at the message on his phone, the ambiguousness of it, the double-entendre meaning; if anyone else saw their exchange, they wouldn't have a clue what they were really talking about. It seemed whatever she said could be taken in one of two ways depending on either his or her mood. He readjusted himself slightly as he took it the way he hoped she'd meant. It was pretty clear she was up for some fun so he replied back excitedly.

I've got a trip out to LA so I'll be gone a week or so. But maybe we could grab that drink when I'm back? Would that work for you? Be good to catch up again in person.

Frankie couldn't believe her luck that he wanted to meet so soon. She'd only been watching him and chatting with him for a few days, but was pleased that he seemed keen. And she'd made it easy for him, after all: most men liked to be teased a little, and she had been doing a fine job of getting his attention so far. But was she ready to do it all again just yet? Should she let the dust settle a little first, take the heat out of current goings-on? Or was it best to go with the momentum, strike while the publicity was hot and her mission was getting the exposure it so deserved? Surely the murders must be making others think about their bad choices in hobbies, reflect on it at the very least? Even if it stopped one person from taking up the sport, it was worth it—and it was definitely worth it to the animals involved. She looked at the tiny screen in her hand and pondered what to do. Moments later, momentum won out.

Sounds good, she typed back. *Tell me where and when and I'll make it work.*

Perfect. I'll work on it. What time do you finish work usually?

It varies, but around six, so I'll dash home and change, then be on my way.

Frankie wasn't intending for anything to happen on their first meeting, and even though she'd been the essence of a flirt, she needed to work on Aaron a little more. If she was infiltrating his life on the side, she needed him to want her, and chase her, just a little, to give her time. The fact that he was married with children didn't bother her. They were collateral damage as far as she was concerned. It was Aaron and Aaron alone she was interested in, but not in the way that Aaron hoped she was. Still, the plan was working out just fine so far.

Can't wait to see you again after so long. You've not changed a bit—still looking great.

What bull, she thought, but replied in a similar fashion. *Me neither, and you're as dark and handsome as you were back then. Until then, toodle pip.*

Aaron closed the app down on his phone and smiled to himself. The sound of Stephanie moving around upstairs brought him back to reality and he slipped his phone back into his jeans pocket and headed upstairs, where she was just slipping into her nightdress. He sidled up to her and gently kissed her neck, whispering breathlessly into her ear.

"Why don't you leave that off, and I'll join you shortly?" He pecked her neck again.

Dropping her head back with pleasure, she smiled knowingly and he left her to grab a quick shower.

Not ten minutes later, Aaron was back, a fluffy towel tied around his waist, his broad chest tanned and muscular from working out three times per week. He liked good-looking things and he added himself into that folder. He took the time and effort to look his best, for himself and those he cared for. And Stephanie appreciated his effort, and he hers.

But it wasn't the beautiful Stephanie Galbraith that filled his head that night as they moved together: it was someone else, someone else with long brown hair. And her name was Frankie Green.

On the other side of town, Frankie certainly wasn't thinking of Aaron, well, at least not in the same way he was of her. Her desires were somewhat different, more deadly as she percolated the plan in her head. She had chewed through several small packets of cashew nuts, and a glass of red wine had since turned into three. Nibbling helped her think, get the pieces of the puzzle right. She'd been lucky so far, but she wasn't going to become complacent: that's where errors occurred and she'd no desire for time inside sharing a cell with a serial killer. Aaron would be easy to get on his own, she was sure—he'd made that pretty damn clear—and that would work in her favour. Finding him through Fiona Gable had been a stroke of luck, and as she nibbled and sipped, she wondered idly if either of them had known Sebastian Stevens too. It wasn't such a farfetched thought: like-minded people, those who shared the same interests, particularly something so expensive, could well have crossed paths at some point. The thought amused her as she tossed the last of the nuts into her mouth and took the little empty plastic wrappers out to the kitchen.

Chapter Seventy

"COFFEE, BABE?"

He always made sure when he was about to leave on a work trip that he paid a little extra attention to her, like he had last night, and Stephanie appreciated the thought. And had enjoyed it. She had hated spending the evenings alone in particular, but Aaron had been a pilot for as long as she could remember and they'd easily slotted into a routine. Like today. The whole family was at the breakfast bar, the boys with pancakes and maple syrup made by their father and Stephanie about to be served coffee. She smelled bacon cooking as she sat on a vacant stool.

"Perfect. Love some. And that bacon smells good too." She leaned over and kissed both boys on their cheeks, though at age seven they found pancakes far more interesting than their mother's love. Neither of them stopped chewing, though they at least smiled through full mouths. Mornings when they were all together as a family was Stephanie's idea of bliss, and when Aaron left in a couple of hours, the house would feel quite different until he came back towards the end of the week. He poured her coffee and set it down in front of her. He had used the 'I love Mummy' mug, her favourite. Life was indeed good.

"What have you got planned this week while I'm gone? Anything exciting?"

Stirring a little cream in her coffee, one of life's luxuries and one of her few vices, she smiled at her husband affectionately. "You really do have a memory like a sieve, don't you? The builders are here most of this week, doing the new en suite, remember?"

Aaron was busy putting eggs and bacon onto a plate for each of them and still not really focusing on what she was saying. The hot bacon fat stung his fingers as he picked pieces out of the pan without the aid of tongs.

"Hmm? Okay," he said absentmindedly, picking up the plates up and taking them to the breakfast bar for them both. "Sounds like fun. You finally chose something you like?"

Stephanie rolled her eyes at the two boys, who both giggled, knowing full well what their mother was thinking. It was a bad habit, she knew, but they always found it amusing, so she indulged them every once and a while. Aaron very often missed the whole story because he wasn't fully listening. How could he forget the builders were due in? His memory had more holes in it than Swiss cheese.

"Yes, I did, it's all sorted and by the time you get back from LA, it should all be finished and looking pretty cool. Then we'll be able to have a soak in the tub together when they've finished the main bathroom next." She leaned forward and pecked him lightly on the neck, just like he had done to her the night before. "What time are you leaving?" she asked, changing the topic and licking her lips at the same time. The builders were due around eight, but the boys had to get to school. "What I mean is, are you able to drop the boys off this morning or not? Just thought you might if you can, so I can be here when they start."

"Absolutely I can take them. I'm not due to leave until around ten, so plenty of time," he said, chewing on a piece of buttered toast. There was a blot of egg on his chin. She leaned over and dabbed at it with her napkin.

"Great, though you know what builders are like. They'll probably turn up at nine thirty and want a cup of tea before they start, then it'll be lunchtime before you know it. That's why I want to be around while they're here, keep them moving so it's done before you get back."

Aaron smiled at his orderly wife. She could be so bossy at times, just the way he liked her, and even before her morning shower, hair all mussed up, sat drinking coffee and eating breakfast in the kitchen together, she was drop-dead gorgeous.

"I expect you will. They'll be wondering what they've let themselves in for after a couple of days of you being Sergeant Major Galbraith," he said with a mock salute, making the boys giggle.

She looked at the clock on the cooker. "Eat up, boys. You need to leave in ten if you're going to be at school on time. And that goes for you too, Mr. Driver," she said, and saluted Aaron back.

Within a couple of minutes, everyone's empty plate was abandoned in place, stools were vacated, and young fingers pushed toothpaste-y brushes around their mouths before the three of them left for the car in one giant noisy rabble. The door slammed behind them and peace descended on the house. Climbing the stairs, she could just hear them outside as car doors banged and excited voices rose and fell. Stephanie grinned at just how lucky she was.

Chapter Seventy-One

AARON ALWAYS MISSED his family while he was away, but it came with the territory and he loved his work. While the actual flight to LA wasn't that long or arduous, there were strict rules that stated how much rest time a pilot was to have before flying back again, and the time differences played havoc with a pilot's body. Better to be safe than sorry, but this trip always meant several days away at one time to comply. He'd been working for the same airline for some time and that loyalty gave him certain perks, so he could pretty much pick the routes and days he wanted to work and let the others fight it out for the less popular ones. One of his perks was his own loyal team, and one woman was particularly loyal to him. They'd been working together for the past five years and while they didn't see each other outside of work, they made the most of their time together when they were away. While Valerie would undoubtedly have liked more, Aaron was a married man, as he gently reminded her from time to time.

The door opened to the cockpit and Valerie popped her head inside.

"Coffee, gentlemen?" she enquired, smiling a little more directly at Aaron than at his co-pilot.

"Please. Any sandwiches going?"

"I'll see what I can find. Was lunch not enough for you today, then?" Valerie winked at him behind his co-pilot's back, their quick lunch encounter still wonderfully fresh in her mind.

"Got to keep my energy up," was all he said, and Valerie knew exactly what he was referring to—their upcoming time together later. She couldn't wait. While they could only see each other at work, she was beginning to get a bit down about it, and wanted more. The thought of him going back to his wife and young family after they'd shared their time together was getting to her, but she knew it would always be the same way. They'd talked about it briefly a couple of months ago when she'd become tearful at the prospect, but he'd told her straight out he would never leave Stephanie and the boys. He hoped she understood.

And right at the beginning of their relationship, that had been fine. She just wanted to have fun too and they did, together, but as time went by, she'd developed deeper feelings for him. He, unfortunately, didn't feel the same. So, she took what she could and enjoyed the time they did have and suffered the hurt at the end of each trip. Checking her wristwatch, she reminded herself that she could have him all to herself in five more hours and headed back to the galley in search of sandwiches and coffee.

"What you two up to tonight, then, Val? Room service or a night out?" Amber knew all about Valerie's part-time love life, and she also knew it was starting to bother her, though wondered why she didn't do something about it—like dump him. She was a popular and beautiful woman and deserved a full-time partner of her own, not just the sneaky bits on offer from a married man with sex on his mind.

Deep down, Valerie knew it herself. "Well, I'm voting for room service, that's for sure! I'm in need of some alone time and I plan on making the most of the next few days, though he mentioned going out to Venice Beach. How about you?"

"Venice Beach sounds like fun. You should go, get wild with the locals a little, though I prefer Santa Monica myself, or better yet, Malibu. But no, no real plans, and I'm not in a rush to pick up any more strangers for a while, so I expect I'll go off with the others bar hopping by night and beauty sleeping by day." Amber still had the mental scars, and several actual ones, from when she'd picked up a *gentleman* on a flight and taken him back to her hotel room for a quick hook-up. What she hadn't banked on was his needs and his peculiar, downright scary, tastes. It had certainly made her think twice about casual liaisons, which was a good thing, and had slowed her down. While she'd never reported the incident, it had taught her a lesson.

"Sounds like fun," Valerie said, putting sandwiches on a plate for the men. "If I ever see that mean, animal of a man again, I'll put something in his coffee for you. Just you give me the nod and consider it done." She, too, remembered him well, had felt his eyes burning into her backside as she'd worked first class with Amber when he had been on board. She had also seen the news about him afterwards with the hunting auction video debacle.

"If I see him first, he'll be getting more than something in his coffee from me," Amber said, her lip curling. "More like a swift kick where it hurts then a baseball bat round his head. Probably get me sacked though," she said almost mournfully, and both women laughed. It would never happen.

"Let's hope someone else does him in first, then. Otherwise the pair of us could be in trouble," Valerie finished, giggling. She set the coffees and sandwiches on a tray.

"I'll get the door for you," said Amber, and the two friends headed out towards the cockpit.

Chapter Seventy-Two

THAT NIGHT, Stephanie put the boys to bed as usual, then made herself comfortable on the sofa, a glass of white wine dangling between the fingers of her right hand, the remote idly flicking through channels in her left, in search of something to prick her interest. She wasn't one for much television, preferring the comfort of a good book, but she wasn't in the mood for that. She wanted something mundane that would wash right over her, take no effort to think about. Taking a long sip, she stopped at a news channel. There was a picture of a good-looking blond man on the screen, and he seemed familiar to her. Turning the volume up, she tried to work out what had happened and where she thought she knew him from. The reporter was broadcasting live from outside a tall building somewhere. Stephanie managed to deduce that Mr. Handsome had been found dead, and it seemed he was the second victim, the first having been killed in the same grotesque way, throat slit and photos of the corpse posted online for all to see.

The reporter went on to say the blond man had recently been the target of public outrage after bidding on two white rhinos to hunt in a Zimbabwe reserve. A man well known in many circles, particularly in business, he had had his share of fans as well as enemies, and police were continuing their investigations into his death. The name of the victim moved on ticker tape across the bottom of the screen: Sebastian Stevens. Stephanie sat up straighter as she remembered where she knew him from, although they'd both been about fifteen years younger when she'd come across him and she'd never learned his name. Feeling herself lose colour, she downed the remainder of her wine in one go and turned the TV off, sitting back into the sofa and closing her eyes to regain her composure. Her head started to pulse and she rubbed her temples to push a headache away.

"So he's dead then. And good riddance. I hope it hurt."

Aaron had never asked about the little scars on the backs of her legs, now faded and about a centimetre long, and she'd first explained them away as nicks from getting stuck in brambles when she was young. The topic had not been mentioned since; there was no need. What the animal had really done to her that night she had no idea, though she remembered getting painfully drunk with him back in his room and awakening with a throbbing headache which she'd assumed was from a hangover. It was only when she'd got back to her own flat the next morning that she realised he must have spiked her drink. She'd surely have felt those little cuts had it only been booze in her stomach.

That was the first and only time she ever saw him, but now his stupid face and blond locks were stuck in her head, the question of what exactly had happened to her that night fresh in her mind once again. She had not bothered to report the incident; she had been too embarrassed. Yes, she'd gone there for sex, and they had had fun together, but when she'd passed out... Well, she'd just been mortified. She had had no idea what he'd done to her, and still didn't.

And now he was dead.

Stephanie took her empty wine glass into the kitchen, poured milk into a pan, and made herself a soothing mug of hot chocolate to take upstairs to bed. While she wished Aaron was lay beside her, she was also glad he wasn't there to see her reaction, not that he could do anything about it. But it was a comforting arm she needed right now, and there wasn't one available. He'd only ever been a pilot, and she'd known what she was taking on when they first got together. But that didn't mean she liked it.

With the last mouthful of chocolate gone, she slithered down under the duvet and fell into a fitful sleep, dreaming of Aaron and Sebastian as they floated randomly through her head, combining in one unsettling dream.

Chapter Seventy-Three

THE MORNING BROKE with bright sunshine streaming in through the front bedroom windows, waking her early, the light fiercely bright with no curtains to shield it away. She opened her eyes slowly and lay there on her stomach. The clock read 5.45 am and Stephanie groaned. Her head felt heavy as she lifted it off the pillow to turn over onto her back. The sun made an odd pattern as it shone through the patterned holes on the lightshade. Little flower shadows danced all around the top half of the wall and she watched them, her head empty. A noise in the hallway brought her back into the moment, as she realised one of the boys must be up and about. She grabbed her robe off the end of the bed, and fastening the sash loosely around her waist, she headed out to see why he was up so early.

"Hi Mum," said a little voice as Josh came out of the toilet, drying his hands on his PJ bottoms instead of the hand towel by the basin. She could never figure out why he did that, and had given up asking, hoping he'd stop it before he grew much older.

"You're an early bird," she said, tousling his hair. "Want some tea and toast?"

"Yes, please."

"Then grab your robe—it's still a bit chilly yet—and I'll see you downstairs. Is Jasper awake too?"

"Nah, don't think so," he said, and sauntered back to his room to get his robe. Stephanie made her way downstairs, smiling at the way he had about himself. The two boys were alike to look at, but in personality and behaviour they couldn't have been more different. Jasper would lie in bed until noon if he thought he could get away with it, while Joshua had always been an early riser, though not as early as today normally.

She smiled as he padded into the kitchen and climbed up onto a stool, his hair messy and his thin legs hanging like pipe cleaners inside his tartan patterned PJ bottoms. He'd fill them out one day.

"Are the builders coming back today, Mum?"

"I hope so. They should be here every day this week to get it finished before your dad gets back. Why do you ask?"

"Just wondered. Will they be taking the wall down today, do you think? I'd like to watch."

"I expect so, but you'll be at school, so I doubt you'll see it. You want me to take a couple of photos of it for you instead?"

"Can't I stay home and watch? Please?" he whined, but she stood firm. There was no way he was staying home if he wasn't ill. She slid a small plate of buttered toast towards him.

"Sorry, buddy, no can do. You have to go to school so you can be clever like Daddy, and if you want to be a pilot ...." She let the sentence hang, knowing just how badly he wanted to be just like his dad when he grew up. It usually did the trick when he didn't want to go to school for some reason. He was airplane mad and desperate to follow in his hero's footsteps. Jasper, on the other hand, had no clue what he wanted to do when he grew up but at aged seven, Stephanie wasn't concerned just yet. There was plenty of time for career planning.

"I've got to go out myself today, but I'm sure one of the men would take some pictures if I'm not back in time. I don't know what time they will be taking it down and I can't really wait." She watched as he nibbled the edges off a slice of toast, not really that interested in it. "Would you like some cereal instead of toast? A growing boy needs fuel."

Looking thoughtful, he replied "No, I'm fine thanks. Perhaps I'll have some a bit later before I go."

She smiled to herself, wondering just what went on in that young head of his. He was so deep and thoughtful at times, and so similar to Aaron in many ways. Another face appeared in the doorway. Jasper had joined them.

"Morning, Jasper. Toast or cereal? And how come you're up this early? It's not like you."

"I heard noises, and cereal, please." Jasper climbed up onto a stool next to Joshua, his PJ bottoms hanging just as loosely.

"The wall is coming down today and Mum's going to ask the builders to take some pictures of it. It's going to be so cool!" Joshua said excitedly. "I wonder if there are any dead bodies behind it like in the movies!"

"Maybe a dead rat, more likely. This house isn't that old, you know, Josh, not like the really old ones in London. They have dungeons and tunnels underneath them!" Jasper made a shrieking sound at his brother, trying to scare him, his hands and fingers working in the air like something from a horror movie. Joshua screamed.

"Stop scaring your brother, Jasper, and eat your cereal," Stephanie scolded as she put a bowl of Shredded Wheat down in front of him. "There'll be no dead bodies of any kind, not even a mouse, I'm sure. There will be more likely a lost toy or something from the previous owner, definitely nothing to get excited about. Now both of you, eat your breakfast while I go and shower, then because it's still so early, we can call at the park on the way to school for a few minutes if you like."

Cheers went up around the kitchen and both boys got busy with spoons and fingers, looking forward to a bit of stolen time on the swings and slide.

"In another couple of years, it won't be swings and slides," Stephanie mused as she climbed back up the stairs. "Better make the most of these years while I can."

Chapter Seventy-Four

WITH THE BOYS safely dropped off at school, Stephanie headed back home to greet the builders, though she really just wanted to see what time they arrived, let them know she was around so they didn't slack off all morning. After errands later that morning then an hour or so of shopping, she was going into town to meet a friend for lunch, before heading back in time for the boys arriving back. She was happy being a full-time mum and housewife, and with Aaron away so much, she'd had to step into the role, not wanting her boys to be brought up by a nanny. Initially, she'd baulked at the notion of being home all day and losing her career in marketing, thinking she'd go back to it when the boys were older, but the truth was, she loved her life, *their* life together, and for as long as her husband worked away, she'd continue to fulfil her role as the household's 'go-to woman.' She turned the key in the front door and was pleased to hear banging already going on upstairs. As the front door slammed shut behind her, she heard footsteps coming down the stairs, and turned to see Bill, the builder in charge of the project.

"Morning, Bill."

"Morning, Mrs. Galbraith. Lovely morning for it, eh?"

"Glorious, and please, call me Stephanie."

"Okay, Stephanie, will do," he said, smiling a heavy smoker's grin, with tar-stained teeth peeking out. "It's going to be a noisy one today,

I'm afraid. We're taking the interior wall down so it's likely to be very dusty too. I'll be putting plastic sheets up, but you know, dust gets everywhere so it's best if you keep all the other doors closed. Minimise it as much as possible."

"Thanks for the heads-up. I'll do that. I'm out for most of the day anyway, so don't worry about the noise. Let's just get it done. Oh, and before I forget, would one of you be able to take a couple of pictures of it coming down? Only Joshua wanted to see it."

Bill smiled. "Sure thing, not a problem. Fancy himself as a builder one day, does he?"

"Pilot, like his dad. Well, that's his plan, but at seven, that could well be musician by the time he's fourteen."

"Well, I'll get some snaps for the lad, then I'll email them to you when you get back. Right, better get back to it," he said, and headed off back upstairs.

A quick change of shoes for Stephanie, and she was on her own way. She planned to head first into Richmond town centre for errands, then jump onto the train and into London for lunch with her friend Ruth. It had been a few weeks since their last lunch date and they had lots to catch up on. Ruth doted on the two boys and treated them like family, even though they weren't, and was always keen to hear about what they'd been up to. They'd been friends since their later school years.

Her offices were just around the corner from the Green Park tube station, where Stephanie was exiting now. She always looked forward to her lunch and dinner dates with Ruth, and usually her partner Amanda, who also doted on the twins. She could see the building just up ahead. A young man stood outside, a cigarette between his fingers, a leg bent behind him, foot resting on the stone wall. He looked like most young men in their early twenties—jeans, hoody and overgrown hair—but that was fashion and no doubt he would have looked at her choice of dress in her own twenties and thought it bland. She smiled at him as she entered the front doors, and then took the tiled stairs up to the second floor where huge glass doors led the way to Ruth's empire, McGregor & Co and the techy world beyond.

Ruth was floating round reception and spotted her immediately.

They embraced, both women grinning fondly at each other and planting real kisses on each other's cheeks.

"I'll just grab my bag," said Ruth. "Fancy Turkish or Thai for lunch? Or something else? You choose," she called as she dashed over to her desk.

"Turkish sounds good to me," said Stephanie when Ruth returned, "and since Aaron is away, that will keep me going with no need to cook tonight."

"Excellent. I know just the place. Particularly good at lunchtime, but busy, so we may have to have a glass of wine while we wait. You in a rush?"

"Heavens, no, as long as I'm back for the boys, but I've plenty of time."

The two women linked arms and made their way out of the building towards the little Turkish restaurant a couple of streets over. With the warm sun on their faces and laughter in their hearts, they looked like the close friends they were, without a care in the world.

But that was all about to change for Stephanie. Her world was about to fall apart, and she'd need Ruth more than ever to help her through.

Chapter Seventy-Five

SHE FELT the train start to slow as it approached the station, and she gathered her things together and stood and stretched. The train came to a standstill, and she stepped out onto the platform, a stiff breeze catching her around her shoulders as she walked towards the car park and on to school to pick up the twins.

Thirty minutes later, the boys were strapped into the back seat, excitedly replaying the best parts of their day and who had scored what goal in their PE lesson. Music to her ears, she thought fondly.

"Did you get some photos, Mum?" Joshua asked excitedly.

"I asked Bill to take some. I've not been back yet, so it will be a surprise for all of us."

There was a collective "cool" from the back seat.

A few minutes later she parked up in the driveway. Josh and Jasper scrambled out, and she followed them inside. The door was open for the workmen. She dropped her keys into a bowl on the hallway table and followed the boys up the stairs, suddenly aware of the builders' silence and the sound of men snickering.

The boys rounded the corner at the top of the stairs and then stood still, almost falling over each other as they came to an abrupt halt. There was a furtive sound of hurried shuffling.

"Boys?" said Stephanie as she rounded the top of the stairs.

Her hands flew to her mouth and she grabbed Josh and Jasper by the shoulders. In the gaping space where a wall had once stood was one of the workers, his face hidden by a black, shiny rubber-like mask with just a tiny hole for his mouth and two small slits for his eyes.

She turned to Bill, who was looking at something terribly interesting on the floor. "Where did that come from?" No one spoke. "Someone tell me. Now!" She turned Josh and Jasper around and pointed them back down the stairs. "Boys, go to your rooms." Wordlessly, they scurried back down the stairs, aware that something was amiss.

The man in the mask peeled it off slowly. Underneath, his face was beet red. He, too, stared at the floor. "We found them in the wall. I'm sorry. . ." His voice trailed off.

"What do you mean *in the wall*? Whose is it?"

Bill cleared his throat. "Well, um . . . we assumed they'd be yours?"

"What do you mean 'they'?"

"Well, the DVDs and the handcuffs. And the riding whip. They were all together behind a hidden panel in the wall that we were taking down." Bill pointed to a box on the floor.

Stephanie felt her face begin to burn. A cold sweat prickled her neck. "What secret panel?" No one replied. Gingerly, as though picking up dog excrement, Stephanie flicked back the flap on the box and extracted a handful of DVDs. The cases were plain vinyl, but each one bore a woman's name written in black marker and a date. She didn't recognise the names of the first two but she stopped at the third one, which read simply *Val*. She only knew of one Val, Aaron's brief affair last year. But the date marked it as recent.

The colour drained from her face.

Bill cleared his throat again. "OK, lads," he said briskly, "let's leave the lady some privacy now." He turned to Stephanie. "I'm very sorry about all this. We'll be back in the morning to carry on. That's probably best."

"Fine," said Stephanie. Her voice sounded strange in her ears. As Bill and the workers trooped hurriedly down the stairs, she sat down on the dusty floor and leaned her head heavily against the wall, swallowing back the vomit that rose in her throat.

Chapter Seventy-Six

"I'D LOVE to take the boys out; shall I pick them up?" Thank goodness for nanas and grandmas.

"Would you mind? This migraine is almost killing me. I really need to go and lie down." Stephanie hated lying to her mother but under the circumstances, if she knew what was going on, she felt sure she'd understand.

"Of course I will, darling. Why don't I grab their PJs too? Then if you're still not feeling better, they can stay over."

"Thanks, Mum, but I don't want them missing school."

"One day won't hurt, and your dad and I would love to spoil them. We could even go to the zoo or something, pretend it's educational if it makes you feel better."

"Well, I suppose you're right. Thanks again, Mum."

Not long after she'd hung up, they bundled the boys into the back seat, exchanged flurries of hugs and kisses, and then once again, Stephanie was alone.

Nearly two hours later, she finally plucked up the courage to slide the DVD labelled *Val* into the player. For a few moments, there was nothing on the screen then it focused in on a room. The picture was quite dark, though she didn't know if that was bad lighting or on purpose, and she clutched the remote in her hand tightly, as if holding it so would give her strength. Now she could see a room, almost empty save for a large four-poster bed and a few pieces of furniture. It was the bed that had her attention right now: it had half posts and a dark finish with decorative silk tassels hanging at each corner. It was one she herself had lain in. At their cottage. Involuntarily, she covered her mouth with her hand.

Now a man walked into the room, his back to the camera, and lay down on his stomach on that very bed. He was totally naked, wearing a black rubber gimp mask and nothing else. Stephanie paused the video: there was a large mole on his left shoulder, and she recognised the placement immediately, and who it belonged to. *Aaron*. She sat transfixed, staring at the screen. Her husband lay still, arms stretched out towards the top corners of the bed. Then a woman joined the picture. Visible only from behind, she too was totally naked apart from a pair of stilettos, but Stephanie would recognise that long dark hair anywhere. It was Valerie, the woman Aaron had 'once' had a fling with, the woman he'd told her it was over with. The time and date stamp in the lower corner of the screen told her otherwise: the recording was less than a month old.

She knew she'd seen enough, but curiosity pulled at her. Tears pouring down her cheeks, she watched as Val picked up a burning candle, straddled her husband's bare thighs and, raising her arm in the air as high as it would go, tipped the candle up. Droplets of hot wax landed on his bare shoulders. He rose to the sensation as best he could with her sitting on him, then slowly lowered himself back down, presumably as the initial sting left his skin. There was no sound to the homemade movie, but Stephanie didn't need to hear to understand what was going on. Pleasure and pain all mixed up together.

Her hand shaking, she ejected the recording and slipped another DVD into the machine. The camera opened on the same room, the same man, though a different woman; she'd no idea who. The scene was much the same, but this woman had a riding crop, the one found in the wall, she guessed, along with the rubber mask. Aaron lay spread-eagled on the bed again; now a redhead was hitting his bare backside with a thick leather thong. His body flinched each time it made contact; welts bloomed on his skin.

Stephanie pressed "open" on and ejected the disc, slipped it back into its case. So her husband was not only still seeing Valerie, but had been seeing others at the cottage too, enjoying his filthy little hobby in the same bed he and Stephanie slept in together as a loving couple.

Loving couple. She smiled bitterly and closed her eyes against the flood of tears that now ran freely down her face.

Chapter Seventy-Seven

STEPHANIE AWOKE the next morning with a banging headache and swollen eyes. It took her a moment to remember she was all alone: the boys would just now be waking up at their grandma's, and Aaron away at work. Or so he said. How many other lies had he told her? She'd been tempted to call him and have it out with him, but she'd restrained herself, figuring she needed to think it through a little more. No, she would wait until they could talk in person, face to face. Like husband and wife. Or not.

She threw the covers back and swung her legs out, then groaned with the pain in her head. If she didn't have one yesterday, she almost certainly had a migraine forming today.

"Serves me right for lying to my children," she said out loud, and went downstairs in search of the kettle and a mug of hot tea. "Tea solves everything, apparently," she muttered. "Let it try and solve this one."

It was strange being totally on her own, and on a school day. It was too early to call anyone and chat, so she typed out a quick text to Ruth for when she was able to reply. Her phone pinged with a reply almost immediately.

Coffee is always welcome, though detect a problem? All OK?

Are you free this morning? Need to talk to a friend. Husband troubles. Send. She waited for the reply.

Oh dear! Say 10? My place easier or town? You choose. Xxx.

Your place. See you then. Xxx

A knock on the back door startled her, but she could see it was Bill through the glass and waved at him to come in. She knew she looked a state, a real sight for sore eyes, mainly her own.

"Morning," he said gently.

"I know I look a state this morning," she said, touching her wild hair. "I'll go and make myself presentable, though that might take me a while longer than usual."

Bill forced a weak smile in response.

After a shower and some time in front of the mirror with her cosmetics, she looked and felt almost human again. Amazing what putting some war paint on could do to your spirits, she thought wryly. Her stomach rolled with hunger, and she decided on a plate of scrambled eggs and a whole lot more tea rather than her usual muesli and yogurt.

"It's not called comfort food for nothing, and right now, I need comfort." She busied herself with the task of cooking and then ate in silence. After a chat with Ruth, she'd feel better she was sure. She pulled the door closed behind her and left to the sound of a hammer banging upstairs in the new en suite.

Chapter Seventy-Eight

THE LAST OF the passengers had disembarked off the plane and Amber, Valerie and the rest of the flight crew were finishing up with their final tasks, getting ready to leave themselves. They were always happy to be landing back home at Gatwick, to spend a few nights with their friends or family, and, more importantly, sleep in their own beds.

In one cluster, they moved into the airport terminal, through passport control, and made their way outside, chatting amiably with each other. Most of them held smartphones in their hands, idly scrolling through emails and checking voice messages Suddenly Amber stopped dead on the pavement, all colour draining from her face.

"Amber?" said Valerie, turning back to her friend. "You look like you've seen a ghost. Are you alright?"

"Remember that handsome prick of a guy from the plane I told you about in Bulawayo? He's dead. Murdered. Look." Amber passed the phone to her.

Valerie's brow furrowed. "Oh my god... Amber!"

"I know, right? What a horrible way to die." She shuddered. "But you know what? After what he did to me, I'm kind of glad. Maybe he got his comeuppance. I'll bet next month's wages he's done to others what he did to me, and I'll also bet no one has ever reported him. Dumb cows like I was."

She clicked the screen off, shivering again as the memories flooded back. Valerie wrapped an arm around her friend's shoulders and squeezed.

"Come on," she said briskly, "Let's get you to the car then you can tell me all about it."

Chapter Seventy-Nine

RUTH SAT WATCHING Amanda finish off the last of the sweet and sour pork like it was going to be her last meal for a while. Little blobs of orange-coloured sauce were still evident on the plate, the only sign that a meal had been there recently. Amanda licked the stickiness from her lips and flopped back with a hearty sigh.

"I'm stuffed! That was just what the doctor ordered. And Wong's is the best for sweet and sour pork balls. No one else comes close. And twice in the space of a few of days!"

"Does that feel better now? Only you didn't really come up for air once you started—did you not get fed today?" Ruth smirked approvingly.

"I did, but you know what it's like when you're tired. You do eat more, carbs particularly. You hanker after heavier food, and this damn case is keeping me awake at night. I'm barely functioning without the aid of coffee as it is. *And* I've started hitting the chocolate bars from the vending machine."

"Ouch! You'll need to accompany me running, then, or you'll become a bit of a piglet," said Ruth, playfully making a fat blown-out face, puffing her cheeks out to demonstrate her point.

"Running is not my thing, thanks all the same."

"Talking of coffee, I met up with Stephanie today. She texted me, needed a girly chat. It seems Aaron has been up to no good."

That made Amanda sit up straight in her chair. "Oh? In what way?"

"In the 'I've-been-meeting-up-with-other-women' way, behind Stephanie's back. At the cottage. I didn't quite know what to say when she told me. She just poured it all out. And it was really embarrassing for her the way she did find out." Ruth told Amanda the whole story, about the secret panel, the builders finding it, and Stephanie watching the distressing DVDs on her own.

"Oh why has he been doing that? I thought he was a decent one, one of the really nice ones. Just goes to show, you never know what goes on behind closed doors."

They sat thoughtful for a moment or two in quiet reflection. On the surface, Aaron and Stephanie had the perfect marriage and family life together.

"And when's the dickhead back home?" Amanda spoke first.

"Friday. She's desperate to talk to him about it but she wants to do it in person, not long distance while he's away. She wants to talk face to face, watch his reaction, I guess. Which is fair enough. I've told her to call me if she needs to chat again. I don't want her suffering in silence."

"No, absolutely. Does she want to come over, stay a night or two?"

"I offered, but no." Ruth picked up her glass of Pinot and drained the last mouthful. "I hope she's not downing much of this in his absence," she said, indicating her glass. "She looked like she'd cried all night when I saw her. The rims of her eyes were nearly scarlet."

"Well, let's hope they sort it when he gets home, and be here for her if the proverbial hits the fan. Not much else we can do, really." Amanda stood, picked both their plates and cutlery up, and carried them to the dishwasher. She called out to Ruth, who was heading to the lounge. "Need a top-up? There's only a drop left. May as well finish it off."

She finished loading the dishwasher and then picked up the bottle and followed Ruth into the lounge with it anyway. Ruth hated seeing anything wasted, and that included half a glass of wine.

Chapter Eighty

THE CLICK of his key turning in the door did something to Stephanie's stomach. Only a few days ago, that click had done something to her heart, but not today. Her nerves were jangling like the small tin pipes of a wind chime. She heard his bag drop to the floor and his footsteps behind her in the kitchen.

"Mmm, something smells good! Hello, hun," he said, and turned her around for a kiss. Stephanie offered no resistance, taking the lingering kiss that she always enjoyed, trying to appear normal. She was anything but. He slipped his arms around her waist and pulled her close, nuzzling in her neck. "And you smell good too. I've missed you."

"Me too," she said, not meeting his eye. She turned back to the stove and stirred the bolognaise sauce as the two boys raced excitedly into the room. It was a welcome distraction for her and she took the opportunity to top up her glass of red and pour one for Aaron.

Sipping her wine, she watched as Aaron scooped both boys in his arms together, crouched down on his knees, the sound of their excited laughter and joyous chatter tugging at her heart. Whatever happened from this point on, she knew, she had to think of the boys, and keep her own concerns in perspective. She'd spent another restless night thinking it through and come to the conclusion that there was obviously something missing in their marriage that needed fixing: why else would he feel the need to do the things he'd been doing? But that didn't mean she wasn't going to be soft on him. Not at all: there was a long way to go to sort this mess out and she was going to insist that they have it out, and that he do his part to fix things.

She handed him his glass and he took a long sip.

"Why don't you get changed? Dinner will be ready in fifteen. I thought we'd all eat together early, and when the boys go up, we can have some time to ourselves. I need to talk to you."

"That sounds ominous," he said, smiling brightly and watching to see if she smiled back. She didn't. She turned her back and concentrated on stirring the sauce again. She was holding herself together, but only just, and doubted she'd be able to eat much of the food she'd been preparing. She'd blame it on a migraine, she decided. Again. Perhaps the wine had been a stupid move after last night, but she knew she couldn't get through this evening without something to bolster her nerves.

The familiar sound of his feet climbing the stairs relaxed her. Suddenly they stopped. Would he put two and two together?

"Wow, this looks great!" she heard him call from upstairs. Then silence. Perhaps he was unpacking his case. Perhaps he was getting changed. Or the penny had dropped – the missing wall. She stood motionless at the stove, listening. She took a full mouthful of wine, nearly draining her glass, and waited. Nothing moved; there was not a sound. She laid out dinner on the table, got the boys seated, and called up to Aaron that it was ready. His footsteps could be heard coming down the stairs, slower than usual. He knew she knew.

Her stomach flipped over, and as he came through the door, she busied herself with refilling her glass—again. It was only when they were all seated and the boys were chatting away that she chanced a glance his way and noted with some satisfaction he had lost most of his normally healthy tanned colour. She bit back a smile. Let him sit through dinner and chew things over in his head, just like she'd had to these last few days. Whatever his reasons, whatever the story he was now busily concocting by way of an explanation, it had better be good.

Strangely light-hearted now, she filled a fork with spaghetti and sauce and chewed ravenously, making up for lost time as she'd eaten

Chapter Eighty-One

STEPHANIE SAT in silence on the sofa in the lounge. The boys were safely in their beds listening to the story Aaron was reading them. As she waited for him to finish up and join her, she mulled over for the trillionth time what she was going to say to him, where to start. She hoped that when the time actually came, she could stick to her plan.

Finally, she heard his footsteps on the stairs. He entered the room with their nearly empty wine glasses and handed hers to her. He slumped down in his chair across from her.

"So what's on your mind, hun? What do you want to talk about?"

Like he doesn't know. Give me strength, she thought.

"I want to talk about the secret panel in the old wall, the wall that's now gone. The workers found a few interesting items behind it, items of yours, I assume." She kept her voice level.

"I thought as much. But I can explain."

Oh, the cliché of it. "Then please do. I'd love to know all about it." She couldn't keep the sarcasm out of her voice.

"It's all over now, if I can just say that first. Valerie and I have been over for a long time, over a year probably, just so you know. And it was only ever a couple of times, just sex, nothing more. And the others were both one-offs. There's nothing going on now, I can promise you."

He looked her directly in the eyes as he said the last part. The lie was like a knife slicing into her skin.

"Just sex?" she said, incredulous, "JUST sex?" Though the videos hadn't shown it, she'd turned it off before it had got to that part, she'd assumed they had ultimately had sex. She'd googled BDSM and learned that not all role plays included the actual act itself, but of course now he'd just admitted that his had. At least he had the decency to bow his head at her pain.

"And the riding crop?" she continued. "You enjoy that sort of thing, Aaron? Because you've never suggested we use anything like that when we are together, not even a tiny bit. I had absolutely no idea. Yet you obviously like it."

He kept his face down as she spoke, silent, flinching slightly at the wrath in her voice, playing the submissive role he obviously liked. She hoped it wasn't turning him on. At last he looked up and met her eye. "I'm so sorry, Steph. I really am."

"No! You're not. You're just sorry you got found out!" she yelled. "Did you just forget to take them out of the wall or did you plan for the embarrassment of the builders finding them and giving them to me? Rub it in, why don't you?"

The look on his face told her he had never planned for her—or anyone else—to find his stash.

"I don't know what to say," he said, staring at the floor again. "I never meant to embarrass you. I should have moved them."

"You should have not done it at all, more like!" said Stephanie, incredulous. Anger burned in her eyes, but he couldn't bring himself to look at her face.

They both fell quiet for a moment, each catching their breath and wondering what to say or do next. Aaron spoke first.

"But now it's all out in the open, I have to work on clearing my mess up. Please believe me when I say I'm deeply sorry, Steph. Deeply, deeply sorry."

Stephanie let out a long heavy breath as she gained control of her anger and they both sat quietly for a moment longer.

Calmly, Stephanie said, "I've been going out of my head while you've been gone, tossing it around, so I've had some time to think, and while it's certainly a big surprise and an issue, we've got the boys to think about. I don't want a house filled with tension and accusations, which will only hurt them; they're too young to understand. And then there's the issue of your fetish, for want of a better word, and your need for it. I dare say we can work on that part possibly, it's too early for me to even think about it much. But answer me this. Do you still love me, still find me sexually attractive, not just love me in a good mother way?" She held her breath. Their eyes locked together.

"Yes! Yes, I absolutely do, always have done and always will." The pleading in his eyes told her he was telling the truth now, at least.

"And you say it was over with Val about a year ago, you've not had anything other than a working relationship with her since?"

"I promise you, no, nothing. Not with anyone but you. That's the truth."

Stephanie got to her feet. "Then you'd better sleep in the spare room tonight, you lying piece of shit."

"W-what? What do you mean? I'm telling the truth!"

"Date stamps on films don't lie, Aaron. Remember that if you're going to lie to me about it again. It was only one month ago, Aaron, one sodding month ago, so don't tell me it's over." She spat the last words at him as she left the room and slammed the door hard behind her. Knowing he wouldn't follow her, she stood on the other side shaking, her hand over her mouth to muffle the sobs.

She tiptoed up the stairs so as not to wake their sons, went into their bedroom, and flopped down on the quilt, burying her head in her pillow. Then she sobbed her heart out.

Chapter Eighty-Two

He sat there stunned. How could he have been so stupid, leaving his toys and DVDs in the house? Why hadn't he just left them there in the cottage? She hardly ever went up there. He knew why he'd brought them home: he'd wanted to watch them when the house was empty or take them out in his car with his laptop hidden in a rucksack, park in a quiet spot, relive the footage, the experience, over and over again. Who'd have thought his secret panel in the wall would have been found? But it had. And he was going to have to pay the price.

Muttering to himself as he sat alone in his chair, he berated himself for his stupidity. Why was there never any whiskey in the house when you wanted a glass? He saw his phone vibrate on the coffee table and reached for it. A smile spread slowly across his face: a message from Frankie. It simply said 'Welcome back to England.' He sat for a moment with his phone burning a hole in his hand, wondering what to message back. Her timing amused him somewhat.

Thanks. Long trip but home safe and well. What you up to this weekend?

The little Messenger bubbles bubbled and he waited for her reply.

Thought you might be free sometime for that catch-up coffee or a wine. Find the time?

Something stirred inside him and he smiled at the screen. Frankie certainly was keen.

I'd love to. Just not sure when I can get away, that's all. Can you leave it with me until tomorrow?

After Stephanie's bombshell, he had to be careful. Besides, he wanted to spend some time with the boys, take them to the park for some kick-about.

Of course. No rush, and I've no plans at all so whenever you're ready. Be good to see you again!

She added an emoji blowing a kiss and he blew one back. What the hell, he thought. If I'm in the doghouse, I may as well do what I want. It's not like anyone is going to be checking in on me at the moment. He sat back in his chair and closed his eyes for a brief moment, taking a deep breath, shoulders settling a little looser. He'd been surprised at Stephanie's reaction, couldn't understand why she'd gone off the way she had and was now upstairs, obviously upset. Crying irritated him somewhat, and he never encouraged the boys to cry, preferring to teach them to be strong, not nurture their weak sides. The only time he ever showed his weak side was when he was being dominated by a sexy woman, but that was different, of course. Then he could be as weak as any man could be.

With their brief messaging finished, he took the empty wine glasses out to the kitchen, and made sure the house was locked up before heading up to the stairs to bed. As he rounded the corner at the top, he saw the closed bedroom door and his pillow on the floor outside it, waiting for him.

"Spare room it is, then," he said under his breath, then picked up his pillow and headed to the guest room. He stripped and climbed in; the bed covers felt cold to his skin. He'd had a tiring week, and he closed his eyes, expecting sleep to come immediately, but after twenty minutes of tossing and turning, he knew it was going to be futile. The time zones and the row were messing with his brain.

The moon shone through the open curtains, and he lay staring at the ceiling, thinking. Was this just a blip or was it going to be something much bigger? Was Stephanie going to blow it out of proportion, or would it all be over by the morning? He hoped the latter, but she'd caught his lie out: Valerie and he were still very much on, never mind finished one month ago. She gave him what he desired, though it didn't stop him wanting the safe and loving relationship he had with his wife and kids. He just needed the extra spice in his life, and he wasn't willing to give that part up. No, he'd just have to get better at being discreet; he'd been doing it too long to not have it in his life, now or in the future.

His mind wandered to Frankie and he wondered what she might be into, a good-looking woman like her, and single too, and getting a tiny bit flirty, although it was early to be reading anything into it. He reached for his phone and re-read her message. Maybe he wanted to read more into it. He tapped a quick one out.

What are you up to right now?

Send. A minute or so passed.

Lying in bed. You?

Same. On my own. Why had he typed that? he wondered as he waited for her reply. Simple—he'd wanted her to know.

Oh? How come?

In the doghouse. Had a bit of a row.

No one to keep you warm and toasty tonight then. She was definitely flirting with him now.

No. You offering?

Don't think you'd get away with that one. A winking emoji.

Shame. Could use the company.

He waited, had he pushed it too far too soon? He hardly knew the woman. It seemed an age before her response came but it was loud and clear.

Then get away sometime over the weekend....

He re-read the message then read it again, felt himself harden at the same time. There was no doubt what Frankie was implying, the little dots leaving things up to his imagination. The question was, should he indulge? He could always tell Stephanie that they both needed some space to think and he was heading out for the weekend. Not that he had anything to think about, of course; nothing was going to change for him in that regard. He had an idea, and Stephanie would just have to like it.

I was thinking about a trip north, actually, to the cottage. Want to come up to Windermere tomorrow? Bring your toothbrush.

Oh, sounds good. Love to! I'll check the trains.

Takes about three hours. You'll be there for lunchtime.

Aaron smiled to himself in the moonlit room. No, he'd never give up fulfilling his needs, and he needed the comfort they brought him even more now. If he wanted to indulge himself this weekend, that was his right.

You're on, if you're sure. I'll message you when I know my ETA. Pick me up at the station?

Will do. Won't be a problem this end, so see you then. Can't wait.

Frankie clicked her phone off with a smile. Oh yes indeed. She couldn't wait.

Chapter Eighty-Three

HE WAS SITTING in the kitchen, a steaming mug of hot tea in his hands, staring out at the garden, when Stephanie entered the room. He turned towards her and smiled, hoping she was feeling a bit better this morning and he would receive a welcome smile back. But no, her face was void of emotion and void of colour save for the red rims of her tired eyes. He felt a pang of guilt for upsetting her, making her cry, that she'd even found out, but there was no going back now. The cat was well and truly out of the bag. The pang soon left, but he had to be seen to do the right thing. She managed a weak 'good morning.' He stood, and went over to her, rested his hands on both her shoulders and pulled her close. He placed a light kiss on the top of her head.

"I'm sorry, Steph. I know I've upset you."

She wrapped her arms loosely around his waist but didn't say a word in reply.

"I've been thinking. I'm going to go up to the cottage, give you some space, and do some thinking myself. Just overnight—I'll be back tomorrow sometime. The break will do us good, take the tension away from the house and the boys. Just a few hours alone each."

"Really?"

"Yes, really. I think it's best, and like I said, just a few hours alone."

Tired, she nodded in agreement, even at the mention of the

cottage, the scene of his crimes. While she'd had all week to think about it, he hadn't: he'd been blindsided by her last night. And then there was the matter of his lie to deal with, and that was what had hurt her, probably more than actually finding out about his antics. She was wondering just how much she did know him. The door burst open and Joshua hurtled in.

"Daddy! Daddy! Are you making pancakes this morning? Please?"

The two adults pulled apart slowly and focused on their enthusiastic young son.

"Sure will, buddy," said Aaron brightly. "Will you help me?"

Stephanie took the opportunity to leave them to it. "I'll go wake Jasper," she said, and headed upstairs. Maybe Aaron was right: a bit of thinking time each would do them good, though mainly for him. And it was only until tomorrow; he wasn't away again until Thursday so they'd have plenty of time together afterwards. Opening Jasper's door, she stood and watched him, the weak morning light streaming through a crack in the curtain, the silhouette of him so beautiful and still so small in his bed, his hair all mussed up as usual. Whatever happened between her and Aaron, they had their precious family to think about first and foremost. She wouldn't allow the boys to be hurt. Jasper stirred, aware that someone was close by, in that place somewhere between sleep and surfacing to the real world for the day. She sat on the edge of his bed as he came round, stroking his hair gently.

"Morning, sunshine. Want some pancakes? Joshua is up and helping Daddy make them. They may eat them all if you lie here too long." She kissed the top of his head and he smiled up at her.

"I'll just be a minute," he said, tossing his quilt back. "Don't let them eat them all. I'm on my way." He bounded out of bed, and Stephanie left him to pee and find his bathrobe.

She returned to find the kitchen a hive of activity. Joshua stood on a low stool, watching batter form into pancakes in the hot pan under Aaron's watchful gaze.

"Mummy, I've made one all by myself!" he said, with a smile as wide as his head.

"You eat them up with Daddy," she said fondly. "I'm going for a shower and Jasper is on his way, so make sure you save him some." She headed back up the stairs.

Aaron flipped a pancake over and felt his phone vibrate. Discreetly, he pulled it out of his pocket and checked the message.

All sorted. Be in at 12.30 lunchtime. Windemere.

He quickly tapped out a reply: *Pick you up then. If I'm a little behind, wait there.* He hit send. He checked the time on his screen: he'd better get a move on himself.

Joshua flipped the small pancake and they both cheered at a successful attempt just as Jasper came in and sat down.

"Morning, buddy. Sleep well?" asked Aaron.

"Yes, thanks." He peered at the pan. "Did you save me some?"

"Of course we did. You get the second one—be ready in just a minute," he said and he slipped Joshua's helping out on to a plate. Joshua helped himself to more than enough maple syrup.

"Listen boys, while you're both together. I know I only came home yesterday, but I have to go off again this morning. But I'll be back again tomorrow afternoon."

There was a chorus of disappointed groans.

Aaron soldiered on. "But when I get back, why don't we arrange to go ten pin bowling after school on Monday and pizza afterwards? How does that sound?" By the noise that erupted in the kitchen, it was a resounding yes.

"Great. That's settled then." He flipped Jasper's pancake out for him, adding more batter to the pan for one for himself. He checked his watch while the boys ate and he cooked. He needed to leave within the next thirty minutes if he was going to get there in time to meet the 12.30 train.

Stephanie entered the room, dressed and looking much better than she had earlier, a little make-up giving her more colour.

"You look nice. Want a pancake before the boys eat them all?" She shook her head 'no' so he served it up for himself, drowning his in maple syrup too. Like father, like son.

"I'm taking the boys out on Monday after school—pizza and bowling. Want to join us men?" He winked at Joshua and Jasper and they both giggled. While they loved their mother, they loved 'man time' with their dad, goofing about.

"Thanks, but no thanks," she said, smiling. "You men go off and have fun together." Her voice became a little more serious and she asked, "What time are you leaving this morning?"

"When I've eaten this and grabbed an overnight bag, so pretty soon. Is that okay?" It would have to be: he was working to a plan now.

"Yes, of course. Text me when you set off back home tomorrow, would you? Just so I know roughly what time to expect you for dinner."

Picking his plate and cutlery up, he pecked her on the cheek as he passed her, headed for the dishwasher.

"Will do. Now, I'm off to get cleaned up," he said, and left them finishing their breakfast. As he headed up the stairs, he wondered if he was doing the right thing. It had seemed so last night, with Frankie's flirty messages exciting him. But now? Tossing his toiletries back into the bag he'd only just unpacked, he reconciled it in his head: a little time apart to think was probably what they needed. Though he'd be thinking about something else entirely.

Chapter Eighty-Four

PHILIPPA GOT on the train at London Euston, found herself a vacant seat and made herself comfortable for the journey ahead, glad the train was half empty and she hadn't got to make polite conversation with anyone. Spreading out, she put her overnight bag on the seat next to her and placed her hot latte on the table in front, along with her Kindle and phone. It was nearly time to go.

Making use of her downtime to relax a little, she scrolled through her newsfeed, following what was interesting in both her and her friends' worlds. It was while she was sitting there that a message came through from Georgia. It had been fun bumping into her after all these years, but Philippa couldn't see a way to keep their friendship alive after what she'd done to someone so close to her, like murdering her boss. How could she look her in the eye ever again? Although she was sure she'd never make the visit back to Manchester or even halfway to meet her... She'd toyed with un-friending her online, but how could she without reason? That seemed mean. So they were both still connected and Georgia wanted to chat.

I'm bored. Tell me something interesting. What are you up to? Georgia typed.

Philippa smiled at her phone. Georgia hadn't changed one bit.

Actually, I'm on the train at Euston, heading north shortly. New boyfriend invited me away overnight. Winking emoji. Send.

Lucky lady! Where to? Anywhere nice and warm?

To the Lakes, so not sure about warmth. Well, not with the weather, anyway! Another winking emoji. Send.

Oooh, naughty! Who is he? Tell me more.

Sexy pilot friend. Home for a few. Send.

And? Does he have a name? What does he look like? I need more info.

Philippa debated what to say but kept it light, just in case. There was no way she was going to mention his name; that would be a stupid thing to do.

He's spoken for, so I can't say much more, save to say he's tall, dark and gorgeous. Send.

You're kidding me! Well, have fun. I'll just hang out on my own, maybe find a crappy book to read .... Sad emoji.

Philippa couldn't help chuckling to herself as she posted a smiling one back. Emojis did much of the work for you it seemed. She picked her coffee up and sipped it as the train gently pulled out of the station, bang on time. At 12.30 pm, she would be stepping down onto the platform at Windemere, and into the arms of her next victim.

Georgia marvelled at how natural her friend sounded, how absolutely normal, and again, the doubt crept in; she wanted so desperately to be wrong. She checked Google for Saturday trains headed to the Lakes out of Euston at that hour; it wasn't hard to find. And now Georgia knew just where her old friend was going for the weekend. Philippa was going to Windemere.

Chapter Eighty-Five

THE DRIVE UP to the Lakes went without a hitch. The traffic was light for a Saturday morning and after stopping for a latte halfway, he arrived in good time at the cottage a few miles outside Grasmere Village. He'd spent the time alone wisely, and had put some effort into thinking about his needs, his relationship with Val and his relationship with his wife and boys. Could he possibly love them all equally, at the same time? Stephanie gave him love and stability and a beautiful family, but Val gave him something else he yearned for, food for his fetish. And yet here he was, driving up to the cottage, on his own, to meet a relative stranger for the weekend. While neither of them had planned anything to happen, he'd be surprised if it didn't, though in what form he'd have to wait to find out. And neither Stephanie nor Val would know anything about it. If he wanted all his needs met, he'd just have to be better at concealing his activities, and he would probably have to stop keeping DVDs of the events at the house or cottage. But that was the easy part to change: he'd just use a file in the cloud or a discreet USB drive on his key ring so it would be with him the majority of the time. There were ways around every problem if you just thought about them in a different way.

He flicked his indicator to turn left down the unsealed track, though there was no need, really; he hadn't seen another vehicle for the last twenty minutes. The cottage stood off in the distance, looking like a much smaller version of the mansion in *Skyfall*. It looked lonely all on its own; the grass around it was a little overgrown, but the sun was out, warming the dark stone walls and making it feel more welcoming.

Grabbing his overnight bag, he trotted up the front path, unlocked the front door and stepped inside. The small cottage had been shut up since his last visit about a month ago, the recording of which had started the fallout of his secret life, his secret tastes and the now not-so-secret Val. And here he was again—about to meet someone new. He threw open the front windows to let the sunshine in and the unused smell out. It would still be chilly at night, so the wood burner would be needed later. He checked the wood supply that lived just to the side of the backdoor out back. There was plenty. He loved spending time at the cottage, and considered it his place rather than a family place, although they were always welcome, but because he liked to hunt, Stephanie wasn't that keen on being around when he did it. There were four trophy heads mounted, looking down from the walls of the main room, three he'd hunted in Africa and had flown back, and a stag's head he'd hunted locally. He was proud of them all, each one telling a story, an experience that meant something to him, an experience many others didn't understand, his wife one of them. She hated seeing them mounted, fearing it would scare the boys, but he'd held fast. Where else was he supposed to display his hobby? So it had become more his place and now she knew he also used it for another of his hobbies.

He began to unpack the few supplies he'd picked up in the village on his way in. He placed red wine in the wine rack and left fresh bread and crackers in the cupboard. While there was a pub nearby, he had prepared ahead in case they didn't feel like going out for something to eat. The cottage was about ready for his guest, and with no need to lock it back up, he left the curtains billowing in the breeze through the open windows to circulate the air while he drove to Windemere station to meet the 12.30 train. And the woman who'd recently entered his life.

Chapter Eighty-Six

He spotted her immediately. Her long brown hair was unmistakable, shining in the sunshine as she walked on the platform, the train pulling out slowly as she moved towards him. She looked radiant, though he still had no clear recollection of where he knew her from, although he didn't much care either. She was here now, and for the rest of the weekend.

"Aaron! Lovely to see you again!" She hugged him tightly like a long-lost friend

He caught the perfume of her hair and breathed it in deeply. "At last, Frankie! It's been too long!" He gently pushed her to arms' length and looked her up and down. "And you haven't changed one bit. Still stunning. How do you do it?" The lies came easily to Aaron, and he played along with it, not wanting to admit he was still clueless. She laughed lightly at his compliment and he bent to take her bag, steering her towards the exit and his waiting car.

"Hungry?"

"I am, quite. I keep away from train sandwiches if I can help it."

"Well, I bought a few supplies but depending on whether we go out for dinner tonight or not, we may need to get a few more." Frankie smiled, a little seductively, Aaron thought, or had he imagined it? "Perhaps we should stop in the village anyway, then we have the choice for later. He put her bag on the back seat as she took her place in the passenger seat and fastened her seatbelt.

"Good idea. I brought a bottle of wine in my bag so I guess it depends how much we drink whether we can drive later or not," she said, and laughed, her head back slightly, eyes twinkling at him.

There was no mistaking now what the woman beside him was hoping for at the cottage and he smiled appreciatively, patting her knee in agreement, leaving it in place for a long moment, further testing the waters. There was no resistance.

"In that case," he said, turning to her as he drove out of the station car park, "I will pop back into the village and grab us some supper. Do you eat venison?"

"Love it, and it will go well with the red I have in my bag."

"Perfect. I'm pretty good with venison and a few trimmings," he said. A moment later he pulled up outside the local store and added, "You stay here. Back in a tick."

Frankie had no intention of getting out of the car and being seen anywhere. It was bad enough she was sitting outside the village store in the first place.

He returned in no time at all and they were soon on their way to the cottage. In the quiet of the car as they drove through the empty countryside, she ran through in her mind the few items she had hidden in her belongings behind her. Everything she needed for Aaron was safely packed away, to be brought out when it was the right time to do so. While it was not long after Sebastian, the opportunity had presented itself and she'd taken it.

Aaron the Third. It had a certain ring to it.

Chapter Eighty-Seven

THE HOUSE SEEMED SO quiet and empty without him. Even though the boys were making enough noise for all of them put together and she'd just spent a week without him, she couldn't shake the feeling. The boys had played together all morning, not needing anything from her apart from a snack, and she'd moped around the house trying to find something to take her mind off events—nothing had worked. Her head was all over the place, one minute angry and upset at him, the next desperately wanting to talk to him, to hold him, to be with him. It was going to be a long wait until he returned. Her phone buzzed, interrupting her thoughts. It was a message from Ruth.

Convenient to chat? Just checking in.

Yes, perfect timing. Call me? May as well talk than type if Ruth was able to and someplace where they could talk easily. The phone rang immediately and Stephanie tapped the green icon.

"I was just sat moping," she said. "Perfect timing."

"I was afraid you might be. How did it go? Did you two talk? Are you okay?"

"Yes. I suppose. He didn't deny it but I did catch him in a lie. He said it was over months ago with Val, but date stamps don't get it wrong. I think that's what hurt me the most. His lie."

"Are you both speaking?"

"Yes, sort of. He suggested he go up to the cottage, just overnight. He'll be back tomorrow. It'll give us both some time to think, though I've had all week. Apart from knowing his lie, that is."

"So you really are moping about the house on your own. Where are the boys? And how is Aaron?

"They're here, playing, good as gold. And Aaron is fine too. I was just thinking how quiet it is though, without him. I really could do with talking to him, being with him, even though he's upset me. I'm missing him already. Aren't I stupid?"

"Not at all! We all react to things differently and he *is* your husband, for goodness' sake. You don't stop loving someone overnight, not usually. What will you do, then?"

"I'm thinking of going up there, to the cottage. He won't mind, since it's him that's caused all this upset. He'll probably be pleased to see me."

"Then what's stopping you?"

"Not sure, really. Don't want to make a fool of myself, or let him off the hook so easily. Plus, it's a long drive, and I'd have to leave the boys with Mum so it would be late when I get there after I've organised everyone. That is, if she can have them. She might be out this evening." She was beginning to sound a bit whiney, but then she felt whiney. And a bit lonely.

"Look, ring your mum and see. That's the first thing. Then, if she can, why don't we all drive up, keep you company? Amanda and I can drop you off and find a nice pub for the night to stay in, and drive you back tomorrow or later today, depending on how it goes. He can bring his own car back, maybe with the two of you in it. What do you reckon? Sound like a plan?"

Stephanie let out a sigh, and then stayed silent for a couple of beats. It made sense, really: drop the boys off, drive up with friends, and if it didn't work out, drive back with friends. If it did work out, then she'd come back with the man she loved. On the surface, nothing could go wrong, so why not give it a try?

"Well, if you're sure? Shouldn't you check with Amanda first?"

"She's right here, nodding her head at the idea, listening in. She's a detective, remember. She knows what's going on, long before she's been told much." The two women laughed a little. It was true. Amanda did tend to know things long before anyone else even suspected.

"Right, let's see if Mum can take the boys—again. Call you back in a minute." Stephanie hung up, then stood staring at the phone in her hand for a moment longer, wondering if she was doing the right thing. Yes, she wanted to see him, but what if he needed the time to think? It *had* been his idea. Doubt started to swim around her head but before it had chance to settle, she pulled her shoulders back and found her mum's number in her phone. The call connected almost immediately.

"Hello darling. What a lovely surprise!" Her tone was always warm and welcoming. Stephanie wouldn't have minded a cuddle from her mother right about now.

"Hi, Mum. I wonder if I could impose on you again, to take the boys? Overnight."

"Yes, of course you can! Your father and I always love having them. But is everything all right? It's not usual for you to drop them at short notice and this makes twice of recent. Not that I'm complaining, mind, just asking." Her mother should have been a detective too. Not much escaped her radar.

"Everything is fine, Mum, or it will be. I just need to do something that doesn't involve the boys. All be back to normal soon."

"Sounds ominous. But if you're sure?"

"Thanks, Mum, I am. Can I drop them pretty quickly? I've got to be somewhere."

"Ready when you are, darling. I'll see you soon."

"Thanks," she said, and hung up. She quickly called Ruth back and gave her the news and they arranged to pick her up an hour and a half later, which would give them time to pack a few things. As she hung up, Stephanie once again stared at her phone, wondering if it really was such a bright idea.

"I guess we'll soon see," she said to herself, and headed off to tell the boys.

Chapter Eighty-Eight

"WELL, THIS IS LOVELY," Aaron said. They were sitting on the rug in front of the fire they'd lit in the wood burner. The late afternoon had turned chilly and they'd lazed around chatting in front of the flames. A nearly empty bottle of red wine sat on the hearth close by, ready for the last of the top-ups when needed.

"I brought some cheese to go with the crackers. Would you like some to soak the wine up with? I know I would," he said, laughing a little, "Perhaps I should have had some *before* I started drinking. I wouldn't like to drive right now!"

"Me neither." Frankie giggled from where she lay stretched out on the old comfy sofa, a hand-knitted blanket covering her feet. "And yes, I'll have some, please. I might not make it to dinner at this rate. And, there's another bottle to drink yet!" She watched him as he rose from his place on the floor and wobbled a little, trying to make his way to the kitchen door on slightly unsteady legs.

"Heavens!" he exclaimed, "I must be getting old. I can't hold my drink anymore." He put his arm out to grab the doorframe before he banged into it. Frankie felt the effects of the wine dulling her own senses—she'd drunk more than she should have under the circumstances. The lion's head mounted on the opposite wall reminded her of why she was there, what the task was and the reason she'd fabricated her story to get into his life. But there was still time to do that yet, and despite trying hard not to, she was enjoying the company of this attractive man. *Very* attractive married man, she scolded herself through pursed lips.

"Here we are! Crackers and cheese await you, Madame," he said, and mock-bowed at her feet, like a butler.

"Why, thank you, Jeeves. Splendid," she mocked back, and sat up fully to take a couple. She put one straight into her mouth and crunched loudly, holding the second one ready.

"My, what big teeth you have!" Aaron stood there smiling at her appetite.

"All the better to eat you with," she replied, trying her hardest not laugh and splutter crumbs. But it was no use; they both burst out laughing. The floor was showered with little golden bits of cracker.

"Oh dear! Now look what I've done," she said, horrified at the mess she'd made in front of her, but Aaron was too busy holding himself from the fits of laughter that were wracking him. His hearty laugh was probably audible back down the quiet lane. They were having fun, and Frankie was conscious of the fact that things weren't quite moving in the direction she'd originally planned. She'd thought they'd sit quietly and have a coffee or two and dinner; she hadn't banked on having so much fun, with a man she barely knew and was planning to kill.

Aaron, after managing to bring his laughter under control, refilled both their glasses and handed hers back, a little more serious than before. She immediately detected the shift in his mood.

"Are you okay, Aaron?"

"Yes. I'm having a good time, that's all. I've not laughed so much in a long time. It's been good hanging out with you," he said, and he bent to his knees, gazing straight at her, their eyes making contact and holding. She knew she should look away, but it was too late. His lips connected with hers, and while initially she didn't move, she felt herself cave in and returned the gentle pressure, enjoying the softness of him. This was not what was supposed to happen. But it was happening, and Frankie was letting it. She pulled him in closer, and he responded by increasing the pressure as they kissed, adding more passion.

Outwardly she seemed calm, but inside Frankie's head, it was a different story. Two stories in fact, and they were fighting for her attention, each one calling for her to act on two quite different outcomes. Yes, it had been a while since she'd had a lover in her life, and she found Aaron extremely attractive, but the taskmaster in her head was pulling her in quite a different direction, the real reason she was there. Could she have both? Could she get what she wanted from this man on both counts, could she be so greedy? Or would her DNA all over him be what got her caught? There was no evidence of her being at either of the other victims' apartments, of even knowing them, but there was plenty of DNA here already, and she'd have to clean up a lot better after this one to ensure the place held no clues. All this was hurtling through her mind as Aaron pushed her gently back onto the sofa, ready to take things to the next level.

Their lips parted for a moment and Frankie took the opportunity to speak. "Why don't I slip upstairs for a moment, and I'll call you back in here by the fire, when I'm all set? How does that sound?" she asked in a low, sexy voice. "I'm sure it will be worth your while," she added, teasingly.

He smiled in agreement, knowing he was going to be getting her, what he'd suspected he'd get all along. Had hoped to get.

"Don't be long, then," he said, and stood to let her off the sofa. When she'd left, he added more wood to the fire and refilled their glasses once again, and waited anxiously in the kitchen for her to call him back through. It wasn't long before he heard her returning footsteps, and he waited eagerly for her call.

"I'm ready," she called huskily.

Chapter Eighty-Nine

"WELL, for what it's worth, I think you're very brave, Stephanie. For confronting him, and for coming all the way up here to claim your man, as it were."

Amanda was talking and driving, Stephanie in the passenger seat, Ruth leaning forward between the seats in the rear, trying to listen to their conversation and add her thoughts where she could. Even in modern cars, the back always seemed far noisier.

"I've got the boys to think about, and that's a big motivator for me doing this. Otherwise I'd probably be sat rocking backwards and forward in a corner somewhere, slowly going out of my mind drinking, wondering what to do. At least this way, the problem will *have* to be solved so we can all get on with our lives. Get back to some semblance of normality and hopefully the boys won't even notice."

Ruth added from the back seat, "And they love going to your mum's, so that's a plus. And the other positive is Amanda and I get a night away in the Lake District," she said, smiling.

"Well, if it was a night at the Lakes you wanted, there were simpler ways of getting it. You only needed to say," Stephanie said, and grinned at her friend. "Let's hope we've not had a wasted trip."

"Well, we'll be there in a few minutes, so I guess you'll soon find out. I think we'll drop you at the cottage, then we'll wait a while in the car, say ten minutes? Just to make sure it doesn't go horribly wrong and you come running back out." Amanda was the planner, the thinker, the sensible one.

"Oh, great! What do you think is going to happen in there, exactly?"

"No, I only mean if he does want some time alone and he's not happy you've shown up out of the blue."

"Right."

"That way, if you need a lift instantly, we're there. If you don't come out during that time, we'll set off back towards the town, and you can just call my mobile. We can either come back and get you, or Ruth and I will have a night in Grasmere. Either way, let us know if you need a lift back or not." Amanda grinned at her friend. "Hopefully you won't, you'll work it all out."

"Well, I guess we'll soon see, like you say. Can it be that easy? Can I get over his lies? And more importantly, can we deal with his other needs? Because going forward, he's going to want to continue with it. He obviously gets something from it, and I don't want him going behind my back."

"You'll work that out over time, I'm sure. That's not something you'll figure out today." Ruth was now the extra voice of reason. "That's a biggy to work on."

"I agree," chimed Amanda as she turned left into the unsealed lane. The cottage was visible in the distance, Aaron's car parked in the drive out front.

"Now I'm here I'm not so sure!" Stephanie suddenly felt panicked. "Pull over!"

Amanda did as she was told, and left the engine idling as they all sat there in silence. Stephanie stared straight ahead at the cottage, a frightened expression on her face.

"I'm not sure I can do it," she said, so quietly she was barely audible. "What if it backfires, and he's angry I've shown up. He wanted the time apart. It was his suggestion."

"You said yourself you thought he was doing it for you and the boys, take the tension out of the house. He's the one at fault here, remember, not you." Ruth spoke calmly but firmly. "He'll be glad to see you, that he's not upset you too much, that you've come all this way to sort it out with him. I'd be surprised if he was angry."

Stephanie glanced over at Amanda, who was gently nodding her head in agreement.

"I'm with her too, Stephanie. It will all work out just fine. You'll go in, stay and talk, and we won't see you again until we get back to London. You've just got to get over that threshold first and say hi."

The three women sat back in silence as Stephanie mulled it over again, plucking up the courage to go ahead and make amends with the man she loved. Thoughts of her two young sons eating pancakes for breakfast with their daddy filled her head and sealed her resolve. With renewed determination, she turned to Amanda and said, "Then let's get this show on the road, driver." Amanda and Ruth both cheered as they pulled away on the track.

"Would you let me out just before the house? The bit of fresh air will do me good, maybe fill my lungs with some extra strength."

"Okay, and we'll wait there too, so if you need us, just walk back to the car. We won't leave for ten minutes."

They travelled slowly over the rough lane, tyres crunching in loose gravel, a light dust billowing up from the rear of the car as it passed over the dry track. Amanda pulled to a standstill and Stephanie opened her door to get out. The night air was chilling, and she pulled her cardigan closer round herself. The temperature in the north was a few degrees cooler than she was used to. The cottage looked warm and welcoming; the curtains were still open, and there was an orange glow from the wood fire. She looked back at the car and saw Amanda and Ruth watching as she approached the cottage. It was pitch black outside, just the weakening light from the car's headlights showing her the way and the dim light coming from the cottage up ahead showing her destination. It was incredibly quiet. Underfoot, her boots crunched lightly over loose stones as she passed over them, her heart picking up pace with each step. Why was she so nervous? At worst, they would have a screaming row about her turning up, but at best, he'd take her in his arms and nuzzle into her neck, just the way she liked him to. Aaron was her husband and the father of their two boys, and she loved him deeply—no matter what.

"You can do this, Stephanie. Pull your big-girl pants up," she muttered, and took the last few determined steps forward to the front door.

Chapter Ninety

AARON STOOD IN THE KITCHEN, listening, wondering whether he was doing the right thing. Was about to do the right thing. Or the very wrong thing. Frankie had made no bones about it: she had gently chased him, flirting with him, leading him on, and he'd invited her to the cottage—overnight. Hadn't he learned his lesson? Hadn't Steph only just found out about his affair, his fetish? Hadn't he come away supposedly to think things through, try and repair some of the damage and go back home with a plan to make things right? Yet here he was, stood in the kitchen of the cottage he'd used so many times for his other interests, with a woman undoubtedly looking hellishly sexy on the other side of the wall, waiting for him to pleasure her. And her him.

She called again, bringing him back from his thoughts, to the moment at hand. He moved out from the kitchen and opened the door back into the lounge, the warmth from the wood fire brushing his face after the coolness of the other room. Walking into the room fully, he couldn't help the jolt he felt in his groin, taking in the scene before him. There, stretched out on her back on the soft old sofa, was Frankie, looking every inch the sexy siren she was, wearing nothing but an alluring smile.

His mouth felt dry.

"Don't just stand there. Come on over," she said, fluttering her eyelashes gently, the tip of her tongue dancing on her upper lip.

Damn, she looked as sexy as hell. All previous hesitation and thoughts of doing the right or wrong thing left him abruptly. He slipped his feet out of his shoes, unbuckling his belt at the same time, not taking his eyes off hers as he did so, then with swift nimble fingers, he pulled open the buttons on his shirt and threw it to the floor.

"You've still got too much clothing on. Why don't you take it all off and join me," she purred. It wasn't really a question, more a demand, and since he liked receiving demands from a woman at times like this, he savoured it as he fully undressed. He waited for further instruction, the warmth of the fire dancing on his naked skin.

"Now, slowly, come here and kiss me." Frankie had picked up his vibe, what he liked by way of direction or not, whether he was the dominant type, and was thrilled to find he was going to obey her. It was going to make what she was about to do next a whole lot easier. He followed her command and stood at her shoulders looking down at her.

"Do you like what you see, Aaron?"

"Yes, I do."

"Would you like to touch?"

"Yes, I would."

"Then lie on top of me." He didn't need asking twice, and he gently positioned himself on top of her, taking care not to squash her slim frame underneath his firm male body. She spread her legs slightly so the sofa could take some of his weight.

"That's nice, isn't it," she purred, and ran her fingernails up and down his back lightly, waiting for the right moment.

"Kiss my neck," she ordered, and Aaron quickly obliged, leaving soft kisses dotted up and down her neck. Frankie let out low moans of enjoyment.

That's what his ears heard, what his brain registered, but that wasn't what was really happening. Frankie was making all the right distracting sounds, but they weren't for real. She was acting her part out, the sexy siren, the sexy killer. Her left hand rubbed his back gently, but her right hand was preoccupied with the syringe she'd placed down the back of the sofa cushion, in just the right place.

Flipping the cap off the top of it, and with Aaron completely distracted, she raised her right arm up in the air ready to bring the whole thing down with a slam into his shoulder. But the moment had other ideas.

Chapter Ninety-One

THE TWO WOMEN watched on as Stephanie finally reached the cottage and hesitated outside the door. Suddenly Amanda's phone filled the car with sound. As a detective, she knew better than to dismiss a call; she had learned the lesson the hard way some years back.

"Damn. Sorry, Ruth, I'd better answer it." She pressed 'accept.' "Amanda Lacey speaking." There was silence at the other end of the line. "Hello? Lacey here. Who's calling?" She heard a faint gasp, possibly a woman's, and waited a moment longer before trying again. "It's okay to talk. I can hear you're there."

A woman's faint voice filled her ears. "I'm sorry," she stuttered. "Maybe I have this all wrong."

"Why don't you tell me anyway? Perhaps I can help you," Amanda said gently. It wasn't the first time she'd received such calls, had someone on the other end unsure of what to say or do.

"It's Georgia here."

"Hi, Georgia. What can I help you with? Have you thought of something?"

"I think I might know who you're looking for, who was with Sebastian that night, when he was murdered. I've been thinking about all the pieces fitting into place but I don't want to drop the person in it if it's nothing."

"I understand, Georgia. Are they a friend of yours?"

"She was. Is. I mean, we were friends a long while back and lost touch. Then she suddenly came back into my life about a week ago. And she has a scarf, like the one with the poppy on. She's a vet too, with short hair. Oh my god!" Georgia started to break down on the other end of the phone and Amanda did her best to console her and keep her talking.

"Shh, Georgia, you're doing the right thing. Just try and stay calm and talk to me, okay?" A slight gulp confirmed Georgia was still there and listening. "What is your friend's name and where is she now, do you know?"

Georgia sniffed loudly. "Philippa. Philippa During. A vet in Rickmansworth, but she's not home. I believe she's away this weekend, up north with her boyfriend." Another gulp, this time with a half sob mixed in. "Oh dear. What will happen to her now I've told you?"

"You've done the right thing, Georgia," Amanda said again. "Leave it with me. We'll need to ask her some questions and look a bit deeper. No one is in any trouble right now. Do you have an address or a number for her?"

"Yes, I have her number. It's in my phone. What will happen now?" Georgia sounded more and more distressed with every word that left her mouth.

"We'll talk to her and take it from there. If she isn't who we are looking for, nothing will happen to her, but we have to investigate first. You've done the right thing, Georgia. Thank you. Now, take a moment and find the number in your phone, and I'll hang on here."

A rather nervous "Okay" came from Georgia's end of the line, and Amanda waited uneasily, hoping she didn't hang up beforehand. A moment later, Amanda was writing the number down.

"Thank you, Georgia. You're very brave. Now, we'll follow this up right now and see what we can find out. Don't worry. I'll be in touch soon. Before you go, do you happen to know where up north she may have gone, or the boyfriend's name? Did she say?"

After a brief silence, Georgia said, "The Lakes somewhere, maybe Windemere. She wouldn't tell me his name but he's already spoken for, and a pilot."

Amanda felt a jolt of adrenaline surge through her body. She hung up the call with Georgia, pressed a speed dial number that went straight to Jack, and leapt out of the car, holding the phone to her ear as she ran forward into the darkness.

A scream came from inside the cottage, shattering the eerie night silence.

"Oh my god! No!" shrieked a woman's voice. The front door slammed and Aaron heard the sound of footsteps running down the path away from the house. "No! No! No!" came the voice again, getting fainter now.

"Stephanie! Stephanie, oh my god! Please wait!"

He tried to scramble off Frankie as best he could without hurting her, and out of the corner of his eye he saw something long, like a pen, fly through the air. He leapt to his feet, unaware of the death sentence he'd just sidestepped, and fished madly for his trousers.

"My wife. Oh hell! I'd better go after her," he said to Frankie, flustered. This was not how it was supposed to be. "Get some clothes on, but stay here!" he said, reaching for his shoes.

"What the?" He bent down, puzzled. There was a syringe beside one of them. It took him a moment to register what it was exactly, and where it could have come from. It certainly wasn't his. He picked it up, taking care to keep the bare needle end away from himself, not knowing what it contained but knowing instinctively that it wasn't a good thing and it had been meant for him. He held it out in his hand and turned to Frankie, a questioning look on his face.

"Care to explain what this is and what you intended to do with it?"

Frankie pulled her silk robe around her a bit more tightly. "Just something to relax us a little," she stammered. "I thought you might enjoy it. It really heightens the experience."

She gave a weak smile, but that wasn't going to work with Aaron now. He had more pressing problem to deal with—his wife. Still holding the syringe carefully in the palm of his hand, he jogged down the short hallway. He reached for the door handle and a figure appeared out of the darkness, blocking his way out.

"Amanda! What are you doing here?"

"Never mind me right now, Aaron. Are you on your own in there or are you with a woman by chance?"

Aaron craned his neck past her; he could see the headlights of a car in the distance, and worrying about Stephanie. The interior light was on and he could see Ruth and Stephanie in the front seats.

He was aware of Amanda asking another question. "And what's that in your hand. Where did you get that?"

"It's not mine! I've just seen it myself. I have no idea what it is!"

"Open your hand slowly, Aaron, and give it to me." Her voice was deadly calm. "Carefully," she said as he uncurled his fingers.

So Georgia had been right, thought Amanda. She felt ill. In a low voice she asked, "Who gave you this, Aaron?" She kept her voice hushed, suspecting the owner was in the other room—the woman Stephanie had just witnessed with her husband, and Georgia's old friend.

"It's Frankie's, I'm assuming," he said, equally quietly, and pointed behind him over his shoulder with his thumb. "She's in the lounge. Why?"

"Stay here. Have you got your phone handy?"

"No, it's in the lounge. What's going on?!"

"Keep your voice down," Amanda ordered him. "I'll tell you later, but right now, get to the others in the car, call 999 and stay put. Now go."

Aaron jogged down the lane to the car. Ruth saw him coming and got out, reaching him in three long strides.

"You leave her alone," she began.

"Never mind that now, Ruth. Call 999. Amanda needs assistance. And for god's sake, stay in the car, both of you!"

"What? What's happening?" Ruth took a step back.

"Just dial the police, would you?"

Aaron's voice was a squeak of fear. He left Ruth fumbling for her phone and jogged back to the house in case Amanda needed his help. If he wasn't in trouble before with Stephanie, he most certainly was now.

Chapter Ninety-Two

AMANDA ENTERED THE LOUNGE, not really sure what she'd find. It was times like this she wished she was armed. While she'd instructed Aaron to call the police, the cottage was out in the middle of nowhere and the police could take a while—and then send what, exactly? A beat bobby on his cycle? This wasn't the Metropolitan police in Croydon, no armed response unit here; she'd have to do the best with what she had.

In the lounge, a woman was sitting in an old chair, wrapped only in a flimsy robe, the wood fire her only protection from a chilly night. She kept her head down, looking at the carpet, and didn't speak a word. Amanda wondered what she was thinking about. Did she know her game was up? That Amanda was a detective, that she knew about the syringe and its lethal contents? Or was she hoping that she could get away with a tale of a party drug perhaps, or a sleeping drug.

"I'm DS Amanda Lacey. And you are?" She waited for the woman to raise her eyes and say something, but she stayed mute and still. Trying again she asked, "What's your name?"

Still nothing. Amanda kept her distance, not knowing if the woman had any other weapons close at hand, like a hunting knife.

"This would be better for you if you fill me in a little. The local police are on their way and I know exactly what is in that syringe. Were you about to use it on Mr. Galbraith?"

The woman's head flew up now, and a volley of words spewed out of her mouth.

"He's no Mr. Nice Guy, you know! He hunts for fun, kills big game for fun! How can any decent person do such a thing?" Anger flared in her eyes now, and her voice rose. "Look around you, at these so-called 'trophies,'" she said, wafting her arms around the room. "They all died at his hands, for fun!"

"Is that why you wanted to hurt him, because he hunted? Is that why you killed the others, because they both enjoyed the sport too?"

"Yes! They deserved to be taught a lesson! Gloating to the world about what they'd killed, their sick pictures of themselves with their kill. I thought I'd do the same to them. Nice touch, didn't you think? Let *them* be someone's trophy, *my* trophy."

"Seems a little extreme, if you don't mind me saying so."

"I couldn't care less what you think! I'd have had another trophy if you lot hadn't turned up and interfered. He'd have been dead shortly and another trophy photo posted, showing the world what happens to those who hunt big animals. But you've screwed that up now. He goes free, gets away with murder!"

"Unlike you, though."

"If it's my price to pay for cleaning them off this earth, then so be it. I didn't do it for malice. I'm not a cold-blooded murderer. I didn't get enjoyment from it." She lowered her voice and added, "Quite the contrary, actually. It really upset my stomach, made me sick."

"If you're looking for sympathy on that score, you'll not get any from me."

The reflection of blue flashing lights was just visible on the walls as the police vehicle came to a standstill outside. There was the sound of car doors slamming shut, boots on the wooden floor. Amanda turned to the men in uniform and introduced herself, all the time keeping one eye on the woman in the chair.

"DS Amanda Lacey, Met, Croydon.

"Sergeant Carl Blake, Windemere. Care to fill me in?

"Sure will. Quite by chance, even though we have two other

victims, I came across this woman after driving the cottage owner's wife up here for the weekend. This woman was with the owner's husband, and had this with her." She showed him the syringe. "It's filled with a lethal substance that will kill in seconds if it's administered. It's my belief she intended to use it on her victim, Aaron Galbraith, then cut his throat and post the images to social media like she has the other two victims. One in London and one in Manchester. She has admitted as much while we waited for you."

"I'd heard about that, seen the photos. Quite a way to publicise your crime," he said to Amanda, then turned his attention to 'Frankie.' "So, care to tell us anything more?"

"I've said all I'm saying for now. I'm just sorry I didn't get to finish him off. He gets away with it."

"So you've said," Amanda said disdainfully. "Can you tell us your name or have we got to search for your wallet?"

"Philippa During."

Blake stepped over to her and got right to the formalities.

"Philippa During, I'm arresting you for the attempted murder of Aaron Galbraith and the murders of," he looked at Amanda who filled in the names of the two victims for him, "Sebastian Stevens and Fiona Gable ...."

Amanda stood quietly to one side as he read Philippa her rights, cuffed her and escorted her outside to the waiting police car out front, where more units were now arriving. Another officer took the syringe, now in a plastic evidence bag, the needle secured so as not to prick anyone accidentally. With the murderer now out of the house, the lounge and the rest of the house had become be a crime scene. The local police would have to process it and catalogue the evidence. But there was no doubt about what had gone on that night, and what Philippa had planned to do. Aaron Galbraith had been one lucky man, she mused, though when Stephanie got hold of him, he might think otherwise. What a sorry state of affairs for her friend to be mixed up in.

Out of her jurisdiction, there wasn't much more for Amanda to do at the scene. She made her way back up the lane to her waiting car.

Aaron, wisely keeping his distance, sat on an old fallen tree nearby. She walked over to him.

"You'll need to go to the station, too," she told him. "There will be further questioning in the morning, but they have their suspect and she's not denying anything, though they'll want your side of things." He nodded. "Best you stay local tonight, though not here at the cottage, obviously. The police will give you a lift when they're done, I'm sure. And you might want to get dressed again. They'll sort you out a blanket or something." He nodded again, too numb to add anything. "We're all staying back in the village, though as you can imagine, Stephanie is pretty distraught. You might want to leave talking to her until she's calmed down a bit. We'll drive her home tomorrow if that's what she wants. I'll let you know."

"Thank you, Amanda. What a bloody mess I've made." He hung his head in shame; it was going to be a long road for them to get over this, if they ever could. He watched glumly as Amanda went over and got in the driver's side of her car and put her arms around his wife, pulling her close.

He wished he could have done the same.

Chapter Ninety-Three

RUTH, Amanda and Stephanie had finished breakfast and were chatting over warm milky coffee in the dining room at the hotel. The room was half full of weekend visitors all ready and raring to go on a day of discovery, nature, great walking tracks and, of course, stunning lake views. And that was exactly the opposite of how Stephanie was feeling. Red-eyed from a night of horrendous tears, she sat at the breakfast table feeling numb all over, too broken to cry any more. Not for herself so much, but for her two young boys back home and how they were going to take the news of their breakup. The two people they loved and trusted the most were about to go their separate ways. She could see no other way forward.

"You don't have to do anything yet, Stephanie—no rash decisions, nothing," said Ruth. "Aaron has betrayed you, I get that, and more than once, I get that too, but just wait a while before you mention anything and upset the boys." She thought for a moment and then added, "Would it be helpful if I called your mum, asked her to keep them for another day or so, and we'll stay here? Or I can go—whatever you prefer. Give you some time."

Stephanie shook her head slowly, almost trance-like. "No, I should go back, pick them up, and try and get on the best I can until I've spoken to Aaron. Where is he, do you know?"

"Well, he's not at the cottage, that's for sure. He's probably wrapped in a blanket, somewhere not too far away. The police will have sorted him out somewhat, I expect." While it wasn't time for laughter, the thought of him still in a blanket eating breakfast somewhere amused her and she smiled despite herself.

"What are you smiling at?"

"Sorry, Stephanie. This is not the time or the place. I'm sorry."

"No, tell me. I could do with the distraction."

Ruth had no choice not to tell her now, and Amanda eyed her partner warily.

"I was just thinking about him sat in a café eating breakfast nearby, but still wrapped in a blanket. Look, totally inappropriate, I know. I'm sorry," she said again.

Stephanie stared directly at her, giving her a look Ruth couldn't quite fathom. Had she now made matters worse? Suddenly Stephanie exploded in a fit of laughter, throwing her head back, laughing loudly and catching stares and scowls from diners at nearby tables. When she didn't immediately quiet down, Ruth stood, laughing a little herself, and went round the table to her friend, crouching down to hug her. Then as suddenly as it had begun, Stephanie's laughter stopped and she burst into tears.

"Oh no! Honey, what's the matter?" Ruth cried, holding her friend closer.

It was all too much—the upset of recent events and the recollection of distant ones. Through her tears, Stephanie told Ruth and Amanda about the events from years ago, the scars on her legs, about that one terrifying night with another man, long before she'd ever met Aaron. That man had enjoyed playing with a knife, and he had drugged her and abused her all through one endless night of unspeakable horror. The recent upset with Aaron brought the unwelcome memories back. She'd never known his name that night, but she did now. His name had been all over the news: Sebastian Stevens. The coincidence wasn't lost on Amanda.

Chapter Ninety-Four

LATER THAT MORNING, Rick, Duncan, Amanda and DS Carl Blake sat in the squad room of the police station in Windemere, beige plastic cups filled with machine coffee in front of each of them. It had been an eventful night, and even though neither detective had jurisdiction officially, Amanda had called Rick who'd in turn called Duncan, and they'd driven up that morning.

Ruth was still at the hotel with Stephanie. No one was quite sure exactly where Aaron had crept off to, but he was still in town; the police were not finished with him yet. Philippa, was somewhere in the back of the building, safe and secure in a police custody.

Carl Blake began the debrief. "Her full name is Philippa Jones, though she goes by During, her mother's name. You may have heard of her father, Tony Jones, currently inside for his part in a dog-fighting ring in Kent."

A bell rang in Amanda's head. "He's her father? Really?"

"Afraid so," said Blake. "You know of him, then?"

"You could say that. He very famously got a slap on the wrist and a few lousy months inside for his part in that organised hellhole. I was there the night it got busted. It was one of the cruellest things I've ever seen, and thank god we intercepted before the actual fighting started. A lot of dogs were spared that night." Amanda shuddered involuntarily.

"Well, he's still inside, you'll be pleased to know. Apparently, our prisoner says her dad's sentence after what he did was one of the reasons she's been doing what she has. That and ridding the country of big-game sport hunters. His sentence was way too light for her liking, and seeing her first victim with her kill set her off thinking that she could dish out stronger sentences. Which she did. Daddy dear had made her work with the dogs for pocket money when she was a kid, feeding them and cleaning them out, getting rid of the dead ones, that sort of thing. She'd hated every inch of the place, apparently, but couldn't do much about it. Daddy had to be obeyed or else there would have been strife. Her mother had taken her father's side, not wanting to cause trouble in the house, I guess."

"A bit extreme, don't you think, doing what she's been doing?"

"Probably, but who understands criminals' reasons? I know I never will. She's just another weirdo, in my book. The funny thing is, she's so detached from it all, like she's not the one that's been committing the crimes, even though she is."

"But she's talking and still admitting it, then?"

"Yes, like the proverbial singing canary. Shown no remorse, no regrets. Knew she'd probably get caught at some point, but didn't think it would be quite so soon. Apparently, it made her physically sick, the actual act. Didn't enjoy it all. Can you believe that?"

"So that's okay, then? She didn't enjoy it?" Amanda was incredulous. She thought for a moment. "Hang on a minute. I'm betting she wasn't physically sick in the victims' toilets or sinks. There would have been traces left behind. We found a bag of vomit in a rubbish bin near the first victim's home, and there was another not far from the second victim's, left in a doorway."

"I remember one of ours finding it. What are you getting at?" It was Rick's turn to speak.

"Nothing, really. Just tying up loose ends in my head, and the two bags of vomit were still loose. Assuming they were both hers. A bit of a coincidence if not, wouldn't you say? Proves she had a weak stomach for it but I doubt the judge will take it into account. Both took some considerable planning, premeditated for sure. She'll go down for some time, a lot more than her dad did." Thinking again, she asked, "Do we know yet how she got into their lives, all three of them?"

"Used social media to make friends and dig from there, though not with her second victim, Sebastian. He wasn't particularly active like the other two, and he would have been much harder to infiltrate, I suspect —not your average man. She says she got into his laptop and pretended to be one of the girls he paid for regularly. Philippa intercepted the booking somehow and pretended to be her. That was the other woman you saw entering and leaving his building that night, the real escort."

Rick picked it up. "Did she say if she still has his laptop? It was missing and he definitely had one, but it's never surfaced."

"I would doubt it ever will. She's been real careful so far, apart from telling someone she was with a pilot up north, that is. No names, no definite locations. Could be wrong, though. It could be under her floorboards at home. No doubt the search will find it if it's there."

"Hmm, shame. I'd like to look into Sebastian Stevens a little more if I could, separately from this. And his search history might be useful, searches he particularly made from a computer at home rather than the office." Amanda chewed her bottom lip and screwed her face up as she thought.

"What are you thinking, Amanda?" Duncan asked.

"It seems he had some rather eclectic tastes in the bedroom department, namely blood and knife play, if you've ever heard of it. Apparently, your partner makes little slits with a sharp knife, mainly into the thigh area, drawing blood. A type of BDSM practice which he was obviously into. Not sure you could pay me enough to have that done, and from what I can gather, he didn't always pay. I know of at least one victim that suspects he drugged her and then took his knife to her, so there could possibly be more. And of course, if you don't know what you're doing, it can be horrendously dangerous. Cut a main artery by accident and it's all over."

"But the guy is dead. Why bother?"

"Because if he was part of something bigger, a dangerous fetish ring perhaps, he could afford to be selective about who he did it with and pay the women off easily, keeping them quiet. It was fifteen years ago for the victim I know of, so things may have progressed somewhat from there. Doing it with a willing partner, fair enough. But drugging someone for your own pleasure? That makes it a crime. His web history might help with that."

Duncan scratched his head. "You thinking something on the dark web, then?"

"Maybe. A character like Sebastian Stevens wouldn't get what he wanted from regular sources, though when we contact the agency where he hired the woman he was supposed to meet on the night of his death, they might be able to tell us more." Amanda looked around at the blank faces of the other three men. "Look, call it women's intuition if you like, but I sense there was something going on in the back of his life. Something we don't fully know about yet, something that may hurt others, even though he's gone. I'm just saying, humour me for now, let me ride with it for a while."

Duncan, Rick and Carl all looked at one another and shrugged their shoulders in passive agreement. If Amanda wanted to go digging, it was no skin off their noses.

"That's settled, then," she said. "If you find anything, particularly a laptop, just let me know. That's all I'm asking."

"Thing is, if it is on the dark web, you'll never find it via the browser history. It's a lot trickier than simply typing in a URL. You'll need something or someone else other than that. But go ahead, knock yourself out." Rick was trying to be helpful and it set Amanda thinking. Maybe Ruth could give her some pointers before she made a fool of herself and went to computer forensics.

Changing the subject, she said, "Right, well, I'm off to get some lunch. Anyone care to join me before we head back?"

Rick and Duncan both stood, smiling at the thought of good food. And decent coffee.

Epilogue

"SHAME it all turned to custard up there," said Ruth. "I was quite looking forward to a weekend away with you after we'd dropped Stephanie at the cottage. But it wasn't meant to be." She stroked Amanda's blonde hair; Amanda was using her thighs as a pillow as the two of them shared the sofa back at her place. "Maybe we can go again, just the two of us—walk the hills and look at the Lakes, do the touristy thing."

"Hmm?"

"Tell me you heard all that, or were you miles away thinking about work still?" Ruth was used to Amanda not always being present at quiet times like these. It was one of her foibles, but one that made her a decent detective. When a case went on without a result, it played on her mind, and Ruth was glad that the latest crime had all been wrapped up.

"I did, and to answer your question, which wasn't actually a question I should add, yes, it was a shame. A walk in the fells would have been a welcome break, but it was a stroke of luck how we ended up solving the case at the same time—and that we were nearby. If Georgia hadn't seen that blurry face shot on the CCTV footage, and noticed the scarf and overheard Rick's vet comment, we'd probably still be hunting the hunter. She might have gone on to kill even more after

Aaron. We got lucky, and Aaron certainly got away with his life. Perfect timing all round I'd say."

"It can't be nice dropping your friend in to the police, though. What if Georgia had been wrong? Imagine the mess—her friend being put under the microscope. It would have destroyed their friendship if she'd been wrong. It would be tough to ride that one out. She really is a brave one."

"Let's not talk about it anymore. It's over with. I just hope the walking wounded can get their lives in some sort of order. Poor Stephanie has been through the wringer, and she's decided to give him the boot. It will be tough on the boys, I expect, but the slime-ball couldn't help himself. How can you come back from that and work it into something loving and trusting? You'd need a miracle. But to each their own. They may find a way in the future. Too early to tell. For now, they're going to exist in separate lives."

Ruth carried on stroking Amanda's hair; the soothing tones of Sinatra played quietly in the background, and a breeze filtered through the open window. Summer was starting to make itself more comfortable, each day and evening warmer than the last. It was such a welcome time of year.

"That feels good. It's so relaxing here with you, Ruth." Amanda fell silent, reflecting. "That was another stroke of luck," she said at last, "working on that dog-fighting case. If not for that, I'd never have met you." Lifting her head up to face Ruth, she asked, "Do you remember the little terrier with his tan-coloured patch across one eye? Jack, he was called."

"Of course I do. You'd just dropped him off back to his owners before coming round to my place for tea and toast, if I remember rightly. Why do you ask?"

"Just that he was the catalyst in us getting together, my excuse to call back round here. I knew you'd want to know he'd been returned safely, and yes, I could have called on the phone but, well, in person did the trick," she said, smiling sheepishly.

Ruth bent forward and planted a kiss tenderly on the top of her head. Amanda sat up and turned properly to look up at her best friend. Their eyes locked.

Ruth spoke first. "Then we should ask him to be a page boy at our ceremony. He could wear a little bow tie around his neck."

For a moment, neither woman said a word. Then Ruth spoke again, her voice deadly serious and full of love.

"Amanda Lacey, will you marry me?"

Want to continue on to the next book in the series? Click here to start reading.

Or you could save money and purchase a book set, here's the next one for you: Book set 3

Also by Linda Coles

Jack Rutherford and Amanda Lacey Series:

Hot to Kill

The Hunted

Dark Service

One Last Hit

Hey You, Pretty Face

Scream Blue Murder

Butcher Baker Banker

The Chrissy Livingstone Series:

Tin Men

Walk Like You

The Silent Ones

The Will Peters series.

Where There's A Will

What Will Be

Will Stop At Nothing

More by Linda Coles

If you enjoyed reading one of my stories, here are the others:

The DC Jack Rutherford and DS Amanda Lacey Series:

Hot to Kill

When a local landscaper vanishes, Madeline Simpson knows she was the last person to see him alive – because she killed him.

With a serial sex offender on the loose, Detectives DC Jack Rutherford and DS Amanda Lacey already have their hands full. It's only when another death occurs that a link between the two cases comes to light, and Madeline finds herself the focus of their investigation.

While attempting to keep her deadly secret, Madeline stumbles upon clues that point to the true identity of the sex offender. She's closing in when tragedy strikes, and the death toll increases.

But DS Amanda Lacey has no idea how close she is to the killer as her work and personal lives collide.

How long will she have to wait to find out the full truth?

If you like interesting characters, imaginative story lines, and British crime drama, then you'll love this captivating story.

The Hunted

The hunt is on...

They kill wild animals for sport. She's about to return the favour.

A spate of distressing big-game hunter posts are clogging up her newsfeed. As hunters brag about the exotic animals they've murdered and the followers they've gained along the way, a passionate veterinarian can no longer sit back and do nothing.

To stop the killings, she creates her own endangered list of hunters. By stalking their online profiles and infiltrating their inner circles, she vows to take them out one-by-one.

How far will she go to add the guilty to her own trophy collection?

Dark Service

The dark web can satisfy any perversion, but two detectives might just pull the plug...

Taylor never felt the blade pressed to her scalp. She wakes frightened and alone in an unfamiliar hotel room with a near shaved head and a warning... tell no one.

As detectives Amanda Lacey and Jack Rutherford investigate, they venture deep into the fetish-fueled underbelly of the dark web. The traumatized woman is only the latest victim in a decade-long string of disturbing—and intensely personal—thefts.

To take down a perverted black market, they'll go undercover. But just when justice seems within reach, an unexpected event sends their sting operation spiraling out of control. Their only chance at catching the culprits lies with a local reporter... and a sex scandal that could ruin them all.

One Last Hit

The greatest danger may come from inside his own home.

Detective Duncan Riley has always worked hard to maintain order on the streets of Manchester. But when a series of incidents at home cause him to worry about his wife's behaviour, he finds himself pulled in too many directions at once.

After a colleague Amanda Lacey asks for his help with a local drug epidemic, he never expected the case would infiltrate his own family...And a situation that spirals out of control...

Hey You, Pretty Face

An abandoned infant. Three girls stolen in the night. Can one overworked detective find the connection to save them all?

London, 1999. Short-staffed during a holiday week, Detective Jack Rutherford can't afford to spend time on the couch with his beloved wife. With a skeleton staff, he's forced to handle a deserted infant and a trio of missing girls almost single-handedly. Despite the overload, Jack has a sneaking suspicion that the baby and the abductions are somehow connected...

As he fights to reunite the girls with their families, the clues point to a dark secret that sends chills down his spine. With evidence revealing a detestable crime ring, can Jack catch the criminals before the girls go missing forever?

Scream Blue Murder

Two cold cases are about to turn red hot...

Detective Jack Rutherford's instincts have only sharpened with age. So when a violent road fatality reminds him of a near-identical crime from 15 years earlier, he digs up the past to investigate both. But with one case already closed, he fears the wrong man still festers behind bars while the real killer roams free...

For Detective Amanda Lacey, family always comes first. But when she unearths a skeleton in her father-in-law's garden, she has to balance her heart with her desire for justice. And with darkness lurking just beneath the surface, DS Lacey must push her feelings to one side to discover the chilling truth.

As the sins of the past haunt both detectives, will solving the crimes have consequences that echo for the rest of their lives?

Butcher Baker Banker

A cold Croydon winter's night and pensioner Nelly Raven lies dead and naked on the floor of her living room. The scene bears all the hallmarks of a burglary gone wrong.

It's just the beginning.

Ron Butcher rose to the top of London's gangland by "fixing things". But are his extensive crooked connections of use when death knocks at his own family's door?

Baker Kit Morris will do anything to keep his family business alive. Desperate for cash, he hatches a risky plan that lands him in trouble. As he struggles to stay out of prison, he forges an unlikely friendship with an aging local thug.

And then there's the Banker, Lee Meady, a man with personal problems of his own.

Just how does it all fit together?

As DC Jack Rutherford and DS Amanda Lacey uncover the facts surrounding the case, the harrowing truth of the killer's identity leaves Jack wondering where the human race went so badly wrong.

The Chrissy Livingstone series:

Tin Men

She thought she knew her father. But what she doesn't know could fill a mortuary...

Ex-MI5 agent Chrissy Livingstone grieves over her dad's sudden death. While she cleans out his old things, she discovers something she can't explain: seven photos of schoolboys with the year 1987 stamped on the back. Unable to turn off her desire for the truth, she hunts down the boys in the photos only to find out that three of the seven have committed suicide...

Tracing the clues from Surrey to Santa Monica, Chrissy unearths disturbing ties between her father's work as a financier and the victims. As each new connection raises more sinister questions about her family, she fears she should've left the secrets buried with the dead.

Will Chrissy put the past to rest, or will the sins of the father destroy her?

Walk Like You

When a major railway accident turns into a bizarre case of a missing body, will this PI's hunt for the truth take her way off track?

London. Private investigator Chrissy Livingstone's dirty work has taken her down a different path to her family. But when her upper-class sister begs her to locate a friend missing after a horrific train crash, she feels duty-bound to assist. Though when the two dig deeper, all the evidence seems to lead to one mysterious conclusion: the woman doesn't want to be found.

Still with no idea why the woman was on the train, and an unidentified body uncannily resembling the missing person lying unclaimed in the mortuary, the sisters follow a trail of cryptic clues through France. The mystery deepens when they learn someone else is searching, and their motive could be murder...

Can Chrissy find the woman before she meets a terrible fate?

The Silent Ones

An abandoned child. A missing couple. A village full of secrets.

When a couple holidaying in the small Irish village of Doolan disappear one night, leaving their child behind, Chrissy Livingstone has no choice but to involve herself in the mystery surrounding their disappearance.

As the toddler is taken into care, it soon becomes apparent that in the close-knit village the couple are not the only ones with secrets to keep.

With the help of her sister, Julie, Chrissy races to uncover what is really happening. Could discovering the truth put more lives at risk?

A suspenseful story that will keep you guessing until the end.

The Will Peters Series:

Where There's a Will

A dog walker discovers the body of a young homeless man in Hunsbury Hill Country Park. It carries a message: 'your move'.

Part-time grave digger and cab driver Will Peters knows just what it's like living on the streets and vows the young man's death will not be brushed aside during the mayor's re-election campaign. Forging a relationship with local detectives, Will gets creative and acquires information any way he can. With the help of ex-con Birdie Fox and elderly hard-nosed trade unionist Stanley Kipper, Will sets about bringing the killer to justice.

But as the case unfolds, and the death toll rises, the police uncover corruption on a massive scale, and it appears the murders are far more personal than anyone could have possibly imagined.

Where There's a Will is the first book in an exciting new crime series.

(Will Peters first appeared as Billy Peters in Hey You, Pretty Face, a DC Jack Rutherford story set during the winter of 1999.)

What Will Be

A brutal murder. A friend in jeopardy. A steadfast sleuth.

When a new cold case initiative is launched, cab driver and gravedigger Will Peters has no idea how close he is to a crime committed nearly twenty years ago.

A man ferociously beaten to death in a derelict shoe factory.

Someone knows what went on that night. That someone needs to start talking.

With the help of ex-con Birdie Fox and elderly hard-nosed trade unionist Stanley Kipper, Will sets about finding them.

But it's bittersweet and Will soon finds himself with an impossible moral dilemma. Tell the police what he's uncovered or keep quiet and pray they don't arrive at the same conclusion?

Is he strong enough to decide?

If you enjoy rich characters and a little humour sprinkled through your British crime, then you'll love the Will Peters series. Perfect for fans of Richard Osman's The Thursday Murder Club and The Man Who Died Twice.

Will Stop At Nothing

You can choose your friends, but you can't choose your family.

In a cemetery, the dead are meant to be underground, not hiding in the bushes.

When Will Peters stumbles across the long-dead body of an unknown man, he could never know how the heart-breaking discovery would fit into his own family history.

As he comes to terms with the news, another body is discovered. This time it's even more personal.

As the mystery unfolds, he realises his ties to the victims are connections he'd rather not have.

What's more, a vulnerable friend desperately needs his help. Just how much more can Will cope with? But yet another tragic event leaves him reeling.

And then there's his mother. Will hasn't seen her since he ran away from home over twenty years ago, but there's only one person who can help him fit all of the pieces together.

Join Will, Birdie and Stanley in this final installment of the popular British Will Peters crime trilogy.

In a case that's far too close for comfort and a story of a past he never knew, read Will Stop at Nothing to find out how he reconciles the events that made him the man he is today.

About the Author

Hi, I'm Linda Coles. Thanks for choosing this book, I really hope you enjoyed it and collect the following ones in the series. Great characters make a great read and I hope I've managed to create that for you.

Originally from the UK, I now live and work in beautiful New Zealand along with my hubby, 2 cats and 6 goats. My office sits by the edge of my vegetable garden, and apart from reading and writing, I get to run by the beach for pleasure.

If you find a moment, please do write an honest online review of my work, they really do make such a difference to those choosing what book to buy next.

Thanks, Linda

Milton Keynes UK
Ingram Content Group UK Ltd.
UKHW011956281223
435113UK00001B/79

9 798223 246039